AMONG THE ASHES

C.L. BREES

C.L. Brees

Printed in the United States of America

First Printing: July 2018

Print Edition ISBN-13: 978-0-69-210606-8

Edited by: Ryan Quinn
Cover Art: Depositphoto

Questions unanswered,
and words unspoken,
are the weapons of loss,
that left me broken.

- Jessica Katoff

To my fans: Thank you for motivating me every day to continue sharing stories with you.

ONE

February 7, 2017
Early Morning

OW DID MY LIFE END UP HERE? Caleb sits in his antique rocking chair staring vacuously at the hostile waves smashing against the jagged rocky coastline, and the one thing he can't get off his mind is wondering when and where his life went so far off track. The sun crests the horizon, filling the sky with subdued hues of gold, crimson, and violet that wash across the vast Atlantic Ocean. He blows across the top of his mug, cracking a forced smile at the sheer beauty of his surroundings. And for a moment he stops worrying about everything that's gone wrong in his life.

The past couple of years were heartbreaking for Caleb. There was a time in his life where he'd tell you it was perfect (some would say a little too perfect). It was the life everyone aspires to achieve. But even for those who think they have it all, everything can change in an instant. And that's precisely what happened on a wintry, snow-white February morning in 2015.

What he foresaw as a typical day turned into tragedy. For that was the morning the love of his life, Sebastian, vanished—and no one ever saw or heard from him again. He often uses sunrises to reminisce about their lives together, all the while wondering where he is, what he's doing now, and if he ever still thinks about him. But after wasting countless hours trying to fulfil the answer to one vexing question—*why?*—he can never drum up a rational reason.

Why would he leave me? None of this seems real.

Caleb draws another sip of his green tea and a delicate stroke against his neck startles him. He curls his head and gazes straight into the brilliant, hazel eyes of his new lover, Gabriel, who towers over him with a smile on his face.

"Gorgeous morning, huh?" Gabriel asks.

"Without a doubt. How'd you sleep?"

"All right, I suppose. You worried about today?"

"Nah. It's a straightforward, open-and-close trial," Caleb replies, switching the topic. "You hungry?"

"I could use a little something to get my day started," Gabriel says.

"I'm so hungry; tell you what—give me a few to finish up my tea, watch the waves a little more, then I'll be right there."

"Okay, don't hang out here too long—I can't afford for you to get sick."

"I know, I promise I won't."

Gabriel grins, nods, and turns away back toward the front door. Caleb focuses again on the angry ocean, and his thoughts stray back to Sebastian.

He recalls every detail about the day he vanished; the overpowering scent of citrus cleanser in the air, the roar of the enraged wind blowing the snowflakes across the earth, and the cold vacant spot in the bed where Sebastian greeted him every morning with his radiant smile.

He waited twenty-four hours before contacting the Royal Newfoundland Constabulary to declare Sebastian missing. The constable assigned to the case spent the next year fixated on Caleb. She hounded him but, as the investigation wrapped up, fell shy of naming him a suspect. Finding no evidence of a crime, the constable postponed her pursuit and refocused her energy on newer, straightforward cases to solve.

His mind reverts to the here and now. His tea at this point is tepid, and the elements chill him to his core. He shivers while lifting himself from the armchair and stops a few feet shy of the door. His head swings around and he makes a mental note.

There's something uneasy in the air. I can't put my finger on what, but I can't shake it.

He shakes off the premonition and steps through the front door into the foyer. A few feet away he can see into the living room, and Caleb spots the outline of Gabriel's slender body pass into the kitchen. He grins and moves across the cedarwood plank floorboards. The ricochet of pots and pans banging resonates off the walls; he skulks closer to the kitchen, but guardedly.

Caleb rounds the corner. "Hey, hey, what's all the racket in here?"

"Oh, sorry, I was being loud, huh?"

"Eh, maybe a little."

"I wanted to get things set up for you; I wasn't trying to rush you or anything."

Caleb chuckles. "Babe, it's okay. I hope I haven't kept you waiting long."

"Not long, but like I said, there's no rush. Court starts at nine? You got about an hour before you need to be out the door, right?" Gabriel asks.

"Yeah, but I still need time to get ready. Maybe we should eat first, and I can rush the other stuff."

"If you're sure. I don't want you being late to court."

Caleb shrugs and the conversation goes cold. He opens the fridge and shuffles a few things around before removing what he needs. He bumps the door closed with his hip and gently places the items next to the stove before clearing his throat.

"How do you want your eggs?" Caleb asks.

"Scrambled is perfect, thanks."

Caleb whips into high gear with getting breakfast together. As he cracks the last egg into the bowl, Gabriel scoots behind him and wraps his arms around Caleb's waist. He leans his head back and the scruff of Gabriel's face scratches against his.

"So, tell me the truth—Sanderson, did he do it?" Gabriel casually asks. "I mean, you don't have to tell me."

"Doesn't matter if *I* believe he did it or not—as defense counsel, I have two main responsibilities: first, make certain Mr. Sanderson gets a fair trial; and last but not least, I paint an image of an upstanding citizen, so the jury *believes* he didn't do it."

"I see, dodging the question, are you? Well, gossip around town is he did it; everyone is saying he raped and kidnapped that poor girl."

"Eh, people always speculate around here," Caleb murmurs.

"It's a small town, what else is there to do?"

Caleb shrugs his shoulders. "Something, hell, anything more constructive than gossiping, for a change."

People gossiped a little too much for Caleb's comfort. But being from the area, it was a way of life for most people in these parts. After Sebastian disappeared, the question of what happened to him was at the tip of each townie's and bayman's tongue. Rumors spread; many were certain Caleb murdered him, others claimed Sebastian up and left town on his own accord, but not before accusing Caleb of being an abusive husband.

You name it, he heard it at some point. There were only three people who stuck by his side: his two best friends since childhood, Sam and Susan Butler, and his law partner, Oliver. They pushed back at the locals who ran their mouths in an attempt to paint an ugly image of Caleb. Not one person had the facts, but everybody enjoyed contemplating the unknown.

The butter liquifies and Caleb dumps the eggs into the sizzling pan. He waits, stirring the eggs as Gabriel nuzzles in tighter.

"Everything okay? I get a sense something is on your mind," Gabriel says.

"Just stuff. Nothing to upset yourself about."

Gabriel runs his fingers through Caleb's blond hair. "Ah, come on, I like to make a fuss over you from time to time. Anything I can do to help?"

"Trust me—everything's fine."

Gabriel loosens his grip and pulls away. "Promise."

"I'm positive everything is fine," Caleb says as he drops the spatula in the skillet.

Gabriel leans in, plants a peck on his cheek, and pulls away. A soft scoff falls from his mouth as he opens the cabinet to grab two plates. Caleb has grown accustomed to Gabriel's trivial outbursts and goes on with what he's doing, unfazed by his lover's melodramatic defiance.

Caleb gives the eggs one final fluff and checks on the ham browning on the rear burner. With a fork in hand, he's almost ready to flip them over when the screeching ringtone from the home phone rings. Startled, he drops the fork into the pan.

"It's not my morning."

"Don't worry, I got it, babe," Gabriel says. He disappears into the adjoining room and Caleb tries his damnedest to retrieve the fork without burning himself. "Thanks."

With breakfast finished, he sets up the plates next to the stove as Gabriel reenters the kitchen.

"Who was on the phone?"

"Don't get mad. Constable Dawe needs to talk to you."

Caleb drops the tongs on the counter. His palms turn clammy, and all the color in his face drains.

"Did she say what she needs?"

"I tried to get it out of her, but she refused to say. Sounds important, though."

He wanders toward the archway leading into the living room and squeezes Gabriel's hand as he exits.

"I'll be back in a few. You mind taking over for a minute?"

"Of course. Take all the time you need." Gabriel releases his slight grasp on Caleb's hand.

Gabriel stands paralyzed as Caleb disappears into the living room. He cowers behind the wall next to the archway, standing by to eavesdrop on the conversation.

It has been two years since Caleb's had contact with the constable about Sebastian, and he fears they've run out of fresh cases to work on and now her harassment will pick up right where it ended years earlier.

With his shaky hand, Caleb grabs the phone receiver off the end table, takes a deep breath, and wonders to himself, *What does she want now?*

"Good morning, Constable Dawe."

"Good morning, Mr. Winters—I realize it's been a while since we spoke . . ." she acknowledges.

"Yeah, it's been two years, but not long enough. Is there something I can do for you? Or are you calling to harass me more?" Caleb asks with disdain in his tone.

"It's something more unsettling. Are you sitting?"

Caleb bites his lower lip, shakes his head, and swings his arse around and sits. "I am now."

She clears her throat and continues. "There's been a recent development on your missing husband."

"What development?"

"A couple hiking near Old Pond found skeletal remains in a shallow grave last evening."

"Okay. And the medical examiner has, what, concluded they belong to Sebastian?"

"He's still investigating, but the height, build, and condition of the remains are leading us to speculate it could be him."

Caleb swallows hard and stays silent.

"Mr. Winters, are you still with me?" she asks.

"I'm . . . yeah, I'm still with you—a little shocked is all."

"I didn't call to upset you. It wasn't my intent. Thought you should know before the reporters in St. John's break the story later this morning."

"Well, I appreciate the call. Is the ME sending off a DNA sample or something?"

"He will. They extracted pulp from a second molar and they'll be sending it out for analysis today. His DNA profile is already in the database from the personal items you provided us a few years back," she begins. "As soon as we have conclusive results, I'll be in touch again."

"All right, well, thanks for letting me know. Talk with you again soon," Caleb replies. He sets the phone back on the cradle.

He tries to stand to his feet but straightaway becomes unsteady and collapses back onto the couch. His thoughts race a mile a minute. The adrenaline pulsates through his veins. With his damp hands he runs them against his scruffy face, doing his best to make sense of what he's learned.

What happened?

He closes his eyes and gathers his thoughts before returning to the kitchen. Gabriel will absolutely question him when he returns. He wants to cry, but after over a year of grieving, and plenty of tears, he can't bring himself to muster up the emotional release again.

Caleb exhales one final time before pulling his hands away from his face and standing. He turns toward the kitchen, and Gabriel appears from behind the wall with anxiety painted on his face.

"What's wrong?"

"She called to update me on Sebastian, that's all," he says.

Gabriel charges to his lover's side. "What is it? What did she say? Did they find him? Tell me." The pitch in his voice raises one octave higher, and an onslaught of questions spews from his mouth.

"Calm down, please. She wanted me to know a couple hikers discovered human remains north of here."

"And?"

"And what? It was a courtesy call before the media gets ahold of the story. I'm sure she'll call again soon. Until then, let's try to go about our lives as we always have," Caleb says.

Gabriel wraps his arms around Caleb's neck. "It's gonna be okay, I'm here with you, and we'll get through this together."

"Just one more reason I love you," he says as Gabriel releases his grip and helps him to his feet.

"I think we should get you something to eat. Your face is whiter now than it was when you left the kitchen," Gabriel says.

He nods, and they wander to the breakfast nook in the kitchen.

Caleb takes notice of the clock on the wall in the kitchen as he shovels the last bite into his mouth: seven thirty. The lightheadedness has dissipated, and he quickly leaps to his feet and rushes away. Gabriel stops him.

"Whoa, where are you rushing off to in such a hurry?"

Caleb points at the clock on the wall. "I gotta get showered and dressed if I intend to be in court as scheduled."

"Why can't you call the court clerk and ask for the judge to postpone closing submissions?"

"I wish, but won't happen. Not for a high-profile case like this."

"Look at yourself; you're not in any shape today to get an acquittal for Sanderson," Gabriel says. There is genuine concern in his voice.

"Like I said, kiddo, even though the whole town is talking about this, and the media has coined this 'the trial of the century,' if you ask me, I've wiped the floor with the Crown prosecutor before, and I'll do it again."

"Still—" Gabriel tries to get in a word.

"Stop worrying so much. I'll be home before you know it."

"Still, I wish you'd take a day to gather your thoughts," Gabriel pleads. "Especially before you have to go head-to-head with *him*."

"Him who? Are you talking about Drew Murphy?"

Gabriel nods.

"Please, I'm not worried about him."

"You two have a history together, and he's got something up his sleeve. Maybe call Oliver and have him cover?"

"No way. He's got his plate full this week too. No, work is the best place for me to be right now."

"Always so damn stubborn, just like your mother was."

"See, I get it justly. Besides, it's only one day, and we will have the entire weekend together."

Gathering his thoughts was what he didn't want to do. He didn't want to wallow in the memories any longer. He'd already spent the past twenty months of his life sitting around the house, waiting, expecting Sebastian to walk back through the door and end the cruel nightmare he's been living. But subconsciously he realized after a year that the day Sebastian would return to Torbay was fleeting.

Recently, Caleb hasn't been dwelling on Sebastian as much since he met Gabriel close to a year ago. Sluggishly, he's gotten better, and his life is moving in the direction he wants—but with her call, Dawe tugs at an almost-healed wound and breaks it wide open.

Caleb makes it to the second floor of their modest-sized home and hurries into the bathroom to prepare himself for the big day in court. The bathroom is cold, and a shiver runs up his spine. He turns the faucet to the hottest setting possible, letting the room flood with moisture to increase the temperature. A quick glance at the digital thermometer affixed next to the medicine cabinet sends his head spinning.

Negative six degrees Celsius.

How did I sit outside so long in this cold?

Standing in the middle of the bathroom with his bare body exposed to the chill in the air, he steps into the shower.

Caleb wastes no time finishing up and dressing for the day. Caleb takes one final look in the large rectangular mirror, fixes a stray sandy-blond strand of hair, and dashes out of the steamy room. Racing down the flight of stairs, Caleb snatches his brown leather briefcase from the coatrack in the foyer, grabs his keys, and turns his head where Gabriel greets him.

"All right, I'll see you later this evening," Caleb says as he gives him a kiss on the cheek.

Gabriel still looks unhappy with Caleb's decision and replies with a simple, "Drive safe."

With one foot out the door, he again turns around and makes one final statement. "Ah, shit, I also forgot, Sam and Susan are coming for dinner this evening. You don't mind straightening up, do you?"

"Ah, right, looks like we both forgot about it. Don't worry, I'll take care of the house and getting dinner started." Gabriel gives one of his infamous smirks, the same that caught Caleb's attention when they first met.

He pulls the large, wooden door closed behind him and treads carefully to his Mercedes along the slick porch. Caleb fastens his seat belt and takes one final look at the front of the cabin. He sees Gabriel standing at the window, pulling the curtain back a smidge to watch him leave.

Caleb waves and backs out of the driveway into the roadway. Once the car's out of sight, Gabriel races to the phone and picks up the receiver. He yanks his wallet from his back pocket, pulling out a bi-folded scrap piece of paper. He glances at the seven digits scrawled out and dials apprehensively, tapping his foot against the hardwood floor while he waits for an answer. The plangent, husky voice on the other end answers. "What do you need, Gabriel?"

"We've got a problem."

"Meet me at our usual spot, and make sure you're not followed."

The phone line goes silent, and Gabriel sets the handset back on the cradle. He explores the room; his paranoia is in full control of his brain, and he can't take it anymore; he sprints up the stairs. Once in the bedroom, he grabs a pair of dirty jeans, flannel shirt, and a knitted wool cap from the left side of the bed. As he fastens the final button on his shirt, his head is ringing with his inner voice telling him he must move. He must get out of the house. He's itching at his forearm, and without even stopping to put on a jacket, he snatches his car keys from the bowl and rushes out into the cold.

TWO

February 7, 2017
Morning

THE MERCEDES JERKS INTO A TIGHT parking space along Harbor Drive in the city center of St. John's. The provincial courthouse is two blocks away, which on a beautiful day wouldn't be a noteworthy topic. But it's the dead of winter, and the biting arctic wind makes the short walk unbearable, not only for Caleb, but for anybody brave enough to be out in these punishing elements.

Caleb tosses a red-and-black checkered scarf around his neck, pulling it up to cover his lips and nose ahead of opening the car door. The curse words are already spewing from his mouth before his feet even touch the salt-covered, slushy street, which has already gotten its fair share of traffic.

The car door closes with a thud as the wind batters against his face. Caleb buttons up his long wool jacket over his scarf and pulls the collar of the jacket tighter against his neck.

He rushes along the practically empty sidewalk, fighting the wind with each step. His head turns slightly to his right and he glimpses the snow-covered terrain across the harbor. He takes a moment to pause and take in the beautiful surroundings, but he quickly remembers why he's downtown today.

I must stay focused on Sanderson; the man's freedom is in my hands.

However, still rattled by the unexpected call from Dawe, he can't get his mind off those few words she spoke. Of all days to find out his missing husband may lay on a cold slab in the medical examiner's office, today wasn't the day to learn of his demise during the 'trial of the century.'

He extends his arm, pulls on the handle, and rushes inside the warm courthouse to escape Mother Nature's wrath. Before him is a long line of fourteen people, all waiting patiently to pass through the security checkpoint. Friday wasn't typically a busy day, but with all the media swirling around this case, the courthouse is a shit show, as Caleb expects, with anxious locals lining up to witness closing submissions.

After a brief slowdown, Caleb ultimately gets as far as the X-ray machine where he places his briefcase on the conveyer belt and empties his pockets into a plastic bowl. The machine sucks his belongings inside, all while a gray-haired woman is the only thing standing between him and his escape. She takes her sweet time as if she's on some leisure cruise. Caleb cringes, watching her struggle to grasp orders from the officer in charge of the metal detector.

Jesus, she's gotta be ninety years old. People love a dramatic trial to get the juices flowing.

After the third time the older lady steps through, it beeps again. The crowd is growing impatient, and finally another officer pulls her aside to conduct a secondary screening. A few people behind Caleb clap in exhilaration, knowing the line will finally move again.

Caleb passes through with no problems and recovers his briefcase and items. He knows precisely where he needs to be, and the minutes are counting down until the grand finale.

He stands at the foot of the grand staircase to the second floor, but before ascending he stops to check his phone one last time before switching it to silent.

No texts, phone calls, or e-mails. The only thing on his display is a news alert from his CBC News app about today's trial. He sighs, knowing his future as an attorney rides on winning this case.

He steps onto the first marble stair tread, and the family of the victim, Victoria Wells, brushes past him. They speed by in a hurry to get to the courtroom. Caleb hangs his head in respect, and Victoria's mother, Judith, flings her head back, staring through his soul with her piercing green eyes. Goose bumps shoot up Caleb's arm, her face still transfixed, never wavering. Eventually the skeet walking with her whispers in her ear and her head spins forward.

Caleb respects the law; he put himself through law school, and since the three years he spent there he's had one primary goal: help the accused and guarantee they received a fair and impartial trial. But aiding people, especially the guilty ones, also comes with torment and grief, which he dwells on with every case he works.

The gut-wrenching process sucks, but Caleb recognizes somebody's got to do it, and this path is the one he chose.

After taking his sweet time climbing, he arrives at the second floor but keeps his distance from the Wells family as they hustle inside the courtroom. There's still ten minutes until court begins, and he's in no rush.

His obsession with his phone on this chilly morning has been annoying him. Something seemed off with Gabriel, and he feels the relentless need to confirm he hasn't phoned.

He holds the phone in his right hand and hesitates to dial, but goes ahead anyway. Pressing his thumbprint over the home button, the display comes to life, and staring straight at him is a selfie he took of him and Gabriel climbing a glacier a few months earlier in Iceland.

He searches through the contacts and hovers his index finger over the screen. He gives a glance around before tapping the screen. His heart races. He doesn't even know why he's dialing, but it's too late so he raises the phone to his ear. It rings once and goes to voicemail. He lets out the breath he's been holding.

"Hi, you've reached Gabriel. You know what to do after the beep."

He pulls the phone away quickly before the beep and abruptly hangs up without leaving a message.

What am I doing? Caleb has a hunch something's off, but he also knows how Gabriel is when he's cleaning—music blaring at full throttle—so he relaxes.

He's busy getting things ready for this evening, stop stressing.

Caleb drops the phone into his pocket and heads for the courtroom door. He sighs, shaking his head, and paints the fake smile he has rehearsed so well across his face, even though inside he's distraught and not looking forward to the day ahead.

He whisks through the door to a packed courtroom and trudges along the aisle toward the empty table on the right side of the room. He sees his rival—Drew Murphy, the Crown prosecutor—and sighs.

Caleb touches his hand against the pivoting gateway and shoots a look of death at his foe as he lets his briefcase fall hard against the solid oak bureau. The distraction snaps Drew away from the conversation he's having, and he shakes his head before a huge smirk engrosses his face. Drew's expression doesn't last long, and he focuses his attention back on the associate seated next to him.

Those smirks had become a consistent occurrence over the last few years, but things weren't always this cruel and unstable amongst the two. In fact, Drew and Caleb grew up in the same neighborhood in Mount Pearl, a midsize town southeast of St. John's, and all throughout grade, middle, and high school they spent every waking moment together. There was no better pair of friends in the entire world. But everything changed one spring night during their final semester of law school at the University of Toronto. After graduation, they never spoke friendly to one another again.

Friends and family tried their best to reunite the duo, but with more time deepening their rift, the only thing the help was doing was tearing them further apart.

Graduation day came and went, each of them returning to Newfoundland, but both taking polar-opposite paths in law. The two boys, who always said their aspiration in life was to help those who couldn't help themselves, now couldn't even save each other, and that's when their beautiful friendship ended, and everything became a competition to beat the other.

Caleb pulls out a chair and takes a seat, pops open his briefcase, and removes a few folders. He fans them out in front of him and patiently awaits Justice Julie Rowe to enter in grand fashion.

This wasn't Caleb's first time trying a case before this justice, and although ridged in her style, he found her to be fair and impartial, more than any justice he'd ever worked with. Her no-nonsense attitude complements his, and no one got away with shenanigans while in her courtroom. Of all the justices he might have drawn, she was the perfect fit for this case.

Minutes tick by and Justice Rowe enters the courtroom, which falls silent while everyone raises to their feet. With her presence alone she could command an audience; elegant, but her resting bitch face is dead on. She sits in the oversized, tufted, black leather chair, and the courtroom follows. The room stays silent, and the anticipation mounts as the audience awaits her opening words.

At last, she speaks. "Good morning, ladies and gentlemen."

Caleb and Drew in harmony reply, "Good morning, Your Honor."

"Mr. Winters, is there anything you would like to add before we begin with closing submissions?"

"No, Your Honor."

"Mr. Murphy?"

"Nothing from the Crown, Your Honor," he says.

"Excellent. Bailiff, you may bring in the accused."

The bailiff fetches Sanderson and escorts him in. The clanking of shackles dragging across the marble floor echoes through the courtroom. Sanderson slides into the chair inside the dock, and Justice Rowe gestures she's ready for the jury to enter.

The process takes a few moments, and Caleb sits still in his seat, his head bent forward, reading the words he wants to express to the twelve men and women who will ultimately decide his client's fate.

A thunderous slam of the door closing echoes through the silent courtroom, breaking Caleb's attention. He lifts his head in time to see the jury file into the box and find their seats. A bead of sweat rolls from his forehead and drips onto the side of his face. He wipes it away.

Justice Rowe smiles. "Good morning, ladies and gentlemen of the jury."

They mutter a half-awake response to her greeting.

"Mr. Winters, the floor is yours."

Caleb stands; his knees tremble on his approach to the podium. He sets his speech in front of him and clears his throat.

"Over the past week, you've heard terrifying things about my client, Timothy Sanderson. It's all untrue," Caleb starts. "My client is charged with the heinous act of aggravated sexual assault and kidnapping, and the Crown has done little to connect the dots of how the events transpired."

Caleb's fired up and takes a moment to pause.

"The witness testimony, in this case, has been questionable. Let's begin with the accuser: an ex-prostitute who openly admits to being under the influence of cocaine, ecstasy, *and* alcohol on the night of the alleged assault. This is the same person who has a sordid history of making untrue accusations against associates of my client."

A loud cough from the seating area breaks his thoughts. He takes a deep breath to refocus his mind back on his words.

"Second, if it pleases the court, I want to remind the jury of Ms. Wells's accusation against Mr. Sanderson's business partner, Jeffery Burns, of rape three years ago and that she later recanted her story before it made it to trial."

A soft rumble of whispering voices carried on for a few seconds.

"Ladies and gentlemen of the jury, this will be the final opportunity I will have to speak with you regarding this case. The Crown has given evidence, both testimony and physical, about my client," Caleb continues as he looks around the courtroom. He clears his throat. "Ladies and gentlemen, given the past false accusations from the victim, Victoria Wells, you must weigh her testimony with caution. Also, the physical evidence provided by the Crown is circumstantial. Mr. Murphy and his team have provided no biological evidence to prove with a reasonable doubt that my client sexually assaulted the victim. Given this lack of solid, undeniable evidence other than witness testimony, you must exonerate my client of any wrongdoing in this matter."

Caleb feels another stream of sweat weighing heavily on his forehead. He pulls out a bright white cloth from his jacket pocket and wipes away the sweat quickly before he finishes up his speech.

"To send an innocent man to prison for a crime no one is sure, in fact, occurred would be a grave injustice not only to him but to the entire criminal justice system. Thank you for your time."

Caleb returns to his seat. His short yet powerful statement leaves him confident. But he's also not lying when he accuses Drew Murphy of doing little to prove Sanderson's guilt.

"Thank you. Mr. Murphy, your closing submissions?"

Drew Murphy approaches the podium in his overpriced suit with smugness plastered across his face. Caleb sits with a straight face, but inside he wishes he could stand and slap him. Caleb should pay attention to what his adversary is saying, but the truth of the matter is, he doesn't give a damn what Murphy says. His entire submission will be full of lies meant to make his client look bad.

Caleb glances over at his client across the room, sitting still in the glass enclosure. He despises making his client listen repetitively to the abysmal claims.

Timothy Sanderson isn't a model citizen. The truth is he's ruthless, conniving, and shady in all his business transactions. Caleb knows, however, that through all the despicable events the man has done in his life, rape and kidnapping aren't an expected combination.

After ten minutes of pleading his case, Drew Murphy thanks Justice Rowe and returns to his seat. Clearing her throat once again, the justice turns her attention to the jury.

"Thank you, Mr. Winters and Mr. Murphy, for your closing submissions. Now, ladies and gentlemen of the jury, this now concludes the evidence part of the trial. I will leave you with these words before I release you to deliberate your decision," she begins.

"You must weigh all evidence presented here when you consider your verdict. The Crown prosecutor has presented the court with evidence that looks to prove the guilt of the accused. The defense has provided you with evidence to cast doubt on the prosecutor's series of events. Ultimately, your job as a juror is to decide which side has presented sufficient evidence regarding the law."

Caleb listens, twirling his pen as he waits for her to catch her breath and continue.

"On the first charge in the indictment, aggravated sexual assault, which carries a maximum penalty of twenty-five years in prison, you must consider all evidence presented by the Crown. They must have proven, beyond a reasonable doubt, that the accused, Timothy Sanderson, unlawfully forced himself on the victim, Victoria Wells, against her will."

She pauses again.

"On the second charge in the indictment, kidnapping, which carries a maximum penalty of twenty-five years in prison, you must consider carefully whether the Crown has provided evidence that shows the accused unlawfully confined or imprisoned the victim against her will." Justice Rowe drops her pen in front of her. "Now, I'll excuse the jury to deliberate, and the court shall see you again when you have reached a unanimous verdict," she concludes.

The jury files out through the same side door in which they entered. Caleb leans back in the chair and shuffles all his files into a manageable pile.

All I can do now is wait.

He tosses the files into his briefcase and stands. Almost free and clear of his nemesis, Drew Murphy steps in his path.

With his hand extended and a snarky smirk on his face, Drew speaks, "Good job."

"Go to hell."

Caleb brushes past him and walks through the gate toward the exit.

"Winters, don't be like this, I—"

He swings around faster than he ever has in his life. "You what? Want to throw it in my face? Looking at what you've become makes me sick."

Drew grins proudly, throwing his hands upward. "You haven't changed one bit. Can't even take a compliment anymore."

Caleb scoffs before storming off and there's only one thing on his mind: escaping Drew's presence. He steps into the lively hallway and forces his way through the crowd who stands around chatting about the case.

He pulls out his iPhone to check again for any calls or texts, noting the time, 10:30 AM. A text message from his law partner, Oliver, displays on the screen.

Lunch?

Who can think of food while his client's fate rests in the hands of twelve ordinary citizens? Most of whom more than likely receive their legal and forensics education from the plethora of fictional television shows such as *CSI* and *Criminal Minds*? Things are very different in the real world, but if you try explaining this to people who've never spent a minute working in the field, they look at you like a liar.

He swipes across the screen with his index finger and replies to the message.

Where? When?

His bony fingers stay wrapped around the phone as he
approaches the elevator. Behind him he catches Drew's maddening
voice exit the courtroom with his pack of colleagues. His existence
causes Caleb queasiness and he instead reroutes to the stairs.
Chances are good that if he waits for the slow elevator, he'll end up
sharing the confined space with Drew, something he must avoid at
all cost.

Ugh. God, why are you punishing me?

He descends, rushing to put as much distance between himself
and his foe. As he steps off the last tread, his phone buzzes, and he
reads the response.

Rocket Bakery. Meet you there in five minutes. You won't believe what I
learned.

The theatrical tone implied in the message intrigues him, and the
eyebrow above his left eye lifts subtly. He types out a reply.

Always a flair for the dramatic, eh, Olli?

THREE

February 7, 2017
Morning

C ALEB STEPS ONTO THE SIDEWALK ALONGSIDE Water
Street. The place Olli has picked is a few hundred feet
away, and Caleb wonders along the energetic thoroughfare,
constantly shaking his head from side to side. All he wants
is a warm pick-me-up and a place to escape the bitter cold.

The bakery is in the heart of downtown St. John's, crammed
between an art gallery and a nightclub. Predominantly dotted with
cute boutique stores and a flourishing nightclub scene, Caleb could
never picture himself living in this environment, and it's the exact
reason he built his home near the ocean in the countryside.

Even though a light snow shower engulfs the city, he can make
out the distinctive silhouette of his law partner. The
thirtysomething man shivers while he stands patiently next to the

front door with only a thin fleece North Face jacket covering his
exposed skin.

Caleb approaches and receives a stern greeting from Oliver.

"Took you long enough."

"Where's the alarm? I got here as quick as I could."

"So, you won't believe this news I learned. You ready for this?"

Caleb pulls his scarf tighter around his neck. "Think we can
tittle-tattle indoors? It's cold as fuck out here."

Oliver chuckles and nods.

Once inside they stand in the long line to order, and Caleb
massages his arms with his glove-covered hands, trying anything to
warm himself. He stares at Oliver, who's left him in suspense.
"Man, out with it already. What's this scandalous information?"

"Now, it's unsubstantiated chatter—and none of this fell from
my mouth."

"Oh, for fuck's sake, Oliver—"

"Okay, okay . . . how do I put this?"

"Since when have you ever put anything besides bluntly?" Caleb
asks.

"Hmm, right? I'm always the bearer of unwanted news, aren't
I? It's about Gabriel."

"What about him?" Caleb asks, now worried. "Is everything all
right with him? Did something happen?"

"No, I assume he's fine. But . . . a friend told me this alarming
news."

Caleb's mouth trembles and he presents Oliver with an annoyed
gesture with his hands, the kind that declares: *spit it out already.*

"Let's put it this way . . . old habits are hard to overcome, if you get my drift," Oliver confesses.

Caleb stares vacantly—*What did he say?*

He clears his throat. "So, let me get this straight: the newsflash here is Gabriel's using drugs again?"

"Look, I said it's hearsay, but given his history, I thought you should know. I wanted to wait until after you gave closing submissions to drop this on you. *But* I also didn't want to wait a minute longer either," Oliver says.

"Well, as hard as this news is to receive, I'm grateful you postponed dropping this news on me until now."

"So, what are you going to do?" Oliver asks as the line inches forward.

"The thing I've become good at doing since he and I met; study his patterns, keep my mouth shut, and hope all of this is make-believe. I can't go apeshit crazy on him without tangible proof."

Oliver cocks his head. "Good point. Should I ask my friend to keep an eye on him?"

"Thanks, but I got this."

The line moves again and Caleb's mind spins. Could it all be true? Was Gabriel abusing painkillers again? It's something he doesn't want to think about, let alone deal with again.

Caleb brushes it off—this is St. John's, and many people have too much time on their hands and stick their noses where they don't belong. It's nothing for Caleb to become alarmed about yet.

The cashier gestures for them to approach and Caleb sighs, trying to garner enough strength to refocus his attention on grabbing something to quell his growling stomach.

Oliver steps up first. "Morning. I'll do a small broccoli salad, sausage roll, and the biggest cappuccino you have." Oliver points to Caleb. "And whatever this guy's having, throw it on my tab."

Caleb clears his throat and hesitates. "I think I'll go with a large pasta salad and green tea."

Oliver pays the bill, and the two men slide aside to await their food. Caleb looks around the room for a clock. He spots one. For him, the wait-and-see on when the jury will reemerge from their deliberations begins.

The food arrives, and the two men scavenge the packed restaurant for a place to sit. A two-top table opens in the back of the bistro, and Caleb swoops in like a hawk to claim it.

***

AN HOUR PASSES BY, AND MOST of the patrons have trickled out into the dreary weather to return to their jobs. The waiting for the verdict is driving Caleb insane. He's not accustomed to having to wait this long.

What if he loses the case? Timothy Sanderson is an extremely dangerous man; the whole town knows it. Caleb is sure his client raped and kidnapped Victoria Wells. But Caleb must still defend him, regardless. He took an oath to do so.

He stands. "Another cappuccino?"

"Sure."

Caleb smiles and walks back toward the now-empty counter. Stepping up, the employee takes his order and rushes around, still in overdrive mode from the lunch rush, to make the drinks. Caleb turns his head and catches a familiar face coming through the door.

Drew Murphy.

Caleb's smile turns south, and he taps his fingertips rhythmically across the counter top.

Hustle, little boy.

As the stream of the frothing milk spews into the air, an uneasiness passes over him as Drew inches closer.

Drew clears his throat and the sound catches Caleb's attention. "Winters—they expect a verdict within the next hour. Just wanted to give you a friendly heads-up."

Caleb turns his head. "Thanks for the info."

He returns his attention to the counter in time for the barista to come back with a cappuccino and another green tea. Caleb smiles, takes the paper cups, and returns to his table without another word to Murphy.

Oliver glances away from his illuminated phone. "Thanks, buddy. Did I see Drew Murphy?"

"Yup."

"Did you two speak?"

Caleb huffs. "Unfortunately, he wanted me to know to expect the verdict in about an hour. Olli, I'm nervous."

"You did what you could. Besides, Murphy's 'star' witness is nothing but a manipulator who has a long history of fabricating stories and exploiting men."

"She does, but—ugh, forget it."

"All right . . . I'm not gonna press you."

"You know this is the point where I say I don't want to talk about it, but you're supposed to be stubborn and press me, regardless."

"Fine, you're worse than a woman sometimes. I'll bite—*but* what?" asks Oliver.

"What if this time she's telling the truth?"

"I find it unlikely, but I'll entertain your concern. If Wells is telling the truth, the jury will see it, and your client will go away for a long time."

Caleb quietly listens as he removes the top from his green tea and blows across the surface to cool it.

"And the worst-case scenario here is he didn't do it but they still find him guilty anyhow."

He slouches back in his chair, and his mouth curls downward. *What if he's right? What if I've not done my best and now an innocent man may have to spend the rest of his life in jail?*

Another hour passes, and in front of Caleb sit three empty cups and a law partner who is growing more antsy as the milliseconds tick.

Then it happens.

His iPhone buzzes across the table.

"Winters."

With a few head nods and the traditional "uh-huhs," he ends the call.

"So?" Oliver asks.

"Jury's ready."

"Well, why are we sitting here still?"

"No clue—let's go."

The two men stand and move toward the exit only to have Drew swoop in quickly behind them. Caleb turns his head back over his shoulder and rolls his eyes.

"This man doesn't let up."

"Caleb, let it go—stop letting him get to you."

FOUR

February 7, 2017
Morning

T HE MASSES FUNNEL BACK INTO THE courtroom at fifty-five minutes past twelve, a mere five minutes before proceedings are to resume. The room sits eerily quiet and, considering this is the most significant trial St. John's has seen in a while, Caleb thinks, *Why isn't this place livelier with chatter?* Caleb returns to his seat with Drew hot on his tail. They each exchange cutting looks at one another, and a moment later, in marches Justice Rowe. The onlookers stand to their feet. Her sullen face stares transfixed on the two barristers standing before her. She draws in a breath inconspicuously before speaking.

"You may be seated."

The audience sits, and a low droning echoes unbroken throughout the grand room. A scorned look from Rowe, and suddenly the sound of silence.

"Good afternoon, ladies and gentlemen, I hope everyone had a decent lunch," she begins. "I've been informed the jury has reached a unanimous verdict with regards to *Timothy Sanderson versus Her Majesty the Queen*. At this time, I ask the jurors to be brought in."

A few moments elapse and one by one the jurors file into the jury box while every eye in the courtroom tracks their every move. Caleb turns his head and coughs subtly and catches the bailiff lugging Sanderson into the box.

The jurors situate themselves, but all Caleb can think about is what would become of Sanderson after the trial. Would he walk out a free man, or would he spend the next few years behind bars?

The court clerk stands and faces the jury.

"Members of the jury, it is my understanding you have reached a verdict?" he asks.

A man in his early thirties stands and speaks. His voice booms through the room, "Yes, we have."

"Mr. Foreperson, what is your verdict contrary to section 279, part one of the criminal code with regards to the charge of kidnapping?"

The man clears his throat. "Guilty."

A loud clatter erupts in the courtroom but in true Canadian fashion swiftly subdues.

"What is your verdict contrary to section 273, part one of the criminal code with regards to the charge of aggravated sexual assault?"

"Guilty."

The court clerk directs his attention back to Justice Rowe.

"Both verdicts are guilty, Your Honor."

She keeps a neutral expression and converses directly to the accused. "Timothy Sanderson, a jury of your peers have found you guilty of the charges of aggravated sexual assault and kidnapping. Do you understand?"

Sanderson, appearing dazed, nods his head in agreement without speaking.

Justice Rowe scowls. "For the record, Mr. Sanderson, I will need an oratory answer."

"Yes, Your Honor, I understand."

"Thank you, Mr. Sanderson. At this time, I will call a recess while I deliberate sentencing in this matter. Court will reconvene tomorrow morning at nine."

She exits through a door to the right of the bench, and Caleb hangs his head in disgrace but peeks to catch a glimpse of the bailiff escorting his client from the courtroom.

Caleb wipes his hands against his face before turning his head slightly to look at his foe, Drew Murphy. The prosecutor's face lights up with joy as he elatedly shakes hands with his colleagues.

Caleb gathers enough strength to grunt before pitching the stack of manila folders into his briefcase. The agony of defeat is already upsetting enough, but to make matters worse, his loss is to his worst enemy in the world.

He stands and tries to break away; however, his plan doesn't work out as he hopes.

"Hey, Winters, wait—look, no hard feelings, cool?"

Caleb scoffs. "Right, no hard feelings—no, another innocent man going away for crimes he didn't commit."

"Oh, please. Between you and I, we both know he's guilty. Besides, let's face the truth: I did a much better job persuading the jury."

"If that's what you need to tell yourself to sleep at night, I pity you, Andrew."

"Pity me? You should be congratulating me for getting this scum off the streets."

"Whatever. Look, I have to get back to the office," Caleb begins. "Congrats, though."

Caleb is a few steps away. "See, wasn't so difficult to say, now, was it?"

Caleb rolls his eyes and thinks in his mind of how many ways he could take him out and never leave behind a trace. Nevertheless, he walks back and stands inches from his face. "Ever since we left Toronto, you've changed. I always knew you were shady, but now I'm officially downgrading my opinion even further," Caleb says. "If you'll excuse me, I need to see my client before he returns to jail."

Caleb rushes down the aisle toward the exit, not looking back.

His significant worry has now shifted from Drew Murphy to how his conversation with Sanderson will play out. Even though he lost, and deep down he's witnessed an injustice, he also appreciates that he did everything in his power to get Sanderson aquitted. It's a touching sentiment; however, it didn't change the fact Sanderson would be going away for ten years if the jurors are merciful.

He has the possibility of contesting the ruling, but it is extremely doubtful that pleading would change Justice Rowe's mind.

***

HE HANGS A RIGHT DOWN A CORRIDOR, inching closer to the door where they assemble the accused before trial. He pulls the door open and steps into a confined foyer. He approaches the single corrections officer who is situated in a small office. The only thing dividing Caleb from him is a four-inch-thick reinforced glass window. He retrieves his ID from his wallet and taps on the window. The man eyeballs him, and Caleb drums his fingers on the thin metal shelf while he waits.

"Can I help you?" the officer asks.

"I'm here to see Timothy Sanderson. I'm his barrister, Caleb Winters."

The guard raises a clipboard and runs his pudgy fingers down the list, double-tapping his finger mid-page. "Empty your belongings into one of those blue bins along the wall, and see me when you're finished."

Caleb follows the direct instructions given to him by Officer Sunshine. He drops his wallet, cell phone, and a few one- and two-dollar coins into the container. He returns to the window, where this time the guard speaks no words. The drawer extends out from beneath the thin metal shelf, and Caleb places his entire digital life into the custody of this one officer who doesn't look like he gives two shits to be here.

The drawer slams closed, and a loud buzzing echoes from the massive metal door. He pushes against it, and waiting on the other side is a stocky, redheaded, middle-aged woman with a portable metal-detecting wand in her left hand. She doesn't crack a smile or move from her position.

"Extend your arms outward, like this," she says, giving him visual instruction on what to do.

I've done this hundreds of times, lady.

Caleb extends out his arms while she proceeds to run the metal detector along his body, squeezing at his pants pockets concurrently. She finishes her search and steps back.

"Follow me."

She trudges ahead of him along the lengthy corridor. Her bull-legged gait amuses Caleb as he shadows hot on her tail. They arrive at the end of the hallway, and she extends her arm and points civilly into a tiny room with glass substituting drywall on every side. He peeks inside at a single metal table, two metal chairs, and a ring welded into the tabletop for shackles. The room is cold, devoid of sentiments, and a shiver runs along his back. This isn't the first time to step foot into one of these rooms; nonetheless, his opinion never wavers, no matter how many times he does.

"Take a seat," she says. "Your client will be here in a few minutes."

Caleb pulls out the chair and slouches. He clasps his hands and rests them above his stomach. He waits patiently for Sanderson to arrive, but all he craves is to get the hell out of the room and back to his inviting office. The lull isn't prolonged, and before Caleb can gather his thoughts, the door flings open, and in wobbles Sanderson. The shackles around his ankles clank against the concrete floor with every step he takes, but the most prominent thing is the look of rage and disbelief written across Sanderson's face.

Sanderson's appearance has changed. He isn't the same man Caleb saw in the courtroom not even twenty minutes earlier. No longer dressed in his high-end Hugo Boss suit, he's now back in the orange Department of Corrections garbs with a matching set of ankle and wrist cuffs Caleb has grown accustomed to seeing him in.

Caleb jumps to his feet and stares Sanderson directly in the eyes as the guard helps him to the opposing chair.

Sanderson drops down, rolling his neck until a loud popping sound echoes. Caleb slowly lowers into the chair. Although he can't see himself, he's certain the look of bewilderment is now a look of sheer horror. The guard stands in the doorway. "Five minutes."

The door closes, and Caleb clears his throat. "I don't even know what to say, Tim. I underestimated the jury, and I'm don't know how sorrier I can be."

Sanderson stays silent. His watchful eyes scan Caleb from head to torso. He bends his neck to the other side; another loud crack reverberates. "You fucked up, you know that?"

"I know. Look, I'm going to try and convince the judge to review the evidence the jury used to convict you. It seems farfetched, but it's the only chance we have," Caleb says. "Maybe I can convince her to overrule the jury's decision?"

"And? What if she doesn't? What then?"

"Well, I'll appeal your case. Trust me, we have plenty of legal options."

"You better make something work, otherwise—" Sanderson stops short of making a threat.

"Otherwise what? Go on," Caleb says.

Sanderson takes a moment to collect his thoughts. "Forget I said anything . . . don't leave me hangin', all right?"

"I'll do whatever is in my power to make things right. You can count on that."

Sanderson grunts—that type of grunt where you know someone is feeding you a line of shit to buy themselves time. Caleb stretches out his hand across the table and shakes Sanderson's before standing. He strolls toward the window, knocking to alert the guard he's finished. He never turns his back on Sanderson, keeping his eyes on him the entire time. His client sits peacefully in the metal chair, and the look on his face troubles Caleb. He worries that if he can't convince Justice Rowe to review the evidence, things could get ugly fast.

Where did I go wrong?

The redheaded guard returns, and Caleb rushes from the room, gasping for air as he steps out into the corridor.

"I'm all right."

She looks at him with an annoyed look in her eyes. "You know the way out, yeah?"

"Of course."

"Then have a good day."

Caleb nods and takes a few steps toward the exit. His mind is racing amuck, and he tries hard to keep his focus on getting his client a fair trial. But as he leans against the cinderblock wall, the raspy voice of the guard interrupts him.

"Hey, don't feel sorry for him—this man has ruined the tranquillity of our community long enough and all came to a crashing end today."

Caleb doesn't reply to her judgmental statement. What comeback can he possibly summon on the spot to her comment?

She's right.

Sanderson is a menace to the people of St. John's, and even now with him off the streets, Caleb is fairly sure it doesn't matter; the madness won't stop because he's locked up. He still has plenty of people on the outside ready to carry on his work.

Caleb arrives at the oppressive metal door, and again a loud buzz signals he can exit. He pushes the door open and walks back into the vestibule to retrieve his items. It must have been shift change because a new guard sits behind the glass and speaks through the speaker.

"Can I help you?"

"I need to collect my stuff. Name's Caleb Winters."

The man twists around in his swivel chair and scans through the plastic bins that line the back wall of the small command center. He stops searching and lifts the same blue container from earlier. The drawer skids out, and Caleb tosses his belongings back into his pockets.

"Thanks."

"Have a wonderful day," the guard says in return, a 180 from the earlier guard.

The first thing he checks is his cell phone; two missed text messages.

Where are you?

Anyway, meet me in front of the courthouse at 3 o'clock.

Caleb slips his wallet and keys into his heavy wool jacket before replying to Oliver.

Just met with Sanderson . . . on my way now.

FIVE

February 7, 2017
Late Afternoon

C ALEB RACES DOWN THE BARREN PASSAGE in the direction of the exit. Looking at the time on his iPhone, he sighs with relief; four minutes left to spare. He thrusts his shoulder against the door and scans the area. Straight ahead is Oliver, patiently waiting in the middle of the plaza in front of the courthouse. The snow drifts weightlessly through the air, and Caleb waves his hand above his head to get his partner's attention.

"Hey," Caleb calls out.

Oliver's lips turn upward. "How was the visit?"

"Not good."

"What happened?"

"What you'd guess—he's pissed I lost his case."

"Caleb, it's a done deal now. You gotta let it go and move on to the next case."

Caleb looks down. "I made a promise I'd ask Justice Rowe to revisit the evidence in the case. What do you think my chances are of convincing her to overrule the jury's guilty verdict?"

Oliver laughs hysterically. "I think you'd have a better chance of winning the lottery. Look, I've practiced law for fifteen years, and in that time, do you know how many times I've seen such a thing happen? Nada."

"So you're saying I have a chance?" Caleb sarcastically replies.

"Kid, I don't think it's ever been accomplished in Newfoundland and Labrador."

Caleb sighs again. "Always a first for everything; maybe it's worth a shot."

They stroll along the treeless sidewalk that lines Water Street toward their office building. "You want to get out of this cold and grab a drink?" Oliver asks.

"Any special place in mind?"

"After the day we've had, any place I can get a stiff cocktail is all right by me."

Caleb laughs and smiles.

They're about twenty feet away from the courthouse when a lone reporter ambushes them, blocking their path. "Mr. Winters, Christophe DuBois, CBC Radio One, what is your reaction to today's verdict?"

Caleb frowns. "No comment." He brushes around the youthful correspondent and continues walking.

"Our listeners want to know your reaction; can't you say anything other than 'no comment'?"

Oliver interjects. "Hey, the man said 'no comment,' and that's what he means."

They move quicker, and once they are a few hundred yards away, Caleb finally turns to see the reporter standing in the same spot writing something in his notebook with a look of defeat on his face.

"Jesus, this whole town has gone stupid over this case," Oliver says.

***

THEY ENTER A BRIGHTLY LIT MARTINI bar on George Street and approach the sparsely occupied bar top where a few other patrons sit, coolly drinking their worries away. Caleb pulls out a barstool, dropping his brown leather briefcase to the floor.

He glances in Oliver's direction and sees he's already begun scouring the drink menu. Caleb blurts out, "I should have listened to Gabriel this morning."

Oliver lowers the menu and transfers his attention to his partner. "Huh?"

"You know, the news I got this morning from Constable Dawe. The dead body they found near Old Pond? Is any of this registering in your memory?"

"Wait? You never mentioned anything about Constable Dawe or a dead body this morning. Is she harassing you again?"

"Are you even listening, Olli?"

"I am . . . I swear." Caleb gives him the look he always gives when he catches him in a lie. "Okay, I caught two words."

"I thought so. Anyway, she called to let me know they found some human bones in a shallow grave and thought I should know the RNC were running DNA tests to see if it's Sebastian or not. There wasn't any harassment."

"Shit. Why didn't you call me to take over for you in court? I'd have done it in an instant," Oliver replies.

The bartender interrupts their conversation, and they both put in their drink orders right away. As the handsome bartender walks far enough away, they resume their conversation.

"Honestly, I thought I was good; I am in control. Besides, would have looked odd for me to be there the entire trial and you to do closing submissions."

Oliver nods.

"Hell, it might not even be Sebastian. It'll be weeks before they'll be able to confirm the identity."

"Still, I wish you'd told me sooner. How are you doing?"

"Eh, it's been almost two years. I miss him, but I've also understood this day would eventually come."

The bartender returns with two glasses; a scotch on the rocks for Oliver and a dirty martini, three olives, for Caleb. "Anything else I can grab for you gentlemen now?"

Oliver raises his glass in a toast-like fashion. "Nothing I can think of. Thank you, though." He takes a sip.

"I'm Patrick, you guys need anything, I'll be at the other end, so holler."

"Great. Thanks, Patrick," says Caleb.

Oliver turns his attention back to his law partner. "Where were we?"

"I was telling you, eh, forget it—let's sit here, relax, and discuss something besides work?"

"Sure. What's on your mind?" Oliver asks.

Caleb scans through his head for a different topic, anything other than Timothy Sanderson, Sebastian, or Gabriel and his possible relapse. It comes to Caleb, and he speaks, "How's your wife doing?"

"She's been good, busy volunteering at the food bank. I'll tell her you said—" The slamming sound of the front door interrupts his sentence as it whacks violently against the wall.

"Fuck," Oliver says under his breath.

Caleb spins around in the barstool, and his eyes broaden as two well-known faces enter the bar. He clears his throat and steps down from his seat, marching unwaveringly toward the men.

"You two lost? Biker bar's over on George Street."

The men continue approaching but neither of them speaks. The skinnier of the two cracks his knuckles as he edges closer to Caleb.

"Something I can help you with?" Caleb asks.

"Caleb, Caleb, Caleb. Boss sent us with a message."

"And the message is—?" he asks as Oliver stands.

"You better get him off, otherwise you might find yourself like your husband did . . . buried in the woods," the scruffy, heavier-set man threatens. The man takes his index and middle fingers and forms the shape of a gun and places it against his own temple. "Splat."

"Should I take your statement as a threat or an admission of guilt?"

The man puffs out his chest and throws his hands in the air. "I'm only the messenger. But you'd be wise to listen to our advice."

From across the room, the bartender sees the situation and rushes to the end of the bar. "Is there a problem here?"

The scruffy man sneers. "No, no problem here, *sir*. Right, Caleb?"

"Yeah, everything's okay, Patrick. My 'friends' here were about to leave, right, fellas?"

The scruffy man grins and taps his bone-thin crony on the shoulder. "Uh, right. Enjoy your drink in what peace you have left."

They both laugh and turn away toward the door but stop short. The thin skinhead-looking man looks back and can't contain himself from getting his two cents in. "We're leaving, but we'll be watching you."

Caleb doesn't take his eyes off the two men as the door slams against the wall as they leave. Oliver slips behind him, placing his palm on his back. "Hey, everything all right?"

Caleb gasps profoundly and exhales slowly. "Yeah, guess that's what happens when you do business with sleazy people."

He returns to the bar, snatches the half-full martini glass, and takes a huge swig. He drags the barstool across the floor, sits down, and acts as if nothing happened.

"I won't be insulted if you say you want to head home," Oliver says.

"What? And let those two goons ruin the day. Nah, let's finish our drinks, and I'll go," Caleb says taking a smaller sip. "Oh, tell Steph I said hello."

"What?"

"You know, you were about to say you'll tell your wife I said hello."

"Boy, you don't miss a beat." Oliver sets his glass on the bar top. "You sure you don't want to talk about what happened, or are you going to sweep this under the rug like always?"

Caleb twists his head. "Excuse me?"

"Don't act all sanctified now, Caleb. I've known you for over twelve years, and one thing I've learned about you is you keep enough distance between yourself and others. Why is this? Are you afraid of getting hurt?"

"I'm not afraid. When you're me, you know there's no reason to stress out about things you can't control. The only thing tension does is cause wrinkles, heart problems, and persistent headaches." He takes a gasp of air and continues, "And for your information, I do care, I just have a funny way of showing it."

Minutes tick by and the quiet lingers. Oliver tips his head back and quickly chases the insignificant bit of watered-down scotch remaining in the bottom of the glass.

"Well, my friend, as long as you're okay, I think I'm gonna call it a night and get home early for a change," Oliver says while glancing at his watch. "You should get going too; I'm sure Gabriel's expecting you."

"Right. Well, thanks again for the drink."

Oliver smiles and steps toward the door. "Oh, and please pass along to Constable Dawe about the threat."

"What threat?"

"It was clear as day; that skeet said you'll end up like your husband. Seems like it was an admission of guilt to me."

"Nah, he's talking shit. Don't give those guys the satisfaction of letting them get to you."

Oliver shakes his head. "I'm simply saying the constabulary hasn't released the information to the media yet, so how'd they know a buried body was found."

"Olli, relax. You do realize anyone with a police scanner would know what they found."

"I hope you're right about this. All right, see you tomorrow."

Caleb obliges a smile and Oliver walks through the door into the frozen world. Caleb removes the wooden stick from his glass and bites off each olive before taking a final swig. He nods at Patrick before throwing a twenty on the bar top, slips on his jacket, and he too heads for the door.

***

TWENTY MINUTES AGO, THE SUN FADED below the horizon, and Caleb escapes the bar and walks a few blocks through the light snow along the slushy sidewalk toward his car, which sat parked all day along Harbor Drive. After such an upsetting day, he's nearing his breaking point with information overload. Now, a new major obstacle stands before him: how to address the rumor of Gabriel's relapse. He sighs and composes himself.

I merely want to relax with my friends tonight. After today, I deserve at least that much.

He deliberates some days what would happen if he packed up everything and ran away. The prospect of a fresh start sounds refreshing, yet unattainable. There is no place he could go where someone couldn't find him.

He approaches the car and finds it coated in a thin layer of ice and snow. His digs his brawny hand into the outer pocket of his jacket and feels around until the jagged edges of his keys jingle in his hands. After unlocking the doors, he slouches into the cold black leather seat and fires up the engine. He leans his head back against the headrest and closes his eyes. He dreads having to brave the harsh, nasty weather he escaped, but knowing he can't leave until the windshield is clear, he fetches the ice scraper in the backseat and flings open the door, and he ventures out into the winter wonderland.

After spending a few minutes on the back windshield, he bangs the scraper against the curb and walks toward the front of the car. A flapping scrap piece of paper under the wiper blade forces him to stop and assess the situation. He continues and carefully lifts the wiper to retrieve the crunchy paper. He unfolds it and reads aloud the words scribbled across.

Your picture-perfect life is a lie and it's about to crumble before your eyes— be prepare for the unexpected.

His green eyes glance up and he scans the area. All he finds are a few pedestrians huddling together to keep warm, but none look the type to pen such an uncouth message. He refolds the note and shoves it in his pocket before returning to the task at hand.

The car windows are now free of the wintry precipitation, and he scrambles to the lukewarmth of the vehicle and drives away.

Traffic is nonexistent at this hour, and the silence in the car begins to gnaw at his overactive mind: *I need to hear a human voice.* He searches through the radio stations on the hunt for some talk radio to soothe his nerves.

The clock in the dashboard shows five o'clock, so he stops on CBC Radio One. Naturally, their lead story at the top of the hour is the Sanderson trial. He wants to change it over to music instead, because living through the ordeal was enough and he didn't need a recap of events. However, his curiosity stops him.

"Today, in St. John's, the trial of the century closed with a stunning twist. Timothy Sanderson, local real estate mogul and suspected drug kingpin, was convicted of one count each of kidnapping and aggravated sexual assault. The victim, whom court documents obtained by CBC Radio One denote as 'Vickie,' gave a terrifying account of her ordeal only yesterday. Justice Rowe adjourned court until tomorrow morning when it's expected she will hand down a hefty sentence. We spoke with Crown Prosecutor Andrew Murphy, and he had this to say—"

Caleb rolls his eyes and switches the radio off.

I have no interest in anything that asshole has to say.

He speeds down Kings Bridge Road out of town toward Torbay and spends the remaining twenty minutes in silence. The tiny hamlet is his refuge from the hustle and bustle of St. John's, the place where he can sit and reflect in peace. It's the place where he can escape the chaos his job creates daily.

With all the thoughts spinning, he feels the onset of a migraine creeping from the back of his head to the front. He squints his eyes and focuses on the road.

I wish I could cancel dinner, but I know Sam and Susan have been looking forward to this for some time. This note, though—what could it mean?

***

TWENTY MINUTES LATER HE PULLS THE silver Mercedes into the driveway. The house radiates from top to bottom, and he smiles knowing he is finally home to see the man he loves.

Grabbing the briefcase from the passenger seat, he steps out of the car onto the freshly salted driveway and swaggers to the front porch.

The jazz music wails as he inches closer to the front door, and his hand grabs ahold of the handle and he cracks the door. He expects to find Gabriel waiting for him in the foyer; however, he's nowhere to in sight. Caleb grins but also knows Gabriel has undoubtedly spent the entire day working hard to prepare for this evening. He pushes again on the door and it swings fully open. He sets the briefcase on the floor and looks around: the house is immaculate.

After hanging his jacket on the row of hooks, he yells out, "You home?"

The music abruptly ends and around the kitchen archway appears Gabriel. "Hey, you finally made it home."

Gabriel rushes up and gives Caleb a big squeeze and a peck on the cheek. A moment passes by, and Gabriel doesn't let go, but Caleb presses his hand against his chest and pulls away.

"Yeah. House looks great," he says.

"We have guests coming. I gotta make sure everything is perfect. How'd court go? Did the jury come back with a verdict?"

Caleb's mouth turns downward. "You weren't informed?"

"Of what? Something bad happened, didn't it?"

Caleb nods affirmatively. "They found him guilty."

"That's awful."

"Understatement of the year. Ugh, I need a drink."

Caleb removes Gabriel's hand from his waist and brushes past, heading in the direction of the kitchen. One step in and the aroma of rosemary, red wine, and meat saturates the air. He takes in a deep breath, smiles, and opens the refrigerator door.

He assumes Gabriel is still waiting in the living room, but suddenly Gabriel chimes in from behind him. "How could they find him guilty? You said the case was flimsy, open and closed?"

Caleb pops the top from the beer and grabs a gulp before replying to his boyfriend.

"I thought so too. I guess the jury didn't agree."

Gabriel looks toward the ground, and the room falls silent.

"I need to ask you something. It's pretty sensitive, and I know how you hate confrontation, but something was brought—" Caleb's cut off by the doorbell.

"I think they're here. Can it wait until after they leave?" Gabriel asks as he pats Caleb's chest before rushing for the front door.

Caleb sighs and announces to an empty kitchen, "Yeah, it can wait."

Stop putting stuff off. You will talk to him tonight.

SIX

February 7, 2017
Evening

THE DOOR SWINGS OPEN, AND STANDING THERE are Sam and Susan Butler, still outfitted in their paramedic uniforms. The couple are two of Caleb's oldest friends, going back all the way to second grade. Susan crosses the threshold first, seizing the opportunity to give Gabriel a considerable hug, and soon follows her husband Sam, who stretches out his hand and jokes, "Don't worry, Gabriel, I didn't work on anyone bloody today."

Gabriel laughs, smiles, and extends his hand out.

"I think I'll stick to a handshake, thank you," Gabriel says.

"Glad to see you guys made it." Caleb hugs Susan.

"Wouldn't miss it. It smells like our little Gabriel's been in the kitchen cooking again. What smells so amazing?" Sam asks.

"Red-wine-braised short ribs with whipped potatoes."

"I hope you didn't slave away all day."

"Only a little. No big deal," Gabriel replies.

Sam and Susan hang their jackets and slip off their shoes in the foyer next to the door. Everyone shifts farther into the house and finds themselves where most people do: the kitchen.

"Wine okay for you guys?" Gabriel asks.

"Yeah, a glass of red, if you got it," Susan says.

"Coming right up." Gabriel lifts an open bottle of Chianti and pours the glass half full. He smiles brightly and hands it over.

"Thanks." She takes a long whiff.

"Anytime. And for you?" Gabriel asks Sam.

"I'll take whatever Caleb's having."

Caleb laughs as he throws open the refrigerator door. "Help yourself."

Sam sifts through the bottles and finally settles on a Stella Artois. Pulling his keys from his pocket, he pops the bottle cap off. He lifts the bottle to his lips and takes a big swig.

"Ah."

They all stand around watching Gabriel as he puts the finishing touches on dinner, all the while making small talk about mundane subjects until unexpectedly Susan changes the conversation from dull to something a bit livelier.

"So, Caleb, I overheard on the police scanner they found some skeletal remains out near Chimney Gulch. Did you hear this too?"

Caleb nods but doesn't speak.

"Do you think it's him? Do you think they found Sebastian?"

Caleb scowls, groans, and lowers his head. "I'm not sure yet. But, yes, they did locate some bones. Constable Dawe said they won't know until DNA evidence comes in."

"Damn. Well, DNA is king these days. She'll get in touch when they know, eh?"

"Yeah. Couple of weeks, maybe. Takes a while to be sure," Caleb says before taking a swig of beer.

"Well, if it helps, we find skeletons up there all the time. Hikers do get lost, so let's not jump to any conclusions," Sam says.

Caleb raises his head. "Good point. It's sad, but part of me hopes it's him, you know, so I can put some closure on things. However, another part of me hopes it's not. Whatever happens, I hope it brings me the peace I need."

The room gets quiet and everyone tries to process Caleb's feelings. Caleb isn't the kind of guy who shows his emotions much, but when they come spewing out, everyone stops and takes notice.

After an awkward silence, Sam clears his throat.

"Well, my friend, you'll have the answers soon enough, and whichever way things turn out, you'll be able to move on with your life and on to happier times."

Caleb nods.

I mean, what else can I do in this situation? The conversation continues to spiral further into even more morbid subjects, and Caleb sighs and leans against the butcher-block island. He takes a chug of his beer and stands by and listens.

After a few minutes, he can't take the death talk anymore and breaks up the conversation. "This isn't what I envisioned for this evening, but since we're on appalling news—" he says before Susan interjects.

"Oh Caleb, I didn't mean to bring it up. I'm so sorry. After the day you had, I'm sure you'd prefer to talk about something a little more cheerful."

"Don't worry about it, Susan. Naturally, you're concerned."

"Yeah, man, we're only worried about you, that's all," Sam says in a reassuring tone.

"Thanks."

"So, you have more unwelcoming news to share?" Susan asks.

"Well, other than losing the case today, something else crazy happened."

Everyone is on edge waiting to learn what other news he has.

"After court, I met Oliver outside the courthouse where some reporter from CBC Radio One was on my ass for a statement."

Sam shakes his head in disgust. "They never give it a rest, do they?"

"Exactly. So, neither of us was having it, so we duck into a bar to escape the barrage of questions. We sit down, and wouldn't you know it, not even two minutes later, in walk two of Sanderson's goons."

"Seriously? What happened?" Sam asks as Gabriel pretends to stir the stew, but his ears perk up at the hint of gossip.

"They—" Caleb begins, "eh, it's nothing, I don't want to get into it right now. Nothing but empty threats."

Sam stands and shuffles next to Caleb and softly places his hand on his shoulder. "Hey, we're all here for you."

Caleb nods timidly but forces a smile and squeezes his hand. "Thanks, Sam. Ah, looks like it's time to eat."

The attention turns to Gabriel, who begins dishing potatoes onto the plates.

***

THEY SIT AT THE LENGTHY DINING room table eating in silence. The evening hasn't been the laid-back event Caleb hoped for when he made these plans a week ago, but in all fairness, the day wasn't either. The plates sit empty, but no one speaks. Everything feels uneasy, but finally Susan chimes in.

"Caleb, again, please accept my apology for bringing up such unsettled memories earlier."

"There's no need to be sorry. But since we're on it, I should also apologize for being so despondent this evening. With so many things floating around my head right now, I don't even know up from down. And let's face it, when I'm overwhelmed I can't help but be shorter and sassier than normal."

Susan laughs. "Still the same old Caleb we've known since we were kids—but seriously, if you need someone to talk to, both of us are here."

"Thanks, I welcome the sentimentality," Caleb jokes. "But enough depressing talk. How about something happy?"

Their faces light up.

"Gabriel and I have been thinking about a trip someplace warm. You two interested in joining us?" Caleb asks.

Gabriel scoots his chair away from the table and begins collecting the bare plates. "Gabriel, no, you sit—after spending all day in the kitchen preparing an amazing meal, the least we can do is clean up," Sam says.

Gabriel presses the palm of his hand against Sam's shoulder. "You're our guests. I got this. Do me a favor, though, and don't let him convince you Jamaica is the place to go this year."

Susan shakes her head. "Your boyfriend is so damn stubborn."

Rolling his eyes, Caleb says, "You don't know the half of it."

"Anyway, were there some places you had in mind?" Sam asks.

"Well, Jamaica *was* on the list—however, that's been squashed. Maybe Key West? Or the Bahamas?"

"I can feel the warm sun beating against my pale skin already. Tell you what, I'll scope out prices and see which is the best choice," Susan says.

Gabriel reemerges. "Anyone need a refill?"

Sam lifts his empty beer bottle. "Hit me."

Gabriel snatches the empty bottle and smiles. "Sure. Figure out a place yet?"

"Does Key West or the Bahamas sound good to you?"

"Look, if there's a beach, sun, and the temperature is above freezing, sign me up." He rushes back to the kitchen.

"He's so good to you," Susan comments.

Caleb smiles and rests his cheek against his hand. "He is. I'm a lucky guy, and I never realize it."

***

THE EVENING PASSES BY FAST, AND everyone sits around the wood-burning fireplace reminiscing about growing up in Mount

Pearl, a few kilometers southwest of St. John's. After about a half hour of listening to the stories, Gabriel, who immigrated from Florida three years earlier, grows bored with their trip down memory lane.

"Not to sound like a party pooper, but I'm tired. You guys won't be offended if I crash?"

"You've had such a busy day—feel free to crash," Susan says as she glances at her watch. "As a matter of fact, we should get going too; another early morning for us."

Susan nudges Sam in the shoulder, and he flinches. "Ouch."

"Remember, we have that thing in the morning," she restates.

"Ah, yeah, right—the thing. Busy, busy day for us tomorrow. Saving lives, ya know."

Gabriel gives them both a hug before he wobbles to the staircase. With a final wave, he disappears into the darkness. Caleb lowers his head and stares at the floor for a few seconds.

"Psst, everything okay between the two of you? He seems so distant tonight," Sam says.

Caleb tiptoes closer to the staircase. He makes sure Gabriel is out of earshot before saying anything further. "I'm glad you brought it up. I'm a bit concerned about him after I found out something today."

Sam's face lights up with intrigue. "Something serious we should know?"

"I'm not sure. Olli says his friend saw him talking with a known drug dealer in St. John's last week. I hate to say this, but he might be using again."

"What?" Susan shouts.

"Shh," Caleb begins, "look, I don't know which of Olli's friends saw him, but why would someone lie about something as serious as this?"

"Shit, I hoped we'd never discuss this again," Sam replies.

"What should I do? Do you think I should say something or wait until I have some evidence to back it up?"

Sam and Susan exchange glances. "If it's bothering you—say something now before it eats away at your insides," Sam says.

"Don't listen to him," Susan rebuffs his advice, swatting him away. "If you want my advice, wait until you have something more concrete to back up the conversation. I mean, don't go stirring the pot and possibly ruining your relationship over something that's more than likely mere gossip."

"Thanks. The both of you. I'll think about it before I say anything. However, Sam has a point. With so much stuff on my plate, I should get it off my chest."

Sam smiles.

"But, Susan, your point is also valid. Why piss him off for nothing. You guys never make anything easy, do you?"

"If we did, I doubt our friendship would have lasted this long. Best friends always make your life more difficult," Susan says as she yanks her jacket off the hook.

"Sleep on it and make your decision in the morning," Sam says, reaching for the doorknob. He stops and turns around. "Oh, I almost forgot to ask—how's Drew?"

Caleb scowls. "How do you think? Still smug as ever."

"Figures. I still don't get how two of the closest people in the entire world became enemies overnight. Eh, I guess that's a story for another time, huh?"

"Yeah, not exactly happy memories. I'd prefer that I never have to bring up again what exactly happened in Toronto," Caleb says as his lip droops.

"Duly noted. Well, on that note, night." Sam closes the door behind them.

Caleb stands at the window, watching as their SUV backs out of the driveway into the deserted road. He smiles and releases his hold on the curtain. With the flick of his finger, he kills the lights and takes his time walking through the moonlit house to the staircase.

He quietly ascends the stairs and walks into the dimly lit bedroom to find Gabriel lying in bed on his side. He walks up closer to see his eyes still half open, but he's fading fast.

"Thanks for the amazing dinner," he says softly and leans in to kiss him on the forehead.

Gabriel rustles around and cocks his head to have a better look at him. "For you, anything."

Caleb smiles and turns toward the bathroom to brush his teeth, but the urge to say something overcomes him and he immediately stops in his tracks. He runs his fingers through his wavy blond hair. "About earlier—" There is concern in his voice.

Gabriel sits up straight away and pulls the gray duvet across his bare chest. "Right, you said you needed to talk to me about something."

"I do, it's hard to say, because I know we've talked about this before."

Gabriel grunts and pulls the cover farther toward his face. "What is it?"

Caleb senses his boyfriend already knows what will come next. "Do you love me?"

Gabriel lowers the blanket. "Of course I love you. What a silly-ass question."

"And no matter how hard something is, you'll always tell me the truth?"

"Caleb, you're scaring me. What the hell is going on in your head?" Gabriel asks as he yanks the covers from his body and leans forward.

Caleb sits on the edge of the bed. "Look, I got wind from someone you've been acting extremely secretive lately and this person says they saw you in the company of a known drug—"

Gabriel interrupts. "Lies. All lies."

"Please, don't make this more difficult for me with your attitude. I'm going to ask you straight out: Are you using again?"

"I love you, Caleb, and I'd never lie to you. Look into my eyes. I am not using again," Gabriel says, enunciating each word.

Caleb scrutinizes Gabriel's hazel eyes, and for once in a few months, he feels something. He can't tell what the connection is, but it is more than he has sensed the entire time they've been a couple.

Caleb springs to his feet. "Okay—okay, I believe you. I worry about you slipping back into the old lifestyle. It scares the shit out of me."

"You don't need to worry about me, let alone the entire world. That's your problem; you worry so much about stuff you have no control over and you miss out on enjoying your life."

Caleb stands still and lowers his head. He knows what Gabriel is saying about him is true, and he raises his hands against his face and begins to sob. With all that's happened today, from the phone call to the anonymous note left on his car, it has all taken a toll on him emotionally.

Gabriel climbs out of bed and wraps his arms around his lover. "Caleb, everything will be all right—we've been through worse than this, and God only knows we'll go through more. We have each other, and that's what matters."

Caleb cries uncontrollably to the point where any words he attempts to formulate are incoherent. He buries his face into Gabriel's chest, occasionally gasping for air.

Gabriel softly speaks, "I refuse to let you leave this house tomorrow. I'm going to send Oliver a text and let him know to take over for you in court," Gabriel insists.

Caleb nods and sucks up the mucus that flows from his nose. He stands tall, takes a few deep breaths, and wipes his tears from his red face. Two more deep breaths and he responds, "Well, as much as I'd love for Oliver to cover, he can't. But I do promise to come straight home after court adjourns."

"Straight back—I mean it."

"Yes, mom," Caleb replies. He scoots across the bed and slips underneath the sheets, reaches for the lamp on the nightstand, and clicks it off. The only thing he wants now is sleep, and he prays that when he awakes in the morning, maybe everything will have been a terrible dream.

SEVEN

February 9, 2017
Early Morning

C ALEB STANDS FACING THE COFFEEMAKER, WAITING for the pot to finish brewing. The house sits silent, a little too silent for his liking. He tries to keep the ruckus to a minimum, trying his best not wake Gabriel, who lies fast asleep upstairs. Each morning he enjoys the few moments of solitude before he pours the first cup of coffee, and with everything happening so quickly in the past twenty-four hours, the silence is comforting on some level. He knows Gabriel has good intentions by trying to force him to stay home, but the overprotectiveness grows more annoying than concerned.

The coffeemaker beeps, and Caleb pulls the carafe before it finishes dripping the last few drops. He picks up his favorite mug, which his husband Sebastian gave him years ago after Caleb passed the bar exam. He fills the cup to the brim and grips the handle tightly in his hand. He quickly takes a sip and flips the mug around to read the quote, which always makes him grin: "Lawyers: Because people are idiots."

He sniffs the nutty fragrance intensely and beams. He recalls the day before and replays the sentencing hearing in his head. He pleaded with Justice Rowe to review the evidence; however, his plea left her unmoved and her two-word reply echoes around his mind: *Request denied.*

Ultimately, Timothy Sanderson did receive a sentence of ten years for both crimes, to be served concurrently—considerably lighter than the greatest penalty of twenty-five years for each crime, which is what Caleb expected.

He takes another sip. The howling wind beating against the house compels him to approach the oversized picture window to peek outside. The fresh powder swirls about, and he gazes past the trees, hoping to catch a glimpse of the picturesque ocean view he's grown accustomed to seeing each morning, but instead he sees nothing more than a whiteout blur.

He steps away and pulls out a barstool. He stays stout emotionally, but the reality of knowing that any moment he might receive a call from Constable Dawe is slowly driving him insane. It doesn't matter that he knows analyzing DNA doesn't happen overnight; the wait is driving him insane, and he wants to put finality on the mystery of what happened to Sebastian. Until he knows the truth, Caleb can never move on to the future, a situation that not even Caleb has control over.

The creaking from the floorboards in the living room echoes and interrupts his thoughts. He glances up in time to notice a transitory glimpse of Gabriel stumbling, half-awake, toward the coffeemaker. He coughs and lifts his coffee mug to his lips.

"Morning," Gabriel mutters.

"Good morning," Caleb replies, sitting down his mug. "You sleep okay?"

"Eh, so-so. Damn wind woke me up a few times."

"Yeah, the weather reports this morning mentioned a storm's moving in. I hate driving when the weather is like this."

"Huh? You're not going back to work—*already*?"

"I know you don't agree, but it's better for me to go in. It will help take my mind off everything."

Their eyes lock, and Gabriel throws up his hands. "What I think you need is to slow down a bit. But, hey, you're almost forty, and you can do whatever you want with your life." He folds his arms across his chest, gives a disapproving look, and storms off upstairs.

The tension around the house has yet to achieve its peak since the confrontation Tuesday night, but regardless of this new setback, Caleb feels things are gradually reverting to normal.

Even now, Caleb's brain wonders if his decision to confront Gabriel was the right one. Caleb shakes his head.

I need to get to the bottom of what's gotten into him lately.

Another sip before he steps off the barstool. He needs to escape. *Anywhere but here is where I want to be.*

All the drama, pettiness, and arguing makes his head spin. He knows at the office he can evade nonsense and get back to his life's passion: helping people who *want* help. A quick glance at his watch and his eyes widen.

Seven fifteen.

Time flew by quicker than he assumed in his flurry of emotional tug-of-war. If he hopes to make it to the office by eight thirty, he needs to step up his sense of urgency.

He races upstairs and whizzes into the bedroom. Tugging both doors to his closet open, he pulls out a suit and blue Oxford shirt and hangs them from the edge of the dresser. Whirling around he suddenly pauses when his eyes spot Gabriel parked on the edge of the bed. His head droops and he covers his face with both hands.

"Hey . . . is everything okay?" Caleb takes a seat next to him.

"I guess so. I worry about you . . . us . . . a little too much. That's all."

"I don't know why you do this to yourself. I'm fine. I promise."

"Something's changed between us lately, and I don't know what."

"I don't get it. I'm the same guy you met in the drab bar on George Street. Listen, I think this whole Sanderson trial and the constabulary has us on edge."

Gabriel lifts his head, exposing his bloodshot eyes. "Yeah, it has, but something about you has changed, and the sad reality is you can't even see there's a problem."

"No, I suppose I don't see because I don't think I've changed. Look, how about I work a half day and when I get home the two of us can go out somewhere nice for dinner? Just the two of us," Caleb says.

He wraps his arms around Gabriel's chest and pulls him in closer.

Gabriel sniffles. "God, I hate how you always make everything seem okay even when it's not."

"So . . . I'll take your response as confirmation," Caleb laughs.

"Yes. Go, get ready for work so you can come home sooner. I'll think of a couple of places I'd like to go."

Gabriel flashes a smile, and Caleb relaxes his hold. Calen steps onto the floor and continues his mission of gathering the rest of his clothes. He thrusts the dresser drawer closed and spins around to take another look at Gabriel, who sits on the edge of the bed, staring off.

"Hey, I love you. You know this, right?"

"I know you do, and I love you too. Now go—get ready, and we'll have a fun night ahead of us."

Caleb disappears through the door to the bathroom but leaves a crack in the door. Gabriel stays still and waits a few moments until the sound of water splattering gives him confidence he's alone. He quietly pulls out his cell from his pajama top, presses his thumbprint against the home button, and the screen comes to life. Scrolling through his extensive contact list, he stops when he reaches the name he hunts. He presses send and walks to the far corner of the room.

The anonymous person answers after one ring. "Same spot as the other day?"

Gabriel listens intensely to the voice on the other end of the line and nods. "Yeah, okay, let's say an hour, give or take a few minutes." He ends the call abruptly and sets the phone on the nightstand.

The splattering sound trails off and Gabriel overhears the creaky glass shower door open. He casually walks toward the bathroom and lightly taps once against the solid wood door.

"Hey, I'll be running into town in a bit. Any special requests?" he shouts.

Caleb peeks his head out of the shower, which billows out steam. "Nothing I can think of, but you'd know better than me what we need. Just make sure we have extra coffee, wine, and beer on hand in case we have visitors over the weekend."

Gabriel fully extends the door open. "I'll make sure we're stocked up." He steps forward and plants a kiss on Caleb's cheek.

Caleb smiles and pulls away to look at Gabriel. "So, I take this as we're past all the tension."

"Well, I still worry about you; however, I can't stay mad forever. Anyhow, let me make a list and I'll head out."

"Okay, be safe out there. Weather kind of sucks."

Gabriel leaves the steam-filled room and meanders downstairs to plan out his shopping list. Meanwhile, Caleb situates himself in front of the foggy vanity and wipes his hand across the glass. He stares at himself in the mirror and reflects on how lucky he is for allowing himself to tear down the walls he'd built around his heart. If he never had, he wouldn't have such an amazing man in his life.

And falling in love again after spending nearly a year in mourning was no easy feat. Not knowing where Sebastian went haunts him every day, but having Gabriel in his life now is truly a godsend.

He sighs, smiles, and pulls out his toothpaste from the medicine cabinet.

***

GABRIEL WAITS PATIENTLY AT THE FRONT door for Caleb to return downstairs. Caleb walks into the foyer and sees Gabriel standing with his hand on the doorknob.

"Waiting for me?"

"I wouldn't leave without a proper good-bye."

"I hope not."

With a quick movement, Gabriel kisses Caleb on the lips and hurries through the front door into the winter wonderland. To an outsider, Gabriel's appearance looks more fitting for someone going on a hike in the woods during a blizzard than a quick trip to the grocery. But when the temperature outside hovers around negative three Celsius, fashion goes out the window in Newfoundland.

Caleb stands by at the large picture window in the foyer, watching Gabriel back out of the driveway and into the deserted road. He waits for the silver Mercedes to disappear into the blinding snow.

He backs away from the window, allowing the curtain to flutter. He walks away, and a strange sense shoots up his spine; however, he lets it go. He wanders into the kitchen to grab a snack and a refill for the road.

He snatches his keys from the side bureau and ventures out onto the porch.

EIGHT

February 9, 2017
Evening

CALEB ENTERS THE DARK HOUSE AFTER spending longer than expected at the office. He already knows an earful from Gabriel awaits, but when the front door swings open, the house sits eerily silent. So quiet the ticking from the grandfather clock in the other room beats at a regular pace. He steps inside and flips on the light switch.

Where is he? It's not like him to not be home.

He searches the house from top to bottom, starting his quest upstairs in the owner's suite, the guest room, and eventually finishing in the kitchen. Caleb flings open the refrigerator to find no new groceries inside, and there are no signs Gabriel ever returned from his trip to the grocery. Panic sets in, and he does what any logical person in this situation would do: he bombards Gabriel's cell with calls.

Voicemail. Fuck.

He looks down at the phone but hangs up before the beep.

Searching frantically through his contact list, the first trustworthy person's name he comes across is Sam's. He dials, and after one ring his lifelong friend answers. "Hey, buddy, what's up?"

"Eh, you know, another long day. Hey, have you seen or spoken with Gabriel today?"

"I haven't. Why, what's up?" Sam asks.

"Not sure, but the house is empty, and when he left out this morning he said he was going to the grocery, but it doesn't look like he went or even made it back home. I'm worried; it's not like him to not call if something came up."

"Yeah, that's out of character. Did you try calling him?"

"Repetitively. Every time it goes straight to voicemail, which, again, is odd," Caleb replies.

"Well, listen, I'll keep a lookout for him, and if I do see or hear from him, I'll make sure you're the first person he calls."

"Thanks."

"Oh, by the way—Nicole and I want to stop by in about thirty minutes, I mean, if you're okay with it."

"Oh, she's the ditzy one, right?"

"She's special," Sam laughs.

"Yeah, come on by. Where's Susan this evening?"

"She's off. You should give her a call; maybe she's seen him." The squelching feedback from the ambulances radio reverberates across the line and right into Caleb's ear. "Hey, I gotta go save another life. See you after this call is over."

The call drops and Caleb stands in the middle of the living room. He grips the phone in his right hand and presses the power button to illuminate the screen. Staring back at him is a recent photo of him and Gabriel on a hike, and Caleb hangs his head.

The suspicion in his mind runs amok, but he doesn't dwell on the feelings too long before he decides to phone Susan. After two rings her sweet, gentle voice pierces across the line.

"Caleb, I was thinking about you."

"You were?"

"Yeah. Wondered how the two of you are doing?" she asks.

"I'm good, but I'd be even better if my other half were here."

"Where is he? Something going on?"

"Well, he's not home, his cell's off, and I'm trying hard not to have a breakdown. You haven't seen him around town today by chance?" Caleb asks as he sits down on the couch.

"No, but again, the only place I went was the market this morning. Maybe he's somewhere with no cell coverage?"

"Hmm, maybe. Wait, he went to the market this morning too. You didn't happen to see him there?"

"Don't think so. He would have stopped to chat. I'm pretty sure it was only me and a couple of old folks."

Panic builds, and Caleb's words quiver. "Per-perhaps you two missed each other. Eh, what am I saying? I'm overreating."

"Well, you have been a little on edge lately, but, yeah, you're right," she says jokingly as she listens to Caleb's heavy breathing. "Are you sure everything's okay? I'm getting a sense of panic."

"I think I'm having a high-anxiety day. It only gets worse when I'm confronted with not knowing every little detail of what's going on. But don't worry yet, I'll do enough for the both of us."

"Well, it's best if you take it easy, watch some TV, and if I do hear from our little chef, I'll make sure you are the first person he calls," she replies.

"Thanks, Susan. Okay, well, I suppose I better do something other than phone everyone in Torbay to ease my mind a little."

"All right, if anything changes, call me."

Caleb smiles and hangs up. He lets the phone slip from his hand onto the coffee table, and he plops back against the couch.

Maybe something came up . . . I gotta stop being so wary.

He reaches for the remote, presses the power button, and the television comes to life. He flips through the channels until he comes across a rerun of *Will & Grace* from 2001. It's been ages since he'd caught the show, mainly because cuddling on the couch watching comedy shows was something he and Sebastian always did together, and he could never bring himself to do it with Gabriel. Instead, he and Gabriel cook, argue, and sleep. A mediocre, unexciting life, but that's the way Caleb desires things.

He reaches for the blanket behind his head and snuggles it across his chest. He allows the remote to fall on the sofa, and he lays horizontally on the couch, resting his head against a throw pillow.

***

FORTY MINUTES PASS, AND CALEB has passed out, but a loud knock at the front door awakens him from his light sleep. He chucks the white fleece blanket away, clicks off the television, and jumps to his feet. The banging persists, and in his unsteady condition, it takes him a bit longer to move toward the door.

He unlocks the deadbolt and pulls the door open. Standing before him is broad-shouldered Sam and his partner, Ditzy Nicole (as he refers to her). "Jesus, scare the shit out of me."

"What? I told you we were stopping by. Everything all right?" Sam asks.

"Yeah, sorry, I fell asleep. Come, come in—get out of the cold," Caleb says, stepping aside.

Sam and Nicole step inside and Sam brushes away the thin layer of fresh snow that coats his dark blond hair and his jacket. Caleb smiles and gives his famous goofy smile in return.

"Still no sign of Gabriel?" Sam asks.

Caleb looks around the room. It is still in the same state it was before he nodded off. "I guess not. You know Gabriel. This isn't like him, huh—I'm starting to worry something bad has happened," Caleb nervously says.

"Let's not get ahead of ourselves," Sam replies and points at the couch. "Come, let's all sit down and talk this out."

Caleb doesn't let up with his panic. "I mean, the roads look pretty bad, what if he's driven his car off into a ravine somewhere and no one can see him, or worse, what if—" Caleb's voice trails off.

They sit on the couch and Sam tries to get out ahead of Caleb's incoming panic attack. He rests his firm hand on his back, but it has the opposite effect.

"Sam, do you think something terrible has happened?" Caleb asks.

"What do ya mean?"

"Remember what I told you the other day, you know, about Sanderson's goons?"

"Well, you didn't tell me the whole story, but what about them?"

"You think they could have done something to him?"

Sam takes both hands and grabs Caleb, pulling him to look at him straight in the eye. Sam's lower lip quivers while he thinks hard about the right thing to say. The only way to be with Caleb is as blunt as possible.

"Sanderson's a bully, and we both know it. I don't know what went down at the bar, but don't stress over what those guys said," he begins. "Nicole and I will get back out there and search for him, right?"

Nicole nods, and Caleb tries to slow his breathing, doing whatever is necessary to pull himself out of his panic attack.

Nicole reaches out her hands and squeezes his. "We're gonna find him, I promise. We need a lil bit of time, honey, okay?"

Sam sighs and rolls his eyes. "Look, I realize these past few years haven't been the easiest, with losing Sebastian and all—"

Caleb scoffs. "That's the understatement of the year. I have this gnawing sensation in the back of my mind I can't shake. This all feels so eerily like the circumstances surrounding Sebastian," Caleb begins. "And to top things off, Gabriel and I have been at each other's throats since I confronted him about the rumors of his renewed drug use."

"I'm sorry, you did what?"

"Tuesday night, after you and Susan left, I confronted him. He, of course, denied all of it."

"I don't know what to say, other than I'm shocked you had the balls to confront him. Well, knowing this, is it possible Gabriel took off? You know, take some time away to think about things?"

"Doubtful. First, where would he go? All of his family is in Florida, and they aren't cool with the gay thing. No, no—if he wanted some space, he's blunt enough to tell me straight out and he'd at least tell me where he was going," Caleb replies.

Sam looks over at Nicole and pulls out his cell phone. "Why don't we ring him one more time before we head out, hmm?"

"No argument from me," Caleb says.

Caleb sits next to Sam, bouncing his leg uncontrollably and nibbling at what's left of the fingernail on his index finger. Sam puts the call on speakerphone, and instead of ringing the call goes directly to voicemail—exactly how Caleb described it to him earlier.

"We'll find him, all right? While we're on the topic, has the trifling constable been in touch with you about those remains?"

"Nah, I don't expect to find out anything for a few weeks. We both know DNA analysis takes time. Why do you ask?"

"No reason. I find it strange you get the call a few days ago about some remains and Gabriel starts acting all weird."

Caleb jumps to his feet, looking ready for a fight. "And what in the hell do you mean, exactly? Something you aren't sharing, Sam?"

"Calm down and sit. You're misunderstanding my observation. When did the arguing start? Hmm?"

Caleb takes a moment to think about the question. "A couple of days ago."

"Exactly. The constabulary calls you, you lose the Sanderson case, but also learn Gabriel's possibly doing drugs again. So you, as the loving boyfriend you are, call him out. Clearly, you triggered something in him to make him act out."

Caleb is speechless.

"If you ask me, this is the type of shit people do when they're caught," Sam sternly says. "So, excuse me, but I need you to check yourself before you go freaking out on me."

Caleb cocks his head to the side. He needs a minute to process what Sam is trying to explain. "You're right. I'm sorry. When you put it that way, his behavior's been off lately. Perhaps tomorrow I should pay my client a visit and tell him to back the fuck off. Do you —"

The squelching of the radio attached to Sam's shoulder interrupts his comment. Sam replies to the dispatcher, and the two medics jump from their comfortable positions abruptly.

"Hate to do this to you in your time of need, but we gotta go. Someone slid off the road and into a ditch. Do yourself a favor, relax and watch a little TV."

"Okay."

"I'm entirely certain if you focus on something else for a while, it'll help put your mind at ease," Sam says as they move toward the foyer. "You want me to swing by after my shift is over at midnight?"

"I'm sure I'll need the company, so, yeah, swing by."

"Cool. See you in a bit." The door slams closed, and Caleb stands alone amid the spacious living room. The wind picks up again outside and strikes angrily against the triple-pane windows, and the startling thud sends a shiver down his spine.

***

CALEB RETURNS TO HIS WORN-OUT SPOT on the couch and snuggles back under the blanket. He turns the television back on and glances at the clock on the wall; it's seven fifteen. Not even ten minutes pass before Caleb dozes off again into a light sleep. The easygoing hum of laughter in the background comforts him; however, his relief is again interrupted by a loud thump at the door, and his eyes flicker open.

His body shakes with fright, and he races into the foyer, hoping and praying the person on the other side of the door is Gabriel.

Regrettably, the person who greets him isn't the one he hopes it is.

"Did I wake you again?" Sam asks as he steps inside to get out of the blustery wind.

"Yeah, I sort of snoozed again. Any sign of Gabriel out there?"

"That call took longer than I thought, but the places where we traveled we didn't see his car anywhere. I hate to say this, but perhaps it's time to get the constabulary involved," Sam suggests.

"Tomorrow morning I'll call, if he doesn't show up. Sam, I trust you more than anyone. Tell me the truth—do you think Sanderson has something to do with this?"

"I couldn't put it past the guy. He's ruthless, demented, and psychotic enough to try to pull a stunt like this."

And it's those words that send Caleb's mind whirling. Indeed, it is possible Sanderson got to his boyfriend from behind the thick, impenetrable cinderblock walls of the prison, and there wasn't a damn thing Caleb could do about it now.

NINE

February 10, 2017
Morning

C ALEB WAKES ON THE COUCH TO THE sound of birds chirping outside the window. He slowly sits up and takes a glance in the full-length mirror across the room. His blond hair endures the backbreaking sleep on the hard sofa, but his dress slacks and white Hugo Boss shirt don't fare so well. To an outsider scrutinizing his shallow façade, one would presume he didn't sleep—but Caleb is positive he did, even if only a few hours' worth.

He yawns and stretches his arms into the air. He's parched. And looking at the three empty beer bottles on the coffee table, it's clear why. He sighs and sweeps his fingers against his face, brushing off the stiff drool that clings to the corners of his mouth. The crusty flecks tumble onto his wrinkled pants.

Shit.

With his eyes cleared out, he surveys the room eager to find some sign Gabriel crept in sometime last night. However, he looks to his right, then left, and his optimism instantly sours when he finds everything the way he left it.

Sam left the house around two in the morning, right in time for the snowstorm outside to kick into high gear. And truthfully, Caleb isn't even sure his best friend arrived home safely or not because after three beers, falling asleep wasn't difficult for him to do.

He reaches for his phone, which somehow slipped between the two cushions, and he finds several missed texts from Sam.

> *I made it home safely.*
> *You're probably asleep by now, but everything's going to be okay.*
> *I'll call you in the morning.*

While the messages give him a sense of relief, the sense dwindles when he searches for any other texts or calls; nothing else came in.

He meanders to the front door, cracks it, and takes in the aftermath of Mother Nature's fury. The shining sun is deceptive. One might assume it a beautiful day. Instead, ten inches of fresh powder greet him. And to make matters worse, a three-foot snowdrift towers at the end of the driveway.

He shakes his head back and forth.

I was right; a storm did come.

With a loud thud he closes the door and like a lunatic he races through the house, shouting Gabriel's name. But the desolate aura lingers. *Something far more sinister is going on.* This isn't your typical lover-needing-space situation—Gabriel's disappeared. Though, whether the choice is voluntary or involuntary is still a mystery.

He descends the stairs and stands in the middle of the living room. He inhales deeply, closes his eyes, and gets in tune with his body. His palms are sticky, and he's growing more lightheaded with each passing second he holds his breath. But now the time has come, the thing he dreads doing is about to occur. He must contact the constabulary and issue another missing person's report.

His hands shake. The adrenaline takes over his body. He feels his neck muscles constrict around his windpipe. Not only does the RNC still believe him to be their main suspect in Sebastian's disappearance, but reporting a new disappearance will only thrust him onto their radar again. And the thought of going through another investigation sends anxiety through his mind. Will he survive emotionally?

He doesn't have to search through his contacts, considering Dawe's office number remains etched in his brain. It may have something to do with the fact he spent many sleepless nights phoning her for an update.

The phone rings twice, and with her infamous straightforward voice she answers with one word.

"Dawe."

He clears his throat. "Good morning. This is Caleb Winters."

"Ah, Mr. Winters. You're calling for an update on the remains?"

"Eh, not entirely."

"Oh. Well, since I got you on the line, our forensics team sent off the DNA yesterday. I did put a rush on it, but even so, it'll still be seven to ten days."

"Okay," his voice crackles.

"Is there something else going on?"

He stutters. "Um, my boyfriend," he pauses. "My boyfriend, Gabriel Parsons, he's—"

"Has something happened to him?"

"I'm not sure. You see, he didn't return home yesterday, and I've spent the last twelve hours trying to contact him on his cell, but I always get voicemail."

"Is this out of character?"

"Yes. So, I guess I need to file a missing person's report."

A hush falls momentarily. Caleb stands in the living room, one hand firmly placed underneath his armpit. Those three words, words he never thought he'd ever utter again in his lifetime, haunt him. Dawe coughs and begins speaking.

"Where are you now?"

"Home."

"Okay, I'm finishing up with another matter, but my partner and I will drive out to see you afterward."

"Okay."

"Give us about an hour."

"I'll be right here." He sighs. "See you soon."

"One thing—if he does happen to show up before I get there, can you give me a quick call on my cell? You should still have the number."

"I think so, let me check."

He pulls the phone away from his ear and puts her on speakerphone while he searches his contact list. He explores under

"D," and she's the first name that appears. "I have a number ending in zero, eight, nine, nine. Still the right number?"

"Yup, that's it. Remember, call if he shows up."

"Thanks, I will."

Caleb hangs up and paces. His head floods with a wide range of emotions spanning from anger to fear, sadness to embarrassment. The main thing on his mind is worrying how this same constable turned his life upside down in the past, and now another lover has gone missing, which means one obvious thing: he needs to prepare himself to have his life altered again.

Always surrounded by lawyers, law enforcement, and essentially anyone attached to the criminal justice system, Caleb has a keen idea of how things work: the lover or spouse are always guilty until proven innocent.

If he believes the fifteen months of harassment he endured from this constable, the same one who is about to enter his house again, was bad, this time he's certain it will be worse. He stops pacing and phones the one person he knows he can count on: Sam.

The phone rings twice. "Hey, what's up?" Sam asks with a tired tone.

"I need your help."

"Oh, I was hoping you were calling to tell me Gabriel came home."

Now on the brink of tears, Caleb says, "No, I wish that's why I was calling, but it isn't. Can you and Susan come over right away? I need someone to be here when Dawe arrives."

"Oh, for fuck's sake, Caleb, not her again."

"Please, I beg you."

Sam grunts. "Yeah, we'll be there in thirty minutes."

Caleb's begins to spew out a thank-you, but before he even gets the "T" out, the lines goes dead.

***

AN HOUR PASSES BY, AND CALEB, Sam, and Susan sit irritably in the living room awaiting the arrival of Constable Dawe and her partner. After ten minutes of silence, the awkwardness breaks when a booming knock jolts them.

"That's one hell of a police knock," Sam says jokingly, attempting to alleviate the edgy mood.

"Wait. What does a 'police knock' sound like?"

"Uh, pretty much what we just heard. You two wait here, I'll get the door," Sam insists as he gets up from his comfortable position on the couch.

He moves toward the door and pulls it open. The homely face staring back is one he explicitly recollects. However, just to her side is a fresh face, and it shocks Sam they assigned her a male partner.

"Ah, Constable Dawe, always a pleasure to see you," Sam says, extending his hand to shake. "And this is?"

"Constable Barnes, sir, it's nice to meet you, uh—" Barnes stops short when he realizes he doesn't know who he's speaking with.

"Sorry, Sam Butler, lifelong friend of Caleb's. Please, come in before you catch a cold out there."

Sam moves away to let the constables come in.

"Thanks," Dawe sarcastically replies.

They stand in the foyer of the house, waiting for Sam to make the first move. After hanging their jackets, they walk through the dining room into the living room, where Caleb sits next to Susan. A minute ago, all was good, but now his hands cover his face.

"Mr. Winters." Caleb raises his head and vacantly glares in her general direction, although Sam isn't sure if Caleb even knows where he is.

"Please, constables, have a seat," Sam says. "This is my wife, Susan."

Susan stands. "Thank you for getting here as quick as you did."

"Of course. So, Mr. Winters, you say your partner is missing." Dawe wastes no time with worthless small talk and jumps right into the questioning.

Caleb nods but can't muster up the energy to articulate a coherent sentence. He breathes and clears his throat. "Yeah."

"Okay. By the way, this is my new partner, Noah Barnes."

Caleb extends his hand, and the young man returns his kind gesture. "Nice to meet you."

"Indeed. It's nice to put a face with the name," Barnes replies.

When Sebastian vanished, Dawe worked the case alone. Caleb sits back, coyly sizing up her new partner, but he's unsure of what to make of him. All he sees is a young, fresh-faced gentleman with a slight five o'clock shadow. Barnes keeps a good six inches between him and Dawe. He flips open his notepad and glares at Caleb with his dark, mysterious eyes.

"I'm ready to begin when you are," Barnes directs his statement at Dawe.

Dawe smiles for a split second, but it quickly fades and her usual scowl returns. "So, when was the last time you saw your boyfriend—Gabriel Parsons, right?"

"Right. Um, the last I saw him was yesterday morning around eight. I wasn't exactly paying attention to the clock."

"I see," Dawe replies as Barnes jots a few notes in the notepad.

"What about a physical description? The usual—height, weight, what he was wearing the last time you saw him."

"Well, he's thirty-four, around five feet eleven. Um, let's see, short brown hair, hazel eyes . . . I have a photo, if it helps." Caleb stretches his hand for his phone lying on the coffee table.

"That'll help. You can text it over in a bit," she says while Caleb fidgets with the phone. "Do you know if he had any plans yesterday? Any errands? Work meetings?" Dawe asks.

"He works from home, and the only thing he had on his agenda was to visit the market."

"Which one?"

"The Foodland on Torbay Road."

"Okay, I know it well."

Caleb watches as Barnes scribbles the name in big letters on his notepad and lifts his head to return to the questions.

Then suddenly things turn a bit more accusatory, true to Dawe's way of operating. "How's your relationship been lately? Have you had any arguments or problems?"

Caleb groans while Sam and Susan share a split-second glance at one another. "Of course, you'd have to take things there, huh? But to answer your question, yes, we had an argument on Tuesday evening. But otherwise our relationship is strong, and we don't have problems any other good relationship doesn't. We worked out the issue, and we've been trying to move forward."

"May I ask what led to this argument?" Dawe asks.

"I'd learned from my law partner he might be using drugs again. I confronted him—but he denied it." Caleb hangs his head in shame.

Sam interjects. "He's telling the truth. He asked my wife and me for advice before we left on Tuesday evening."

"Thank you, Mr. Butler—your comment is noted. Now, Mr. Winters, has Gabriel gone missing like this before?"

"No, never, this is the first time. The only people in the area Gabriel knows are my law partner, Sam, and Susan. He immigrated from Florida in December of 2014, so if he went anywhere, chances are good he went back to Miami where his family is."

Constable Barnes chimes in. "But he never mentioned or even gave you a hint he might go back to Florida, correct?"

"No. We don't keep secrets from each another. If he wanted or needed to go back he would have said something," Caleb replies firmly, "but he never made mention of needing to return home."

Barnes writes a few more notes, and Dawe continues her line of questioning.

"Is Gabriel here on a work visa?"

"I don't know much about immigration, but from what I do know he's here on permanent resident status. He has the identification card and such."

"So, his ultimate plan is to become a Canadian citizen?" Barnes asks.

"Yeah, that's the plan."

"I must point out the obvious here; it's like déjà vu. If I can be honest, the chances of one lover going missing are unlikely, but two—I'm sure you see why it's tough for me to wrap my head around this."

Caleb's attitude changes on the spot, going from despondent to defensive instantly. "What are you eluding to? You trying to say *I* have something to do with this?"

Dawe throws her hands in the air. "I'm not jumping to any conclusions. I'm telling you, it all looks strange."

Susan butts in. "Look, you got Caleb all wrong. This man has nothing to do with either of their disappearances. What you should be doing, instead of badgering him, is getting some constables out there and searching for Gabriel."

Dawe rolls her eyes. "Look, here's what we're going to do instead of throwing around accusations: I'll get back to St. John's and get a search party organized."

"About time," Caleb replies under his breath.

"But, I also want you to know exactly where my train of thought is right now."

Susan stands up, her chest puffs out, and she wags her finger like a protective mother. "With all due respect, I think you got this all wrong."

Dawe tilts her head toward Barnes, who struggles to write fast enough to keep up. Her mouth curls upward into a grin almost like she welcomes the hostility. "And, Mrs. Butler, what makes you believe I'm mistaken?"

She scoffs and shares a gaze of concern with Caleb. "You should tell her about the threat you got on Tuesday. She's bound to find out on her own."

Caleb raises his head and looks directly into Sam's bright blue eyes. He wants to send him a message telepathically (if it were a real thing): *You're such a gossip.*

"Aw, fuck, Susan, I told you guys it was nothing."

"Obviously it's worth mentioning—you lost a huge case, and those guys threaten you, and suddenly your boyfriend is missing. I don't know about you, but it seems those series of events are related."

Dawe's interest peaks, and she wants to dive deeper into this additional information. "Mr. Winters, what is she talking about? If you have some pertinent information, now is the time to tell me anything and everything that might be important."

He gives her a glance. "Fine. You know who Timothy Sanderson is, yeah?"

"Of course. Scumbag who is where he deserves to be: jail. What's Sanderson have to do with any of this?"

"Well, not him, per se, but a couple of his hoods paid me a visit after the trial finished."

Barnes taps Dawe's shoulder and butts in. "What exactly did these thugs say?"

"Their precise words were, 'Get our boss acquitted or you'll end up like your husband . . . buried in the woods.' I assumed they were trying to scare me into performing some unrealistic magic. When I met with Sanderson after the verdict, it was obvious he was pissed I lost his case, but I figured he sent his thugs to mess with my head."

Dawe nibbles at her lower lip and turns to Barnes who continues with exploratory questions. "But now—now your boyfriend has gone missing, and you think they may be responsible?"

Caleb doesn't speak, only nods and drops his head once more.

"Can anyone confirm this?" Barnes asks.

"My law partner, Oliver, and the barkeep at Sip witnessed the entire thing."

"And the barkeep's name?"

"I believe it's Patrick."

Dawe breaks up the less-antagonistic banter. "We'll get their information later, but for now we should focus on getting the search party organized. I'll assume you'll all be helping?"

"You assume correct. We'll round up some locals to assist," Sam says.

Barnes closes the notepad, and he and Dawe stand. "We'll also have our constables scour through any CCTV footage, check with customs, and check with the ferries. Give us a few hours, and we'll be in touch about where to meet."

Caleb shakes Barnes's hand. Meanwhile, Dawe walks away without as much as a simple good-bye or thanks. A tear rolls down Caleb's cheek, not out of sadness but because his blood boils from Dawe's lack of empathy. Susan stands next to Caleb and interlocks her arm with his, and she helps him back to the couch. Sam is quiet as he walks with Barnes outside. He doesn't need to utter a single word, because his face conveys his anger.

Once on the porch, Sam pauses at the sight of Dawe standing with her arms folded across her chest, propped against the column. The broad-shouldered medic glances at Barnes and talks with an angry tone. "I don't want to overstep my boundaries, but you're wasting your time fixating on Caleb. So, some friendly advice: concentrate your interest on that shitbag Sanderson."

"Thank you for your opinion; however, I think you ought to leave the investigating to us," Dawe bitchily says.

"Whatever. I still recall how you tried years ago to pin Sebastian's disappearance on Caleb, and what did all your wasted energy get you? Zilch. So, do what you will, but I'm only trying to save you some time and maybe, for once, you can catch the person or persons responsible."

Dawe walks away without gaining the upper hand by having the last word. But Barnes stays with Sam, who now shakes his head and foams at the mouth like a rabid dog planning to jump its prey. Barnes sets his hand on Sam's shoulder and leans in. "I'm fully aware of her past with Mr. Winters. You have my word, this time she'll stay in line."

Barnes smiles, pats Sam on the back, and descends the stairs. Sam stands firmly on the porch and keeps his distrustful eye on the unmarked squad car while it backs into the snow-covered street. He sighs and turns to walk back into the warmth but not before uttering aloud, "I foresee nothing but a witch-hunt about to transpire."

TEN

February 10, 2017
Afternoon

THE GRANDFATHER CLOCK IN THE DINING room strikes twice against the bell: it's one thirty. Caleb paces, waiting impatiently for Sam and Susan to return from changing clothes.

Two minutes later the doorbell rings and Caleb hustles to the foyer. Standing in front of him are his friends, who now stand dressed from head to toe in clothes more suitable for sub-zero temperatures.

"Why haven't you changed yet?" Susan asks.

"I'm such a wreck. The only thing I've been able to do since you left is pace. Why is this happening again? I can never catch a break."

"I mean, you don't work with the utmost clientele. But, hey, we're here now, so get upstairs and get ready. You gotta make it quick. The search party are meeting at two in the Foodland parking lot," Sam says.

"Right. Sorry, guys, again, I'm a fucking mess," Caleb says before darting toward the stairs. His body disappears, but his voice echoes below. "Give me ten minutes."

The couple settle in next to the fireplace and pass the time in silence. The minutes tick by while Caleb changes.

Susan leans in and whispers to her husband. "What do you make of all of this?"

"I don't know—you?"

"We both know Caleb would never do anything to hurt a soul, so to answer your question, I don't believe a single word that crazy constable says."

"Exactly. She's still pissed that no evidence ever surfaced to connect Caleb to Sebastian. I wouldn't put it past her to manufacture evidence to make her theory work. She's seriously on another level of psychotic."

Susan nods, but their conversation abruptly ends when the sound of Caleb tromping against the floor echoes. Soon he rushes down the stairs.

"I'm ready," Caleb shouts but stops on the last step. "Why the odd looks?"

"Nothing—we should get going. They're expecting us soon."

***

AFTER A SEVEN-MINUTE DRIVE TO the Foodland, the SUV skids into a parking spot beside a fresh snow pile. Caleb notices a canopy set up in the corner of the lot where a group of locals and RNC cadets congregate.

From first glance he guesses around two dozen showed up, but they all look cold and huddle together for warmth. Among the unfamiliar faces, he spots Constables Dawe and Barnes hanging around a long table. Caleb sighs before opening the rear passenger door of the Jeep Compass.

For all that is holy, I refuse to work with her—please, God, anybody but her.

He walks ahead of his friends, and as he approaches the outer fringe of the tent a half-dozen heads turn and stare. Caleb doesn't let their accusatory gazes distract his primary goal, so he insistently pushes his way toward the front of the crowd with his head held high. He takes in a deep puff of the frigid air and holds it in a few seconds before exhaling a cloud of mist. Barnes sees him and moves in his direction. As he stands about a foot away, he extends his hand. "Mr. Winters, glad to see you."

"Likewise. Have you learned anything new since this morning?"

"Well, a couple of things: First, I spoke with an old colleague at the airport. He ran a check for me, but sadly, Gabriel hasn't used his passport to leave the country, and the port authority went through their records and could find no match to his license plate."

"So, if he didn't use the ferries or airport, it means he's still somewhere on the island—so this is good news," Caleb says. His face lights up with a glimmer of hope.

"That's what I think too, but let's not get too excited. Our digital forensics team is still combing through hundreds of hours of CCTV footage, and I've made a formal request for the grocery store to kindly hand over their surveillance tapes from yesterday."

"I appreciate your diligence in this matter, constable," Caleb begins. "But I do have one small request."

"Sure."

Caleb points discreetly in Dawe's direction. "I can't deal with *her* today."

Barnes quietly laughs to himself. "Can't say I blame you. We plan to break people up into teams of three, so you and I can go out, if you'd be more comfortable."

"Yeah, a much better idea than sticking me with her heartless—I better stop before my mouth gets me into trouble."

Susan smiles. "Sam, you go with the guys—I'll deal with the Wicked Witch."

"Awe, my wife, always taking one for the team."

"Yeah, for Caleb's sake, I'll do it. But only this once."

Caleb forces a half smile before progressing farther into the crowd. With the briefing about to commence, he finds a quiet spot away from the people who continue to fixate their stare on him. A few faces he recognizes, and in their eyes, he senses their sadness. Others, like the handful of cadets, gawk in his direction with suspicion, possibly due to Dawe spreading misinformation about him.

Either way, Caleb always gets these from the small-town residents, yet he never allows it to bother him. All he cares about is finding Gabriel unharmed and getting back to their life together.

He pauses a few feet shy of the long table, and his friends follow and stand at his side. Susan slides her hand against his and squeezes tightly, and his eyes wander until they meet hers. It's nice having someone on your side during an emotional time. Just knowing someone is there for you means the world, especially when yours is crumbling around you.

Dawe summons everyone to gather around and lays out the purpose of their involvement in the search. She is a bitch, but efficient in not wasting time. It doesn't take her long to organize the teams, plot out the hot spots, and get the mass of people moving. Ten minutes after the briefing began, eight teams spring into action and leave for their designated areas.

Barnes, Caleb, and Sam walk side by side toward the Jeep Compass and head out to their assigned target, a wooded area near Chimney Gulch. This is the exact area where the police unearthed the skeletal remnants only three days earlier, and Caleb can't help wondering if it's not a coincidence.

Meanwhile, Dawe, Susan, and Nicole pile into the constable's unmarked cruiser and set out toward Flat Rock. Dawe does most of the talking as they drive.

The three men jump into Sam's SUV, with Caleb in the backseat. He dangles his boots outside the door to break off the snow from his treads. He bends his foot upward, checking to make sure he's gotten it all off. Feeling confident, he swings his legs inside and closes the door. Soon after, they set off north on Torbay Road. Caleb relaxes; his anxiety levels fade the farther away he gets from Dawe. He rests his elbow on the armrest of the door and sighs.

"You okay back there?" Sam asks.

Caleb turns away from the window. "Hanging in there, as good as it's gonna get."

Caleb takes in the landscape as he sees evergreen trees whiz by through the steam-covered window. The farther they venture away from Torbay, the scarcer the houses become. Having barely survived the search for Sebastian two years earlier, never once did he envision he'd suffer through the same heartache a second time. Yet, here he is. His stomach churns with the thought of losing another lover and, worse, having to live under the microscope of the RNC.

The car is silent. There's no radio blaring, nobody in the front talking, and all the stillness gives him free time to reminisce on the chilly morning in 2015 when he found himself in the same predicament.

Barnes's face says it all: he is reaching an uncomfortable threshold with the silence and turns his head toward the backseat. His emerald-green eyes study the grief on Caleb's face. Still staring out the window, Caleb is unaware of his stare.

Barnes thinks about how to initiate the conversation. And he quickly comes up with something. "You sure you're good?"

Caleb snaps back to reality and tilts his head toward the young investigator. "I'll be good when I wake up from this nightmare."

"I can relate—"

Baffled, Caleb tears into him. "How can *you* possibly comprehend what I'm going through?"

The constable, turned off by the tone of Caleb's voice, mimics Caleb's attitude in return. "Because—my wife vanished two and half years ago, pretty close to the same time your husband did. The police are still hunting after all this time with no luck."

Caleb leans forward, curious to learn about Barnes's story. "Did the police harass you to the point of exhaustion?"

Barnes nods.

"How long have you been a constable?" Caleb asks.

"I've been a constable for ten years, but about six months ago I applied to join the Major Crimes Unit."

Caleb turns away in embarrassment for being so out of line with the constable. As he's about to apologize, the SUV comes to a stop at Pouch Cove Highway. "Constable Barnes, I must apologize for coming off as such an asshole. Everything is so frustrating right now."

"Don't sweat it. I only barked back so you'd tone down your attitude."

"I need to find him."

"We all do. He's going to turn up."

Sam nods. "He's right, Caleb—maybe he's trapped somewhere. The weather lately has been pretty ruthless."

Barnes faces forward, and the conversation in the car trickles back to muteness, something Caleb hates more than anything in the world. Silence is his enemy.

"Do you think I did it?"

Barnes's jaw drops. "While Dawe is an amazing constable, she's also one of the most socially gauche people I've ever met. She distrusts everyone. But to be honest, in this line of work, your faith in humanity quickly fades over time."

"Sounds like you're keeping an open mind, hmm?"

"I'm not as jaded as her yet. I wait to see where all of the evidence takes me before I form an opinion."

"I like him," Sam chimes in.

Caleb relaxes; his anxiety dissipates in this constable's presence. "Thanks. You have no idea how I feel knowing you haven't automatically presumed my guilt."

The constable's tone changes instantly. "Mr. Winters, please don't mistake my kindheartedness for softness. I'm pretty exhaustive in my investigating."

***

SIX KILOMETERS SOUTHEAST, DAWE AND HER group reach the end of the rock-strewn roadway that butts against a dense woodland near Red Head Cove. The three women exit the cruiser and bundle up for the extensive exploration that awaits them.

Susan lags while Nicole and Dawe venture into the untouched snow. After her last encounter with Dawe, when Sebastian vanished, Susan is still distrustful of the redheaded constable. Dawe turns her head and glances over her shoulder at Susan and hollers. "You comin'?"

Susan nods and casually picks up her pace.

This fucking bitch better watch who she's talking to—she doesn't want to fight with me today.

Susan falls in line next to Nicole. If she must choose anyone to stand next to, she prefers Nicole any day (even if she detests the twentysomething, big-breasted, fair-haired woman for being too flirty with her husband).

The three women move farther into the woods and it happens—
Dawe begins spouting off rhetoric.

"So, Susan, I have to ask what your take on all of this is."

Susan pauses. "You have to be a little more specific? What's my
take on what?"

"Gabriel."

"Yeah, what about him? He's a good guy."

"You know what I mean: Do you think Caleb had anything to do
with his disappearance?"

The question has Susan doing a double take.

This bitch is straight-up savage.

How could this woman, someone who barely knows Caleb,
Gabriel, or even Sebastian, be so heartless and blunt in her
questioning?

"Look, constable, with all due respect, I know you've got a job to
do, and part of your job is to make people so uncomfortable they
utter without thinking . . ."

"That's not my—"

"Okay, cut the 'I'm so innocent' crap. You spent the past two
years holding on to the belief Caleb did something to Sebastian.
Now, allow me to be as blunt as you: you're so far off base."

Dawe's eyes widen. No one in all her years with the RNC has
been so candid with her. "Okay, let's assume you're right and Mr.
Winters isn't responsible. Where else should I be looking?"

"For starters, Timothy Sanderson is a pretty good candidate."

"What would Sanderson have to do with a missing person from
two years ago?"

Susan's eyes droop.

There was no ultimate response she could give for what happened to Sebastian. Susan isn't sure if Caleb and Sanderson were acquainted back when Sebastian disappeared. The only thing she's sure about is that whatever happened to him, the same thing is now happening to Gabriel. She recognizes that the two cases are in some way connected.

"I don't know. But I do know this: Caleb is still madly in love with Sebastian. I don't know about you, but if I murdered my husband, I sure as hell wouldn't sit around and mope."

"Maybe it's all an act?"

"Doubtful. If you ever spent time with them you'd know they had the type of love you only read about in fairy tales. Their lives were perfect. And truthfully, I envied them because my marriage would never match theirs."

Dawe shuts up, and the conversation trails off. They continue to trek deeper into the woods, and a brutal, unfriendly gust of wind blows against their bodies.

Susan turns her head to avoid the blowing snow smashing into her face. Dawe, however, picks up the conversation mid-gust like the wind doesn't faze her. "What about you, Nicole? Did you happen to spend much time with Gabriel?"

"I've met Gabriel a couple of times over the past year, so I don't know him too well. But she's right about him and Sebastian. They were the couple who everyone strives to become. I can't see Caleb doing anything to hurt him."

"I know you say you don't know much about Gabriel, but would you say they were as happy?"

"Happy, eh, I think the word I'd go with is 'comfortable.'"

Susan glares at Nicole, and if a picture says a thousand words, well, the expression on her face spoke two thousand, and about 80 percent would be curse words.

Nicole continues, "As you undoubtedly know, Gabriel has a history of substance abuse, and I know sometimes his addiction got in the way of attaining complete happiness for Caleb."

"Do you think maybe Caleb had enough of it and took matters into his own hands?"

"Caleb? No. Like I said, I'm certain he could never hurt a soul. Susan, you know him well—does he strike you as the kind of person who would hurt anyone?"

"I think I've said all I want to say. The constable here is looking in the wrong direction."

Dawe turns to Nicole. "Ms. Bishop, I've been doing this job more than twelve years, and trust me when I say people are capable of inflicting harm on anyone given the right circumstances. Don't ever put anything past anybody."

Nicole hesitates and glances at Susan, who rolls her eyes but continues scanning the tree line of the wooded area in complete silence.

***

SAM PULLS HIS SUV INTO THE parking lot of the Foodland as time inches closer to eight thirty. Night had fallen over the area hours earlier. Being the final group to return, they step out of the car to see everyone huddled underneath the canopy waiting for the debriefing.

Barnes approaches Dawe, and the two speak for a few moments before returning to the table. They stand, front and center, and address the volunteers who spent their evening helping.

"First, I want to thank everyone who took time out of their day to aid in the search for Gabriel Parsons," Barnes says. "While we were not able to find him or his vehicle, we want to extend an invitation to anyone who is able to return tomorrow at ten o'clock to search again."

The soft hum of the crowd lifts as they nod their heads in unison. Sam, Susan, and Nicole stand at Caleb's side.

"You *are* coming back out tomorrow, right, Caleb?" Nicole asks.

"Of course. But for now, I'm emotionally drained. I want to go home."

"Yeah, you look like you need a good night's sleep," Susan says.

Sam cuts in. "Hun, let me get him home. You don't mind catching a lift with Nicole, do you?"

Before Susan can protest, Nicole cuts in. "I'll drive you home, it's not a problem."

Susan stands there, a fake, nervous smirk on her face.

What did I ever do to God to piss him off this much?

Sam gives Susan a kiss on the cheek, pats Caleb on the back, and they walk away. Even though Susan knows her husband is only looking out for their best friend, she's frustrated he left her with his ditzy partner instead of inviting her along.

Sam gets Caleb into the SUV, and not even five seconds later Susan watches as the taillights disappear into the darkness of the rural night. She sighs and turns to face Nicole. The two women smile at each other.

Give me the strength to get through the next twenty minutes.

Nicole flashes a perfect smile. "You ready to hit the road?"

"Yeah. I'm beat."

"The same. Guess we'll all be at it again tomorrow."

"Sam will, but I work at noon. You know I'll have my eyes on the lookout all day."

Nicole frowns. "Well, shit. Looks like I'll get stuck with the nosy constable again."

Susan chuckles softly.

Glad it's you and not me.

She sets her small backpack on the floor of the car and scoots in. She slouches in the seat and tries to come up with something to talk about to make the ride home a little less annoying.

Meanwhile, about a kilometer ahead, Caleb sits in silence while fixating on the blacktop outside the windshield. A thousand thoughts flood his mind, and no matter how hard he tries to make it stop, there is nothing in his power to do so. Caleb's biggest enemy in life is the anxiety he has fought. There are a lot of good days, but some days he struggles to keep it all together—like today.

Sam's eyes shift right. "You're awfully quiet—what are you thinking about in that head of yours"

"Too much."

"You want to talk about it?"

"What's to say?"

"I dunno—how are you? Why are you so damn quiet? It's not like you to be *this* quiet."

"You're right. I'm never this quiet. I can't stop thinking . . . thinking about Sebastian, and now Gabriel."

"I can't imagine what you're going through. I'm here for you, always," Sam says.

"I know. Not sure I'd be this composed if it wasn't for you and Susan. All I want is a logical explanation as to why this is happening again. That's not too much to ask, is it?"

"Sometimes life isn't always logical. Sometimes it's messy, unpredictable, and you gotta stop bearing the weight of trying to make everything perfect."

"It shouldn't be this way," Caleb says.

The car returns to silence, but Sam keeps Caleb talking; anything to divert his attention from dwelling.

"Can I ask you a personal question? And don't get mad at me for this. I gotta know," Sam says.

"I can't promise I won't get mad. How about this—I won't yell."

Sam ponders the counteroffer. "Okay, you seem open-minded. Are you honestly happy with Gabriel? And what I mean is, are you in love with him the same way you were with Sebastian?"

Caleb stays unaffected. Nevertheless, the prying question triggers hesitation. "I suppose you can't link the two relationships with one another. Take Sebastian—when I met him it was love at first sight. He stumbled into my life when I had given up on looking for love. My heart still belonged to my forbidden love in Toronto."

Sam's taken aback: this is the first he's learned of a lover in Toronto. "Wait, what do you mean 'forbidden' love? Would I know him?"

Caleb evades the question. "Now, when I met Gabriel, I wasn't swept off my feet—not like with Sebastian. You're my best friend, so I'll be honest; the first night, Gabriel rubbed me the wrong way."

"How so?" asks Sam.

"Well, for starters, he gave the impression he was drunk or high . . . hell, it could have been both for all I know. Not the type of guy you bring home to your parents."

"True. I should know this, but if he wasn't your type, how did you end up shacked up together?"

"He slipped his number into my jacket pocket and told me to call him—I was lonely, so I called."

"He must have grown on you?"

"Eh, you could say that. I think we both loved the idea of having someone and not being alone anymore. For us, I think we missed having someone to love," he says, wiping away a tear from his face. "Anyway, I don't want to talk about it anymore."

Caleb flips on the radio, and the Jeep coasts along the shadowy highway. Sam pulls into Caleb's well-lit driveway and Caleb flings open the passenger door.

I'd better salt this tonight before I head to bed.

Caleb stands in the ice-covered driveway, contemplating if he has enough salt. Meanwhile, Sam rushes around the SUV, nearly sending himself plummeting to the pavement, ass first. He reaches Caleb, slaps him on the back, and strolls along his side. The gesture, although small, makes Caleb uneasy and helpless.

"Sam, seriously, I don't need you to baby me."

"I said I'd make sure you got in safely. So, for once in your life, let someone do something nice for you."

Caleb crosses his arms across his chest like a spoiled child. He's grouchier than normal but realizes he needs to dial down the bitch factor if he wants to keep his good graces with his friends.

"I'm sorry, this hasn't been my day."

"You're so Canadian."

Caleb stops and glances.

"You know, people say Canadians apologize constantly—it was a joke." Sam smiles and they continue walking.

No matter how terrible things are, Sam always brings a smile to Caleb's face. It's in this moment that he appreciates the veracity of having people who care about him.

Caleb inserts the key into the lock, forcefully pulls the door toward his body, and turns the key. A soft clinking noise rings, and he pushes his shoulder against the door. It pivots open.

"All right, made it safely," Caleb jokes as they move into the frigid house.

"Ever tried heat?"

"These damn thermostats—energy savings, my ass . . . more like 'pain in the ass,'" Caleb frustratingly utters.

"Look, Caleb, I know you're not going to like what I'm about to say, but I brought something along for you in case you need them."

Sam pulls a brown prescription bottle and leaves it on the dining room table.

"What's in the bottle?"

"Well, I know you're not sleeping, and your anxiety is at an all-time high right now," Sam begins. "Only take one when you need it."

"You know my stance on drugs, legal or illegal. I hate them."

Caleb finishes fiddling with the thermostat and sees the bottle still sitting on the table. He steps closer and pics up the pill bottle, twisting it around to scan the label.

SAMUEL BUTLER
Xanax 1 mg tablet
Take one tablet twice daily by mouth for symptoms of anxiety.

"Xanax? Shit's addictive—why would you have something like this?"

"Because, like you, I suffer from anxiety and occasionally have panic attacks."

"You have panic attacks?"

"I mean, it's not something I broadcast publicly, mainly because of my job, but yeah, I was diagnosed with panic disorder."

"Does Susan know?"

"No. No one knows except me, you, and my medical team. I'd be grateful if this information stayed only between us."

"Don't worry, your secret's safe with me."

Caleb smiles as Sam scans the room like a paranoid schizophrenic. "You got any bourbon?"

Caleb points in the direction of the living room. "Liquor cabinet in the corner. Help yourself." Caleb walks away into the kitchen and disappears behind the wall. He isn't gone but a few seconds and returns to the living room with a liter of water in his hand.

"So, these pills? I take one, and what, my problems disappear?"

"Not quite, but I guarantee you'll get the best night's sleep you've had in a long time."

Caleb hesitates but unscrews the plastic cap of the bottle, shakes a pill into the palm of his hand, and tosses the oblong white tablet into his mouth. "Sam—I need a favor."

"Sure."

"Can you stay until I fall asleep?"

"Yeah, of course. I assume it's too hard to sleep in your bed right now, huh?"

"Yeah. I've taken up refuge on the couch, at least until Gabriel returns."

"You'll be back in your bed soon. We're gonna find him."

Caleb smiles and walks to the couch, where he fluffs a decorative pillow and snatches the wool-lined blanket that lies flung across the back of the sofa, right where he left it earlier in the morning.

He sits, twists his body, and lifts his legs onto the couch. Sam gets comfortable a few feet away, and Caleb yawns and stretches his arms before resting his head against the pillow.

"You want the TV on?"

"Yeah, the background noise helps. God, all of this feels like déjà vu."

"I don't know how comfortable I am leaving you here all alone. Maybe you'd be better off staying at our place?"

"Thanks, but I'm better off here—you know, in case he comes home."

"True."

Caleb adjusts his head on the pillow and chats with Sam until his eyelids grow droopy, and eventually he dozes off. Sam finishes his bourbon while watching Caleb peacefully snooze.

He throws back the last dribble left in the glass and quietly sets the empty glass on the coffee table. Resting at Caleb's feet is the blanket he forgot to cover up with before crashing, and Sam gently covers him.

"Sleep well, my friend. Tomorrow's another day."

ELEVEN

February 13, 2017
Midmorning

T HE MIDMORNING SUN CREEPS THROUGH THE windows and Caleb stirs awake. His body aches from another night on the lumpy couch, and as he sits up, he shakes his head. A sharp pain travels across his lower back, and he moans and writhes in pain.

I should sleep in the bed tonight.

He scans the still room and stares at the pile of dirty plates, beer bottles, and glasses that have accumulated over the weekend. The thought of cleaning up is more than he can handle. The only thing on his mind is wanting to see Gabriel's smiling face rush through the front door, but after several sunrises and sunsets, his optimism starts to fade.

Caleb stares at the television screen. The morning news already came and went, but he craves something more mildly entertaining than the boring show he gazes at to keep him occupied. He runs his hand against the couch in search of the remote, but after several swipes he realizes it's not there, so he begins checking other places. With a quick glance below the coffee table he finds the spot where he must have flung it during his less-than-restful sleep.

He switches the channel before standing and staggering to the kitchen. He rubs his eyes, unsure if he's awake or having some hallucinogenic vision from the Xanax. The coffeemaker stares at him and he lets out a sigh.

I need to wake up.

The first few drips of coffee fall from the machine and he returns to the couch, but along the way something sparkly catches his eye through the window to the front porch.

He advances guardedly, slowly slipping his finger behind the sheer curtain. He peeks, and resting in his chair lies a small, thin, rectangular box in silver wrapping paper. Releasing his grip from the curtain, Caleb unbolts the front door, steps one foot out onto the cold reclaimed wooden porch, and stares at the package curiously.

Did I miss a mail delivery?

He squats and gently lifts the package from the chair. Whatever awaits him in the flawlessly gift-wrapped box is light but firm. His adrenaline is driving him to rush inside and tear it open, but the paranoia in the back of his mind stops him. He stands in the cold, holding the parcel in his hand; he flips it over and inspects it closely.

There's no return address, no postage—this didn't come through the post.

He steps back indoors, his feet numb. He stands nervously calm in the foyer, grappling with the thought of opening the package. Is it worth it or not? A few more moments pass, and he inspects it further, ultimately making the risky choice to discover what it holds.

First the note under my windshield and now this? Who keeps leaving anonymous messages for me?

An abrupt ominous sensation washes over him. *What if it's a bomb? Or a deadly insect? Or worse, maybe it's anthrax? Caleb, should you unseal this?*

He takes a few shallow breaths, shoves those worries to the back of his mind, and goes forward. He delicately rips away the paper, exposing a generic, thin cardboard box. On its own, one could say there wasn't anything special about it; however, the fact that the sender spent a tedious amount of time taping the seams with several layers of packing tape gives him the impression that whatever it is, it must be important.

He peels away the top layer of tape, and another, until finally the contents spill onto the floor. He inspects the items that fell: a DVD jewel case and a single sheet of paper torn from a notepad.

Caleb first picks up the letter; it's possible there's a message for him explaining what is on the DVD. He unfolds the note and a crudely scrawled message addresses him personally:

Be careful who you trust—if you don't believe me: watch this.

Now curious as to what's on the DVD that would make him mistrustful of people, he races back to the living room. He

nervously paces in front of the entertainment center, unsure he
wants to know what's on the disc or not.

Am I ready for this? What if it's a ransom letter?

After five minutes of back and forth with himself, he musters up
the courage to pop the disc into the player. Caleb steps back and
stands staring at the screen, which turns blue until a likeness of his
empty bedroom appears. In the lower corner of the screen he sees
the date stamp: January 13, 2015.

He waits patiently for something to happen, but the image of his
bed stays stuck on the screen as time ticks by.

Ten minutes pass and nothing happens.

"The fuck is this?"

He's beginning to doubt anything will happen, but several
questions enter his mind: *Who set up a camera in my bedroom? Why'd
they do it? How'd they do it?*

He fast-forwards, skipping to the thirty-five-minute mark in the
video before, finally, a shadowy figure enters the room. He pauses
and rewinds a few seconds. Before he resumes, he cranks up the
volume to the max and presses play. This time he clearly catches
the inaudible babble of two male voices laughing and carrying on.

At first he sees Sebastian enter, and suddenly Gabriel appears
with his arms flung around Sebastian's neck. Caleb is in shock and
can't take his eyes off the screen. Then it happens—something that
in a million years Caleb would never have suspected his husband of
doing: Sebastian leans in and passionately begins kissing and
groping Gabriel.

Caleb plops on the couch. He's frozen. All he can do is sit and
watch as his husband allows Gabriel to undress him.

Confusion. Anger. Betrayal. All these emotions strike him instantaneously and Caleb drops the remote and leans forward, burying his flushed face into his hands.

He screams. "How could you do this to me? How could either of you do this?"

He snaps from his shell-shocked state and hunts urgently for the remote he let fall to the floor. He holds it firmly, struggling to turn the devastating video off, but as his finger slides to the power button he overhears Gabriel declare: "He'll never find out."

Now he sits with the blue screen glowing at him again. The room spins, he breathes deeper and deeper, and his blood pressure soars. The hurt and rage boil below the surface, and although he's trying his best to preserve a level head, eventually the rage overwhelms him, and he hurls the boxy remote at the entertainment center and strikes a picture frame holding a photo of him and Gabriel.

The power from the strike sends the wooden frame plummeting off the shelf. Caleb watches it hit the hardwood floor and shatter into a million tiny pieces. The briny tears stream against Caleb's face and he gives himself a thrust from the couch. Caleb slowly moves closer to the splinters of glass strewn around the floor.

"How could you do this to me?" he asks as he crouches and picks up the picture.

Whoever left this package had one intention: to shatter his illusion of his perfect life. But now, as he holds the scratched picture, it's vividly clear nothing in his life has ever been perfect.

He fetches a broom and dustpan from the kitchen and hovers over the mess he's made.

How can I go on with my life now? Gabriel better hope he doesn't show his face here right now, otherwise they will have a reason to haul me in.

With the broken glass and splintered wood cleaned up, his adrenaline still throbs, so he reverts to the only thing that calms his nerves: pacing.

He catches a couple of intense gasps, hoping to collect his thoughts. One thing Caleb is notoriously terrible at is keeping his temper controlled when distressing news comes his way. He paces around a few minutes more, but the picture sitting atop the coffee table distracts him from finding peace. He knows it must disappear. He steps closer and picks it up while the tears pour faster. He takes both hands and tears a small slit down the middle. He hesitates momentarily, but resumes, and with one swift motion shreds the picture until there is nothing left to destroy.

After he tears the final piece, his anger subsides, but now he wants answers to two simple questions: *Who wants to destroy my life? Is this Sanderson's doing?*

It isn't obvious who's behind the latest unsigned note, but the most important thing he must do at once is haul his ass to St. John's to pay Constables Dawe and Barnes a visit.

***

HE WHIPS INTO THE PARKING LOT of the Royal Newfoundland Constabulary Headquarters northwest of downtown St. John's. He grips the steering wheel tightly and his fury, while weakened, has not entirely diminished.

He kills the ignition and slouches in silence while three constables meander by his car and into the building. They laugh and smile and Caleb scoffs.

Obviously, their day is going better than mine.

He glances over into the passenger seat where the box and its contents rest. Not only did a stranger decimate his entire reality, but he or she also managed to destroy both relationships he'd ever cared about in his life in a matter of minutes.

He loosens his grip and clenches the door handle with his left hand. His attention span is now compromised. *How do I explain this video to the them? They'll think I took care of the problem out of jealousy.*

Caleb already feels awkward bringing something so repugnant to the surface, but what if this video is some clue to what has become of Sebastian and Gabriel? Caleb should let someone know.

He walks gradually through the parking lot where the snow crunches beneath his feet. He arrives at the glass and metal door where an agreeable constable holds open the door for him.

Caleb looks piercingly at the young constable. "Thanks."

The constable nods, smiles, and continues behind Caleb into the waiting area. The atmosphere is lively, and he finds the information counter where a mousy young woman sits behind a glass partition pecking away at her keyboard. He steps up, and the loud clacking sound ceases.

"May I help you?" she asks.

"I need to speak with either Constable Dawe or Barnes, but only if they're free."

"Your name?"

"Caleb Winters."

"All right, have a seat, Mr. Winters. I'll let them know you're here."

Caleb's lip quivers and he nods before walking away in the direction of a group of chairs that line the glass façade of the building. He's still unsure the choice to come here was the right one, but he lowers himself into the uncomfortable hard plastic chair. His legs bounce as he waits, and he checks his watch sporadically as the minutes tick by. That's another thing Caleb has never been good at in life: waiting.

Around the corner he catches a glimpse of Constable Barnes moving in his direction. A sense of relief falls over Caleb knowing he doesn't have to see *her* face right away.

"Caleb, is everything all right? I didn't expect to see you," Barnes says, extending his hand.

"Sadly, I wish I could tell you everything is good, but it's not," he says, clutching the package against his chest. "Someone left this package on my doorstep this morning."

Caleb holds out the torn-up package and Barnes slowly grabs the box. He flashes a nervous grin. "What is it?"

"My entire life turned to shit."

"Um," Barnes stutters. "What I mean is, what's inside?"

"Ah, sorry, I'm still in a daze. It's video of my husband and boyfriend and their whorish affair they had only weeks before Sebastian went missing."

The Constable looks around before peeling back the flap of the box. "Why don't we get you to my office where you can relax, and I'll run this over to forensics."

Caleb lowers his head and nods.

Caleb follows Barnes through a set of secure doors. The headquarters is an apiary of commotion, and to some degree it makes him uncomfortable.

Is St. John's so violent it needs this many constables?

The walk to Barnes's office feels like an eternity, and when Caleb deliberates if the never-ending journey will end, they get there. He notices the nameplates displayed on the wall outside the door.

Constable Noah Barnes

Constable Gretchen Dawe

He breezes through the door, and the face he didn't need to see sits with her all-too-familiar scowl across her face.

"Hey, make Mr. Winters comfortable—I'm going to run this to the techs."

"Sure." She stands and approaches Caleb. "You look upset, Mr. Winters."

"I am."

She seems puzzled by his brief, direct answer. "Have a seat," she says while pulling out a chair. "What's in the box Barnes took with him?"

Caleb recounts exactly what he told Barnes only moments earlier. She sits in her chair, twirling a pen. There's an expression of disbelief written across her face. "So, you've no idea who left this package for you? Did they leave a note?"

"Yes."

"Has anyone ever left you notes before today?"

"Yes."

She drops her pen on the desk and leans inward. "When?"

"Last week. I came back to my car and found a note slid under the wiper blade."

Dawe's suspicion grows. "And, I don't know, today seemed like the best time to inform us?"

"I didn't think it was important, not until I got this second one."

She scoffs. "Mind sharing what the first note said?"

Caleb thinks back to February 7. He remembers his foul mood from losing the case, how he was annoyed from having to deal with Drew Murphy all day, and he recalls the two thugs showing up at Sip.

He clears his throat. "It eluded to something like, 'Your perfect life is a lie.' I get this crap all the time, especially when I've lost cases."

She picks up her pen and twirls it faster, but instead of replying, she keeps her mouth shut for a pleasant change.

"I'm telling you, someone is out to get me. Some strange shit has been happening over the past week, and I don't know how to explain it."

"Okay, relax. I think we can both agree someone has it out for you. But was someone out for revenge in 2015?"

His blood pressure rises again, and an intense heat flushes his face. His mouth opens, but no words fall out.

What's this bitch alluding to?

He sits in silence; his beady eyes sweep her figure. The anger is fizzing, and when he's about to unleash his aggravation, in walks Barnes.

"So, I had our techs dust for prints and we found a few. I have a hunch those prints are going to come back to you, Mr. Winters."

"Of course they will. I touched all of it. The DVD and the note."

Barnes detects Caleb is growing agitated and quickly de-escalates the tension. "Caleb, hey, look at me. Tell me more about what's on the DVD?"

Caleb sighs at the thought of having to relive it. "At first, nothing except my bed. No sound, no bodies, only thirty-five minutes of an empty bed. But around the thirty-six-minute mark I saw him."

"Him? Him who?" Dawe asks.

"Sebastian."

"And what else?"

"The date stamp was two weeks before Sebastian went missing," he begins as Dawe leaned in closer.

"Okay, what happened next?"

Caleb's voice trembles, and it's clear his adrenaline is kicking in. "There was another male voice talking off camera."

"And what was the voice saying?"

"I couldn't make it out."

"It's okay, our audio techs will figure it out. Let's not get caught up on the trivial details right now."

"Then I saw *them* together."

"Them who?"

"Sebastian and Gabriel. They were kissing."

Barnes glances at Dawe as her eyes widen. Caleb arrives at his breaking point with the blitz of questions and the waterworks take over. Barnes quickly rushes to the office door and shuts it. As he returns to the desk, he snatches a box of Kleenex and pulls his chair closer to Caleb.

"Hey, you're doing great." Barnes places his brawny hand on Caleb's shoulder.

Caleb lifts his head, exposing his bright red, tear-stained face. He sucks in the snot oozing from his nose. "Yeah?"

"Yeah, let's get through this once, okay?"

Caleb nods and wipes away the tears.

"So, you saw them kissing—anything else?"

"The last thing I caught before I couldn't watch anymore was Gabriel tell Sebastian I'd never find out about it. Afterward, I shut it off, threw the remote, and made the hard choice to come see you two."

Dawe's rough tone eases. "Did you set the camera up in your bedroom?"

"No."

"Who would have access to your bedroom?" Dawe continues firing off question after question.

"I don't know. Only a handful of people had keys to the house in 2015. They were—" He pauses and runs the names in his head. "Sam, Susan, Sebastian, Oliver, and Drew."

"I know those first three names. Who are Drew and Oliver?"

"Oliver is my law partner, and Drew Murphy, as in Crown Prosecutor Murphy. We were still sort of friends."

"And you're not friends now?" Barnes asks.

"Far from it. Now he's somebody I must work with. But, you see, our friendship was already broken well before 2015."

The room sits quiet.

"I'm curious, out of all those names, who would have the most to gain by trying to catch your husband having an affair?" Dawe asks.

"None of them. Drew and I might hate each other's guts, but he's the Crown prosecutor. I doubt he'd risk his entire career by breaking into my house."

"In any case, I think we'll still speak with Mr. Murphy and get a statement. Also, you don't mind providing us with a handwriting sample, do you?" Dawe asks.

"Yeah, sure. You're trying to rule me out as the author of the letter, huh?"

"As a defense attorney, you know it's standard protocol," Barnes reassures him.

"I wouldn't expect anything less."

The telephone on Dawe's desk rings and she answers. Barnes helps Caleb to his feet, and when he's only a few footsteps from escaping her negative energy, Dawe covers the phone receiver and whispers, "Mr. Winters, don't leave town."

Caleb scoffs. "Where am I gonna go? My entire life is here."

Dawe keeps her eyes glued to him as he walks out of the office.

***

BARNES RETURNS FROM ESCORTING CALEB TO the exit. Plopping in the chair, he gives a long, disapproving glance at Dawe.

"What?" she angrily asks.

"I think your attitude is a tad unsympathetic toward him, don't you?"

"No. And while we're on the subject, I think you're being a little too lenient with him. Answer me this: What type of person loses a husband *and* a boyfriend within a three-year period?"

"A high-profile criminal defense attorney, that's who. Dawe, you do grasp that he holds people's lives in his hands every day. He sticks up for the scum of the earth whom we work overtime trying to put away."

"So, what, you're saying we should consider his crazy notion of 'the client did it'?"

"Well, you know Sanderson's record: organized crime, drugs, prostitution. Mr. Winters losing his case led him to a lengthy prison sentence. What harm does it do to round up the usual suspects? What're a few questions gonna hurt?"

"You're new, so I'm giving you a lot of leeway here. You want to know what I think?"

"I'm sure you're gonna tell me regardless."

"I think Mr. Winters set the camera up years ago when he realized his husband was having an affair. And now Sebastian has been missing for two years."

"I don't see the connection."

"It's right in front of your face: Caleb killed Sebastian, made his moves on Gabriel after a sufficient amount of time passed by, and then he waited a bit longer before taking out the cheater."

"Sounds farfetched."

"Not really. Anyone is capable of murdering another human being. Trust me. By the way, are we even sure Caleb and Sanderson knew each other years ago?"

"Not sure."

"This is something we should determine."

"All right—I know you're senior to me, but I remind you we need something called 'evidence' before we make outlandish accusations."

"Don't worry—you'll one day understand everyone has something to hide, and those skeletons can come out at any time."

"Well, you do what you gotta do. I'm going to check if Caleb was Sanderson's legal counsel in 2015. If it turns out he was, I'll bring in the aggressors. Deal?"

"Deal," Dawe says. "And while you're chasing your tail, do me a favor and pop into Drew Murphy's office."

"Why?"

"I get a sense there's a backstory there between those two. What it is, I haven't figured out yet. But I want to know everything about everyone he knows before we move forward."

Barnes nervously laughs. "Your imagination is working tirelessly, Gretchen. But, sure, I'll drop in on him. Any specific questions you'd like me to ask?"

"Yes. First, how long have they known each other? Second, what is the status of their friendship in Mr. Murphy's eyes? And lastly, Mr. Winters seems adamant that he hates Murphy's guts. Find out when and why their friendship went south."

Barnes nods. "Got it."

He grabs his jacket, thumps his hand against the doorframe, and exits the office not looking back.

TWELVE

February 14, 2017
Afternoon

CALEB SITS AT HIS DESK ENTRANCED by the energetic city five stories below. The happy couples kissing and hugging on the corner of Water and Queen Streets depresses Caleb. There are couples exchanging chocolates, and a few men even showering their wives or girlfriends with flowers. After being in such a funk, Caleb isn't sure why there is so much love in the air. That is, until he glances at the calendar on his desk: it's Valentine's Day. The forgotten glimmer of love in his heart has been replaced with black coal; the sight of happy couples churns his stomach. He spins around and returns his attention to the laptop.

A soft rap at the office door breaks his concentration. Standing outside the glass he sees Oliver, waiting for the all clear to enter. Caleb forces a smile and waves him in. The door cracks open slightly, and Olli whispers through the crack.

"How are you holding up?"

"As you'd expect—a mess on the inside but doing my damnedest to keep this phony smile on my face and get through today," Caleb says, pointing at his mouth.

"The whole office is here for you," Olli begins. "But the reason I came by is to see if you'd like to join me for lunch?"

Caleb contemplates the offer. "Sure, I suppose a little food wouldn't hurt. When you want to go?"

"Eh, ten minutes or so. Be back in a few," Oliver says, closing the office door behind him.

Caleb forces himself to avoid looking back out the window, but the emotional torture he gets from the happy people below is more fulfilling than staring at his screen, unable to bring himself to be productive. He blinks. Unexpectedly, the phone rings; it's a prompt relief from the boredom.

"Caleb Winters," he answers.

The gruffy feminine voice on the other end speaks, and quickly the liberation he predicted turns into more suffering. "It's Constable Dawe."

"Ah, Constable Dawe, how nice to hear from you," he says, but it comes across more artificial than sincere. "Have you learned any more about Gabriel?"

"In fact, yes, we did discover some additional information. Do you think you'll have some time to drop by this afternoon?"

"I suppose. What's this additional information you found?"

"Eh, I think it's better we discuss the matter in person."

"Uh, sure. I can be by after lunch."

"Um, how about two o'clock?"

Caleb pretends to flip through his calendar. "Yeah, that'll work. See you at two."

"Great," she says. "Oh, and before I forget, I'll be conducting this interview under caution—so I'd advise you to bring legal counsel with you. Okay, bye."

The line goes dead, and Caleb nearly drops the phone in shock. He keeps his composure together, sets the phone back on the cradle, and speaks. "Caution? What a bitch to mention 'caution' and hang up on me."

Caleb leans back in his oversized leather chair, and the blood in his face drains. A second later Oliver returns and sees the unforgettable expression on Caleb's face.

"You look like you've seen a ghost. Something happen?"

"No . . . well, maybe—Constable Dawe wants to question me after lunch. Said to bring you with me," Caleb replies.

Oliver glances at his watch: 12:45 PM. "What's with this woman? Damn, she has a hard-on for you."

"Yeah, not interested."

Oliver snickers. "Yeah, not your type. Did she say what time to be there?"

"Two."

"Ugh, all right, let's eat. We can discuss this impromptu meeting over a salad or something light."

Caleb locks his laptop and closes the lid. "Ready?"

"Yeah, let's move."

The elevator ride is silent, and Oliver watches the numbers on the elevator count down . . . four, three, two, and ultimately they arrive at the ground floor. The elevator chimes, and the two metal doors slide open. They rush into the lobby of the office building where they wrap their jackets tighter against their bodies. It's what you do when it's negative three degrees Celsius outside.

"Where to?" Oliver asks.

"Eh, you pick a place. I'm sure I'll find something on the menu."

"Okay, how about this new bistro over on George Street? Heard the food is amazing."

"With your taste, I'm sure it'll be great."

***

LUNCH IS OVER FAR TOO FAST, and before he realizes, Caleb is again standing outside the police station. He's not looking forward to what looms inside, because he knows today's visit will be drastically different than yesterday's. No sympathy for the grieving companion; instead, he's preparing himself to get the third degree like a prime suspect receives. Caleb's hands tremble and he exhales the breath he holds gruffly. He fidgets with his jacket to take his mind off things.

"Let's get this over with," Oliver announces, laying the palm of his hand against Caleb's back.

They enter the building. The same mousy woman sits at the reception counter. She raises her head as their footsteps echo against the walls of the minimalistic lobby. "Ah, Mr. Winters. You here to see Constable Dawe?"

"I am. I have an appointment at two."

She gives a half smile. "I'll let her know you're waiting."

Caleb nods and turns away from the desk. His head is spinning, and even when Oliver begins speaking, nothing his partner says registers.

His only request now is for somebody to awaken him from the nightmare that encompasses his reality and get back to weeknight dinner parties and staring over at his lover peacefully sleeping in bed.

He stops and finds himself staring at the identical unfriendly seat he occupied yesterday. It's empty and it's calling out his name to fill it. He groans and sits. He gets a sense of déjà vu when he sees the same three constables from yesterday waltz in laughing and smiling.

Everything around him is moving onward, everything except for his own life, which has come to a halt, even though the minutes and hours still pass each day.

His thoughts chomp away at his awareness, so much he doesn't even notice Dawe standing before him.

"Mr. Winters . . . hello?"

A nudge to his bicep arouses him. "What's wrong?"

"You sure you're good?" Oliver asks before directing his attention to Dawe. "Sorry, he's been in and out a lot lately."

"Understandable, you know, given his circumstances. Mr. Winters, shall we get started?"

He agrees and stands out of the uncomfortable chair.

They cross the threshold of the same secure doors and walk along the long, spotlessly clean corridor. They pass by the office that only a day earlier he sat in, balling his eyes out at learning of his husband's and Gabriel's affair. Instead of stopping, they continue and advance toward a small room near the rear of the stationhouse. She stands aside to allow Caleb to enter first, followed by Oliver. The table is set up in preparation for the interview: a video camera attached to a tripod sits beside Constable Barnes, who flips through a manila folder.

Once everyone is situated, Dawe flips the light switch, and a soft yellow glow from the overhead florescent lights engulfs the darkness.

"Caleb, please, have a seat," Barnes insists.

Caleb removes his suit jacket and pulls out the chair. He stares blankly across the table at Barnes, who now shows the most staid face he's ever seen from him. Caleb's heart races and his palms become soaked in sweat as he dishes out the same focused look.

Dawe tactfully drops a stack of folders she carries in her hand onto the large table.

"Shall we begin?" Barnes nods and presses the record button on the video camera.

"My name is Constable Gretchen Dawe, and present with me today are Constable Noah Barnes, Barrister Oliver Taylor from Taylor and Winters Law Firm, and Caleb Winters. This interview is taking place at the Royal Newfoundland Constabulary Headquarters located in St. John's. Today's date is Tuesday, February 14, 2017, and the time is 2:11 PM," she begins. "Mr. Winters, you are here for questioning under caution. This means you do not have to say anything. But it may harm your defense if you do not mention when questioned something that you later rely on in court. Anything you do say may be given in evidence. Do you understand?"

"Yes."

"For the record, please state your full name, date of birth, and nationality," she instructs.

"Caleb Andrew Winters, 22 July 1979, and I'm a Canadian citizen," he replies nonchalantly.

"Now, Mr. Winters, we've asked you here today to question you in the disappearance of Gabriel Parsons. Can you verify the last time you saw him?"

Caleb looks at Oliver for guidance. He gives his approval to answer the question. "The morning of the 9th. I left the house around eight and when I returned home in the evening, he wasn't there."

"And you were expecting him to be home?"

"Yes. The last thing he said to me was he was going to the grocery and he'd see me in a few hours."

Barnes jots notes and never looks up from the notepad in front of him.

"So, everything was fine when you left for work? There weren't any signs of distress?" she asks.

"No. None. I promised him I'd only work a half day. We were planning to have a romantic night out; however, I ended up at the office a bit longer than I thought. Oliver can verify since he's the one who kept me longer."

Oliver clears his throat. "It's true. We had meetings all afternoon regarding a new client."

"I see. So, we followed up on your belief Timothy Sanderson and members of his crew could have had a hand in Gabriel's disappearance. Constable Barnes spoke with several of his cronies. Each of them provided a verifiable alibi for the entire day last Thursday."

"Okay . . . and?"

"And at this point, we've also done more digging into other potential suspects. You know, we like to do our due diligence here."

"Well, constable, I appreciate it."

"While we're on the topic of other suspects, let's look at your boyfriend himself. Were you aware he has a criminal record in the United States and did a stint in rehab in 2013?"

Caleb's expression shifts. "What do you mean?"

"Or did you happen to know he legally changed his name in 2014 only six months before applying for his permanent residency?"

"No. Who is he?"

"His last name changed from Escobar to Parsons. Do you know why?"

Oliver interjects. "Get to the point, constable."

"Could it be possible his past caught up with him and he took off? Or maybe you unearthed all his lies, and things got a little heated?"

"No way. This is the first I'm even hearing of this."

"Maybe he took his own life? Lots of places here to drive a car off a cliff and never be seen again."

"He'd never," Caleb shouts. "Besides, why wasn't any of this caught during his immigration interview?"

"I'm sure someone wasn't working as hard as we do. Let's face it, we can't all be perfect."

Caleb folds his arms across his chest. *Why is she bringing any of the irrelevant information to light? And why now?*

Dawe continues. "So, were you present for this immigration interview?"

"Yes."

"And you assured immigration you'd support him, financially. It's the only way he could stay here, right?"

"Yeah, of course, I did; he's my boyfriend. I'd support him no matter what."

She slams her hand against the table. "Stop lying. I want the truth. How much and how long have you known?"

Oliver again cuts her off. "Constable, please, shouting and accusing my client is not getting us any closer to finding Mr. Parsons. Let's relax for a second." He turns to Caleb. "But, Caleb, if you know something, come clean now."

"Yeah, thanks for the vote of confidence there, counsellor. To answer your questions, if I knew any of this, I never would have asked him out, let alone have committed a felony to get him in the country."

A hush falls over the room, and Dawe sits still, staring through Caleb. She's not twirling her pen as she usually does, not biting her lower lip—absolutely nothing.

Caleb clears his throat. "Can you tell me what else you uncovered in his criminal record? I mean, I've lived with him for sixteen months. If it's something bad, I have a right to know."

Dawe pushes the plain manila folder across the table and Oliver catches it before it slides off. "Let's kick off with the easy ones: car theft, burglary, oh, right, and a couple of drug charges sprinkled in there too."

He flips open the folder, and attached to the left side is an eight-by-eleven mugshot of Gabriel from the Miami-Dade Police Department. He skims through the countless pages and finally glances at Caleb, who's still reeling from the information.

Oliver glances at Caleb. "Swear you didn't know any of this?"

"I swear. If I was aware of any of this I'd never have endorsed Gabriel." His voice climbs an octave.

"There you have it, constables, he had no knowledge of his boyfriend's past. What else you got?"

"Oh, trust me, we're only getting started."

"Well, on with it."

"Constable Barnes had a enthralling chat with your old pal, Andrew Murphy. You remember him, right?"

"You know I do. What's he got to do with any of this?"

"Well, a lot, in fact. See, when you left yesterday, I got the impression you were hiding something about your past," Barnes said, taking over the questioning.

Oliver seems confused and rolls his head at Caleb.

"I won't dignify the question with a remark," Caleb replies crossly.

"That's all well and fine, but let me tell you a story. It's a sad story, one of heartbreak," Barnes continues.

"Caleb, what's he talking about?"

"Don't worry. Whatever Drew declared isn't pertinent to Gabriel, and these good constables are wasting our time."

Dawe drums her fingers and says sarcastically, "You finished?"

He pitches his hands and leans in closer to the table. "I guess so, since you're both so eager to unleash this heartbreaking story."

"Let's go back in time—eleven years, to be exact. A hot spring afternoon, mid-May; an apartment on Beverly Street situated in downtown Toronto, only blocks from the University of Toronto. You remember this place?"

"Of course. I lived there all three years of law school. What about it?"

"You know, I find it strange you didn't mention this the other day when you were so hell-bent on making us aware how much you detested Andrew Murphy. In fact, the two of you shared this two-bedroom apartment, didn't you?"

Caleb unfolds his arms. "Didn't find my previous life in Toronto relevant to the events happening now."

"Hmm. Well, in our world, everything is relevant, and when you hide stuff, it makes us assume there's more you're hiding."

"Again, no comment."

"All right, constables, is this going somewhere?" asks Oliver.

"Oh, it's unquestionably going somewhere. Bear with me a moment more."

Oliver sits back in his chair, anxious of what the following sentences will hold.

"You and Andrew—we're you close?"

"Back then, yeah, we were the best of friends. Hell, we've known each other since we were six years old. Grew up in Mount Pearl."

"But now—you're not on speaking terms? Right?"

"Our lives took different paths."

"How so?"

"We finished undergrad together, came back to St. John's, things were great between us."

"Yeah, yeah, let's get to the part when things went south," Barnes says.

"We both wanted to work in law, so we spent time researching the best law schools in Canada and chose UT. We applied, a few months of nervous waiting passed, until finally, we received our acceptance letters. We were ecstatic we'd both gotten in. So we decided to share an apartment near campus."

"I see. Is the apartment all the two of you shared?"

Oliver leans forward. "I'm sorry, what are you implying?"

"Let me be a bit more direct, since that's how you both seem to like things. Were you and Drew Murphy *more* than roommates in college?" Barnes asks excitedly.

Caleb sits silent, glaring crossly into the constable's eyes. Again, he folds his arms across his chest, takes a deep breath, and ponders.

How do I even respond to this?

The moment passes. He closes his eyes and confesses a secret he's held on to for so many years. A secret so buried he shutters to even say it aloud.

"Yes: we were together, even in love with one another, once upon a time. The problem was that Drew, unlike myself, was too petrified to come out, and after wasting months squabbling about it, our love affair dwindled. And in the end, all the lies and secrets forced me to end our relationship. My anger and bitterness toward him forced a deep-seated wedge between us, and things have never been the same since."

"So, you're still in love with him?" Barnes asks.

"Are you hard of hearing? I told you, *I* ended it when his decision to live straight was worthier than love. So, to respond to your out-of-line question, no, I'm not *still* in love with him. That ship sailed long ago."

Oliver grows beyond annoyed and pushes back. "Look, my client has explained his past relationship, and I don't see how something from eleven years ago has anything to do with Gabriel. Let's move on, okay?"

"Sure. Next item on the list: Forensics examined the security footage provided by the grocery store. Gabriel *did* make it to the store and checked out at 11:52 AM. Although, we did find one thing peculiar that hopefully you can explain, Mr. Winters."

"Sure."

"When he drove out of the store parking lot, he turned right. Yet, to get to your house, you'd go left. Is there some sort of shortcut by going this way?"

"I'm not aware of any shortcuts. I don't know why he'd go the opposite direction."

"We did check all the traffic cameras from the area. However, the Foodland is the only sighting we caught of him. He never heads toward the city. Which without doubt made us believe he went north."

"I assume you're focusing your search there?" Oliver asks.

"We have. And guess what turned up early this morning?"

Caleb's fingers tap his separated lips. "I dunno, you found Gabriel, and kept it a secret?"

"You're warm. We haven't found him; however, we found his car abandoned in Pouch Cove near Old Pond. Any clue why he'd be there?"

"No clue. We have no friends there." Panic begins setting in for Caleb.

Dawe pulls out a set of photos and spreads them out in front of the two. Caleb reaches out and lifts a picture to examine it. He turns to Oliver, who's now sick and tired of the runaround questions.

"All right, I've had enough. I know my client would prefer to be out looking for his boyfriend instead of sitting here for this bombardment of nonsense questions," Oliver begins. "So cut to the chase. Why are we here? Has your forensics investigators made a discovery that gives you any sign he's involved?"

"Maybe."

"And finally, we've arrived at the station," Oliver says.

"Joke all you want. Forensics discovered your prints all over the car: the steering wheel, driver's-side window, and on the door handle on the outside of the vehicle. Can you explain how your prints are all over your missing boyfriend's car?"

Oliver glances over. "Say something, man."

"Of course my prints are all over the car. He's my boyfriend, after all. I moved the car the other night. I needed to pull into the garage, and he was asleep."

"Is this a common habit?" Dawe asks.

"Yeah, I mean, if you dusted my car for prints, you'll find his in there," Caleb says. "This—this is the reason you drug me all the way over here? For some goddamn fingerprints in his car? I always thought you had it out for me, but this . . . this right here is the most despicable thing you could ever do."

The two constables exchange a glance, and Dawe leans against the back of the chair, speechless. Oliver scoots his chair closer to the table and changes his posture.

"Constables, we've sat here and listened to enough crap. Now, I'd like to ask you a few questions: First, why the hell did you bring up Caleb's past relationship with Drew Murphy? What does it have to do with Gabriel's disappearance?"

"Maybe Caleb never got over him, so he murdered Sebastian two years ago in hopes of rekindling the old flame."

Oliver laughs. "First, you have never been able to prove Caleb had anything to do with the disappearance of his husband. Hell, you don't even know if the remains you found are his or not. Besides, you heard it from the horse's mouth—my client was the one to end the relationship with Mr. Murphy, for understandable reasons. Why murder his husband to be with someone he doesn't even want to be with? Your hypothesis doesn't hold water."

Her mouth tics as if trying to speak, but as quickly as it comes on, it fades.

"Which leads me to my next question: Did your forensics team locate any blood? Was there any sign of foul play?"

"It's an ongoing investigation, and we'd prefer not to disclose information," Dawe replies.

Oliver scoffs. "Strike two. Last question: Do you even have enough evidence to arrest, let alone charge, my client with a crime at this point?"

"Not at this time. This was merely a friendly conversation."

Caleb rolls his eyes. "Yeah, okay, questioning someone under 'caution' isn't a friendly chat." Caleb scoots the chair away from the table and stands. "Am I free to leave?"

"I mean, you're not under arrest."

Oliver taps Caleb on the shoulder and signals for him to move in the direction of the door. Caleb wastes no time and makes a beeline to the exit, but Oliver hangs back a moment. "When you're ready to be transparent, you let me know. In the meantime, I recommend you refrain from harassing my client any further. I'm a man who gets things done, and I have no problem filing a complaint with your superiors."

"Understood," Barnes replies.

"If you need anything, you contact me first."

Oliver's threat leaves them dumbstruck, and he leaves through the door and sprints to catch up with Caleb, who is halfway toward the exit and ready to get the hell out. Oliver catches up with Caleb waiting tensely near the front door of the building.

"You okay?"

"I need some air."

Oliver steps in front of Caleb and holds the front door open for him. The walk back to the car across the snow-covered parking lot is silent. They don't exchange a single word or glance throughout the seven-minute drive.

***

RETURNING TO HIS OFFICE, CALEB RUSHES to his desk more pissed than earlier. He stops in his tracks and glances out the window at the snow and fog covering the world below.

How could Drew tell the constables about us when he couldn't even admit our relationship ever happened to the rest of the world? And why now? Why be unashamed about it?

Oliver walks through the open door and folds his arms. "Caleb."

Caleb twists around. "Yeah?"

"Take the rest of the day off, maybe do some work from home. You've had a pretty rough week, and I think the best place for you is where Gabriel would return."

Caleb tilts his head slightly while he ponders the suggestion. "Yeah, I guess you're right. I should be home."

"Listen, you come back when you're ready. Our caseload is light, and I'm sure the interns would jump at the chance to get some real action—for a change."

"I'll keep you updated," Caleb begins. "Oh, and Olli, thanks for sticking up for me today. That interview was a complete waste of time, and those two sure have a set to throw around such outlandish accusations."

"Well, I can assure you they won't be bothering you. Well, at least not for a while. Now, get outta here."

Oliver exits and Caleb packs up. He's inches from the door when his phone buzzes. A notification flashes across his screen: a text message from Sam.

Where are you? We're sitting in your driveway.

Terror overtakes his face. *Did I forget something?*
He quickly shoots a message back.

Leaving work now, be there in twenty minutes. Hang tight.

Caleb slips the phone into his jacket and walks back to the exit. Along the way he passes a few work spaces and waves good-bye to his law clerk and interns. They sympathetically gaze at him, and it's obviously written across a few of their faces they want to console him. However, he knows if he stops, he'll never get out, and the only place he wants to be right now is home.

He dashes into the corridor and finds himself alone in the elevator. Discomfort runs down his spine, his muscles are tense and knotted. He braces himself against the wall of the elevator and sighs, hoping it will release the tension he's built up. After a moment the tightness in his back and shoulders eases, and Caleb separates from the wall and steps ahead to the center of the elevator.

How will I ever face people again? Everyone almost surely believes I'm a two-time murderer.

The elevator glides to a stop, and the doors open. He pokes his head out guardedly, scrutinizing every corner of the garage before stepping out. The vulnerability of being out in public sends his muscles into tense mode again, and the short amount of relief he had—gone in a matter of seconds.

The area is quiet and barren, and Caleb bolts to the protection of his car. With each step, his head swivels side to side, his awareness of his surroundings heightened. Every little noise, every dark corner, sends erratic gushes of adrenaline through his veins. He must be ready for any surprises awaiting him.

He arrives safely at the car with no issues and peels out of space twenty-three, exits the garage onto Harbor Drive, and speeds along the narrow street toward Torbay.

CALEB DRIVES SLOWLY ALONG MARINE DRIVE and catches a glimpse of Sam's SUV positioned in the driveway, exactly as Sam said in his text. After a nightmarish day, the faces of his best friends are exactly what he needs.

Before Caleb can even get the door open, the couple affectionately greet him. The door slams closed, and Susan reaches out her arms and wraps them around his neck.

"How was the first day back?" Susan asks.

"Eh, okay."

"So, not sure if you know, but they located Gabriel's car," Sam says.

Caleb sighs. "I found out this afternoon when Dawe and Barnes gave me the third degree."

Sam checks their surroundings. A neighbor strolls along the snowy terrain. "Maybe we should discuss this inside. Those assholes are after you again, aren't they?"

Caleb's expression closes. He sighs and unlocks the front door.

"You know, you don't have to wait in the driveway for me. You do have a key, right?" Caleb asks as they wander into the warmth of the house.

"We do. But, eh, I don't feel comfortable walking into your house without asking first."

"Well, with everything going on, you have my blessing to wait safely inside."

Susan rolls her eyes and laughs. "All right, Caleb, next time."

"So those constables grilled you earlier, you started to say," Sam says as he closes the front door behind him.

"They did. But, before we get into it, this conversation requires booze—you need anything?"

They nod, and a few moments later, Caleb reappears with a bottle of red wine and three glasses.

"So, what happened?" Susan asks before Caleb has a chance to sit.

Caleb sighs loudly. "Where to begin. Okay, I need to tell you something I've never told another soul."

Sam finishes pouring, and the couple leans forward, expecting some colossal reveal.

"But I need your solemn promise this never leaves this room."

"You can trust us."

"Something regarding my past was uncovered today. I warn you, this is huge and may shock you," he begins. "While living in Toronto, I fell in love with someone, but we were never public about it."

"Okay—and?"

"Hold up, I haven't even reached the scandalous part. The shock is who this person is."

"We already know, it was Sebastian—what's shocking?"

"It isn't Sebastian. We didn't meet until 2008. It was . . . well, someone else." He struggles to get the words out. "Someone who lives in the area, and you both know him."

Sam and Susan turn their heads simultaneously toward one another and slowly turn back to Caleb.

"Well, who was it? We know a lot of people," Sam says.

Caleb bounces his leg and scans the room before blurting out the name: "Drew."

"Drew Murphy?"

Caleb hangs his head and nods. "He's the only Drew we know."

The room goes cold, and Sam falls back against the couch. Susan too is quiet and sits there sipping her wine while keeping her eyes fixated on Caleb. After a moment of silence, she clears her throat. "I'm confused. The same Drew who is, well, was engaged to Edith Blacksmith a few years ago?"

"One and the same."

"So, what, he's . . . gay?"

Caleb shrugs his shoulders. "Who knows what he is, but he *was* in college," Caleb says. He pours his first glass and chugs it without coming up for air.

He pours another glass, but this time he sips slowly. It's clear the onslaught of unhappy recollections, police harassment, and pandemonium has done a number on his mind the past few years.

"Is this really why your friendship disintegrated like a rotting pile of compost?" Sam asks.

"It's the *only* reason. If he'd been courageous, if he'd had the strength to be himself, I'm almost certain my whole life would have gone differently."

"Ugh, stop. You've had one hell of an amazing life."

The rest of the evening involves the three sitting around the living room polishing off two more bottles of wine, talking about Caleb's and Drew's past. The clock strikes eight and Susan looks at the clock.

"We hate to run, but it's getting late. Thanks again for having us over."

"I needed this, so thank you both for everything. You have no idea how getting this off my chest helps."

"Well, I must admit we're both a little dazed. However, when I stop and think about when we were kids, there was always something a little off about him."

Caleb smirks. "Who are you telling?"

"Well, get some rest, and we'll check on you tomorrow . . . okay?" Sam asks.

"Yeah, sounds good. Let Susan drive home since she's had far less to drink than you." Caleb tries to act fatherly.

"I suppose you're right."

"We both know he's right. Hand 'em over."

Caleb stares vacantly forward as Sam lets the keys fall into Susan's hand. The couple stands at the end of the cobblestone walkway, their hands wave good-bye. It's a friendly gesture, but Caleb can tell from his perch in the doorway that their facial expressions don't match up with it. He flaunts a fake smile as they carefully trudge along the slick driveway.

I don't need anyone's pity.

The car fades into the fog and Caleb locks the door. He finds himself standing in the threshold between the dining and living rooms, where he spots the bottle of Xanax resting atop the entertainment center.

His stress levels are at an all-time high, and Caleb battles the impulse to take one, but in a moment of weakness his willpower buckles. He steps forward, snatches the bottle, and shakes the pills around. The noise the pills make banging together is better than the silence consuming the house.

His hands shake as he peels away the cap and pops one of the small white pills in his mouth. He returns to the coffee table and raises his glass of wine to his lips. In one swift move, he swallows the pill with the last swig left in the glass.

My life is falling apart.

THIRTEEN

February 17, 2017
Morning

CALEB AWAKES TO THE SOUND OF his alarm booming beside his head. For the first time in a week, this chilly morning he finds himself comfy in the bed he's shared with so many ghosts. The lumpy couch became a more brutal punishment than losing two lovers, and his body could no longer take the beating. At this point, his physical well-being trumps his mental health.

He twists his head sideways and gazes at the clock: 7:30 AM. He raises his arms and yawns, and his nose gets a whiff of the lewdest stench he's ever smelt. He smells one more time. "Phew. I've truly let myself go."

He throws the duvet and sheets aside and plants his feet onto the cold hardwood floor. His eyes take a moment to focus, and when they finally do, he sees the bathroom no more than ten feet away. But, in his emotionally draining condition, mustering up the energy to put one foot in front of the other proves more strenuous than he could have ever fathomed.

Three days have passed since he last left the house, and if it wasn't for Susan, he'd surely have starved to death.

Trying to rein in his emotions, he trods softly on a direct path toward freshening up and finding some deodorant. As the days without Gabriel elapse, even the meekest tasks like showering and eating become harder to carry out.

He slides his hand around the shower curtain, twists the knob to the hottest temperature he knows his body can manage, and places one foot inside. From the corner of his eye, he sees himself in the mirror and quickly averts his attention. He runs the palms of his hands across his scruffy face and groans.

What am I becoming? I look like a pill-popping, alcoholic junkie who's coming down from a weekend bender.

He brushes off his appearance and steps underneath the waterfall of water, which splashes against his muscular body. In the distance, the faint sound of his cell phone buzzing distracts him, and he pauses for a moment, staring vacantly at the soaked white subway tiles, debating what to do. Instead of rushing to answer, he chooses to ignore whoever it is and gets back to his meager attempt to join humanity.

He wraps up his shower and ties the towel around his waist and strolls to the bedroom. The illuminated iPhone rests on the nightstand and he can see he's missed seven calls.

Damn, must be important.

He thumbs through the call history, and one name appears five times: Constable Dawe. He drops the phone and assumes the purpose of her call is to harass him a little more.

Nope . . . not going to entertain her today.

He feels refreshed after showering and knows his teeth are in desperate need of a good brushing to wipe away the appearance of a down-on-his-luck drunkard. This disheveled look was not befitting of his character. His phone buzzes once more off in the distance, and this time he rushes over to check. A text message from Oliver.

> *Caleb, how are you holding up? Do you think you can come into the office today? If you're not up for it, it's okay.*

He ponders how to reply. *First, he says to come back when I'm ready, now he wants me to come in. Eh, what else am I doing other than sitting around here drinking myself to death.*

He texts back.

> *Yeah, I'll be in shortly.*

A few moments pass, and an answer comes across.

> *Great. See you then.*

He slips the phone into his front pocket, and he makes his way back to put on the finishing touches. With a last glance in the mirror, his appearance bears a resemblance to his former self from a few days earlier. He flips off the light and leaves his bedroom—his self-confidence is slowly returning.

Halfway down the stairs, Caleb feels the vibration of his cell phone against his leg.

Who is it now?

He looks at the phone and sees it's Dawe. Sensing the urgency and frequency of her calls, he decides (against his own better judgment) to answer her call.

"Winters."

"Oh, thank God I caught you. I've been trying to call you all morning."

"Yeah, I saw. What's up? Have you found Gabriel?"

"I have some news."

"What kind of news, exactly?"

"Ah, right—this is about the remains. Unfortunately, there is still no sign of Gabriel, but constables and cadets are out combing the woods near where we found his car," she says.

Caleb's hand wobbles as he slides out a barstool and sits, placing one elbow on the granite counter top. He sits in silence for a few seconds, processing the news. "Wha—what else did you learn?"

"The medical examiner finished his report, and with the assistance of a forensic anthropologist, they established the cause of death."

Caleb remains silent, waiting for her response.

"He died from two stab wounds to the chest. Doc suggests the knife more than likely penetrated the heart."

"Was he able to determine the kind of knife?"

"Doc is thinking a serrated hunting knife. One curious thing in his report, though—the killer is likely left-handed."

"Left-handed? I can't think of anyone left-handed."

"It's some added information for you to consider. So, they've ruled the manner of death a homicide due to sharp force trauma."

"I, I don't have words right now. Part of me feels a sense of relief, yet another part of me is angry at whoever did this. Why would someone want to murder my husband?"

"I don't know. But, if it's of any comfort, Doc says Sebastian's death would have been immediate."

"Doesn't make it any better, but it's consoling knowing he didn't suffer."

"Also, I want to apologize to you for the way I came across the other day. I know you're going through a lot, but as you and I both know, the first suspect in any missing person's investigation is the spouse."

"I know, and thanks. I am grateful for the apology."

"Are there any other questions I can answer at this time?"

"Yeah, one. When will the ME release his body? I'd like to arrange a funeral service, you know, so he can receive the proper burial he deserves."

"The mortuary can stop in anytime."

"Thanks. Oh, and before you go—while I am grateful for the call and apology, my attorney requests any further communication should go through him."

"Right—escaped my mind. I wish you a pleasant day, Mr. Winters."

He hangs up and holds the phone in his trembling hand. He's at a loss for words. He glares at the phone in his hand, uncertain of his next step.

Call Susan or the funeral home?

He glances at the clock on the wall of the kitchen: 8:15 AM.

Too early to call the funeral home—so Susan it is. She'll be able to get me through this.

The phone rings twice, and her familiar, sweet voice answers. "Morning, sunshine."

"Good morning. So, I spoke to Dawe and she gave me some unwelcome news."

"Wait, why is she calling you? I thought she has to go through Olli?"

"She's supposed to, but this time she wasn't calling to harass me."

"Oh, what, she woke up and said, 'Hey, let me call Caleb and say hello'?"

"Not exactly . . . she had a reason for calling."

"I love you dearly, but you are the worst when it comes to getting to the point."

"The remains they found were identified as Sebastian's. She says the ME concluded he was murdered."

She lets out a gasp. "Oh, Caleb, I'm so sorry. Give me like twenty minutes, and I'll drive over."

"Truthfully, I'm still in shock. I don't know why, though. I mean, I've had plenty of time to prepare myself for this phone call. It's not as if he went missing two months ago," he rambles.

"You didn't respond to me. I'll be over in twenty minutes, okay? I don't think you should be alone right now."

"I'm about to head to the office after I make the funeral arrangements."

"Are you sure that's a wise idea?"

"Drowning myself in something other than alcohol might prevent my feelings from hitting me."

"Do you hear yourself? Who are you right now?"

"Caleb."

"Such a smartass. You are aware the police called you to say they have Sebastian and they've ruled his death a homicide?"

"Yeah, I'm aware. I haven't lost it . . . yet."

"Right. Well, I for one, do not think work is where you need to be. Did they at least give you any information on the circumstances of *how* he died?"

"Yup."

"Okay, well, don't leave me in suspense," she says as Caleb overhears Sam in the background.

"He was stabbed," Caleb finally replies with a straight answer.

"Look, I'm on my way over. Do not, and I repeat, do not leave the house until I get there."

"Ugh. Okay. I guess I'll text Olli and let him know I'll be in a little later. See you soon."

He ends the call and takes a moment before texting Olli. All he needs is a moment to think, but the biggest thing on his mind: *How am I going to survive this?*

Sorry, Olli, but there's been a delay, I'll be in around one o'clock.

He drops the phone on the counter and rubs his hands against his face. No tears, no emotions whatsoever. All he feels is numb, and he keeps an eye on the clock ticking by until it hits nine.

Better get this out of the way.

He lifts the phone and searches the web for a local recommended funeral home to use, and after fifteen minutes of debating, he finally decides.

"Good morning, Larson's Funeral Home, how may I help you?" the voice asks.

"Hi, yes . . . I'd . . . I need to plan a funeral."

FOURTEEN

February 17, 2017
Afternoon

HY AM I AT WORK? I SHOULD be more emotional. Why am I not crying? Caleb opens the glass door to the law firm and walks across the lobby, bypassing the reception desk, where the office manager waves and welcomes him back. Caleb stops only for a second but doesn't speak. Instead, he puts on a phony façade and continues through another door, which leads to the staff offices.

He looks up as he steps through the door and sees Oliver leaning against his law clerk's cubicle. It's like he's been waiting in this exact spot patiently for hours. With a concerned expression painted across his face, he rushes across the office and blocks Caleb's path inside.

"Hey, hey. Hold up a sec," Oliver says.

"Whoa. What's up? Can I put down my stuff before we talk?"

"Eh, well—you have a visitor waiting for you. I wanted to give you a heads-up."

Caleb stands on his tippy-toes peeking over Oliver's broad shoulders. There, he sees him: the unwelcome, familiar side profile of his adversary and ex—Drew Murphy.

"You let him in my office? Why?"

"Said he wanted to surprise you. I figured maybe you guys made amends or something."

"Hardly. Damn, Olli, you should have made him wait in the lobby like everyone else," Caleb says, annoyed. "Let me figure out what in the hell he wants, and I'll drop by your office afterward. Cool?"

"Sure, take your time. And, Caleb, be on guard with this guy. I don't trust him."

Caleb sighs. "That makes two of us."

Fuck! Has he come to ruin my day or something? It's not as if I don't already have a million things on my mind.

He firmly grips the door handle, takes a deep breath, and opens the door. "Andrew. This is a surprise. What's the special occasion?"

Drew uncrosses his legs and stands, extending out his hand as he approaches Caleb. "I heard they identified the remains and I had to come in person to express my sympathies."

Caleb can't tell if his condolences are honest or deceptive, but either way, the fact he showed up in person seems like the right thing, given the circumstances.

Caleb replies, "Thanks. It means a lot, particularly coming from you. You know, given our sordid history."

"I'm glad you brought up our history. You got a few minutes to talk?"

Caleb takes off his jacket and drapes it on the coatrack in the corner of his office.

Like I have a choice? Ugh, I wanted to come here and find peace and solitude. Instead, I get this.

Caleb gives his famous fake smile. "Sure. Take a seat." The two men sit opposite from one another across the desk. "Anything, in particular, you wanted to talk about?"

"Look, I'll cut right to the chase—the tension between us has gone too far," Drew says.

Under his breath, Caleb remarks, "No shit."

"And I know it's all because of what I did to you years ago. It was wrong. I was wrong. I let my ego and my fears destroy not only our relationship but also our friendship."

Caleb looks away. "Yup."

"And I know these past few years haven't been the easiest for you, and after everything we've gone through during our lives— well, I should have been there for you."

"You had your reasons, and I had mine. It's all water under the bridge now."

"I had too many excuses, but now I'm ready to make a decision. And it could potentially have a negative effect on my entire life. And the thought of it scares me to death."

"Oh? What kind of decision? Finally thinking about coming out of the closet?"

Drew nods. "I'm seriously contemplating it. I think I've lived a lie long enough."

Caleb sits silently in his chair and his eyes widen.

Where was this guy ten years ago?

Caleb reaches for a bottle of water he always keeps on the corner of the desk and unscrews the top, chugging for a few seconds. "Yeah, I think you've lied to everyone *and* yourself long enough."

"I only wish I had the confidence to do this years ago."

Caleb nods, but he can see there's something else on Drew's mind.

"Something else bothering you?"

"As a matter of fact, yes. A Constable Barnes paid me a visit a few days ago. He asked a lot of questions about you, Sebastian, Gabriel, and, more importantly, he asked me about us."

Caleb rolls his eyes. "Yeah, I know. They threw our secret out in the open."

"Caleb, you're still so dramatic. I tried to say we were only friends, college roommates, but he kept prodding, and he couldn't grasp how two people who grew up together, completed undergrad and law school together, suddenly had such a fallout. But the story I tried to conjure up on the spot, well, he didn't buy it."

Caleb shakes his head. "Well, unfortunately, they took 'our secret' and tried to use it against me. Their claim is I am hiding something from them. Dawe did everything but flat-out accuse me of murdering Sebastian and Gabriel because I'm still secretly in love with you."

Drew laughs. "Nonsense. I read the ME's report, and the killer is left-handed. I think it's pretty obvious to even a blind man that you're not left-handed."

Caleb cocks his head. "How'd you get access to the ME's report already? I found out only this morning."

"Um, hello, I'm the Crown prosecutor—I know about everything anybody does around here."

"Right."

They sit in silence, neither of them sure of what to say next. Caleb breaks the nervous tension; the awkwardness drives him insane. "So, what are you proposing we do? Are you here because you wanted to shoot the shit—or were you hoping we'd make up and let the past remain there?"

"Honestly, I miss you. I've missed you since the day you walked out of the apartment door in tears. Sure, it'll take time, but I'll do whatever I must to have you back in my life."

"You don't have any ulterior motives in mind, do you? I mean, it would look pretty suspicious to the RNC if you did."

"Strictly on a friendship level only. I didn't come here to cause you any grief, Caleb. I know you're going to need support, and if I follow through with my plans to live my life openly, my ass will need someone who can give me guidance. Someone who understands me. Someone who can be there for me when I need a shoulder to cry on. And let's face it, we both know you're the best listener around these parts."

Caleb chuckles. "I hate to admit it, but I am."

Drew's lips curl upward. He tries hard not to, but he stretches his lips apart and flashes his killer smile with perfect, white teeth. It's

Caleb's kryptonite, and every time he sees it his heart melts. Drew could get away with anything at this point.

"So, how about I buy you a drink after work. You know, to bury the hatchet."

"Shame, I already have plans with Sam and Susan for dinner around six-ish."

"Ah, I see. Well, another time then," Drew replies as his bright smile diminishes.

Caleb detects the shift in his demeanor and offers a hasty solution. "On second thought, you haven't seen them in so long, maybe instead of drinks on the town, you should join us."

Drew flips through his phone, conceivably checking his calendar, and deliberates the invite. After a moment, his fingers stop moving and he glances up. "You know what, count me in. It'd do me some good to see those two. God, how long has it been?"

"Since their wedding, fourteen years ago."

"Has it been that long?"

"They married in the summer of 2003, right before we left for law school."

They chat for another forty minutes, and before either of them notice, it's nearing 2:30 PM. Drew jumps from the plush chair. "Hey, I gotta jet. Court reconvenes at three thirty."

"No worries. Thanks for the chat."

"Yeah, was nice. Well, I'll see you at your place around six. Or I could even come by a little earlier to help out."

Caleb smiles. "Yeah, is five too early?"

"I'll be there somewhere around then. See ya."

Drew disappears into the sea of cubicles and Caleb can't wrap his head around what in the hell happened.

I never thought I'd see this day—but why now? All these years he's had plenty of chances to come talk to me, but he never did. Eh, I'm overly paranoid.

He waits in the door for a minute, ensuring Drew has left before heading over to Oliver's office. He's turning the corner and pulls out his phone to shoot off a group text to Sam and Susan, who both deserve fair warning of the extra body arriving for dinner.

After he is confident the message has sent, he flips his phone over to vibrate and softly knocks. From behind the door, Oliver's calming voice shouts out. "Come in."

Caleb twists the knob and peeks his head through the crack. "Hey, you got a few minutes to chat?"

Oliver waves him in, and Caleb pulls out a chair. "I got the official word back from Justice Rowe this morning regarding the evidentiary review you requested in the Sanderson case," Oliver says.

Fear crosses Caleb's face. "She already denied my verbal request, so I assume since you're not smiling, she's now rejected my written one too."

"Yeah, she's not buying your argument of flawed evidence. Therefore, Sanderson's conviction stands."

Caleb lets out a long sigh. "He's not going to like this."

Oliver shakes his head. "Screw him, I'm more worried about how you're holding up?"

Caleb frowns.

"Look, I know I told you to take all the time you need, but after finding out they identified Sebastian I wanted to see you in person."

"I know I should be more emotional, but I think I cried so much when he disappeared I've used up all the tears I have. Sounds heartless, huh?"

"I don't think so. We all grieve in our own ways. You grieved for so many months, maybe now you're relieved?"

"Yeah. It's like the mystery of not knowing is over and I finally have closure, but there's still one more mystery to solve."

"Agreed. I haven't heard any updates on how the search is going from the constables."

Caleb lowers his head. "I have."

Oliver jumps from his seat and slams his hand against the desk. "What? I specifically told them to leave you alone and call me."

"She caught me off guard. Sit, Olli, it's okay."

Oliver returns to his chair and collects himself. "So, did she offer you any insight?"

"Nothing other than telling me the RNC is still searching for him. I know he'll turn up. I am trying to remain optimistic about it."

Oliver's mouth curves into a smile. "I know he will. But you are aware when they find him he'll be deported back to the US."

Caleb lowers his head again. "Yeah, I can't believe he was so stupid to think someone wouldn't catch on."

"Happens all the time. So, what did Murphy want?"

Caleb pauses for a moment, uncertain if he should divulge the entire story or make something up to keep Oliver off his back. "Just came by to talk work stuff."

"Well, not sure it looks good to have him around, especially after how those two constables came at you the other day."

"You're right."

An awkward silence ensues, and Caleb's mind wanders back to "why now?" with regards to Drew's sudden change of heart. Something doesn't add up, but he can't place his finger on what it is exactly. Oliver interrupts his scatterbrain moment with his loud pecking against his keyboard. Caleb snaps out of his daydream and focuses on his partner once again.

"Hey, listen, I should head back home. I need a little more time to prepare for the funeral and finding Gabriel. You don't mind— right?"

"Caleb, I said to take all the time you need. I wanted you to come in so I could see you in person and make sure you're holding yourself together."

"The best I can."

"Well, go home and take care of yourself. Make sure you let me know about the funeral details."

"I will," Caleb says as he feels a vibration from his pocket.

Caleb walks out and returns to his office. The phone vibrates again, but he continues to ignore it. All he wants is to get out of this suffocating building and head back to a place he feels safe.

He stands waiting for the elevator to arrive and another message comes through.

I better phone back whoever called.

Caleb removes his phone and presses his thumbprint against the home button. The screen comes to life, and he sees the notification.

3 Missed Calls & Voicemail
Sam Butler

"Figures, he's calling to give me shit."

The elevator door opens, and he steps in. With the tap of his finger, he calls to listen to the voicemail during his short trip to the underground parking garage.

"Caleb, what the fuck? Why would you invite *him* of all people to dinner? Look, call me back, because we need to talk about this." The message ends.

Wow, he's seriously pissed. I'll call back on my way home.

He shoves the phone back into his jacket pocket and waits patiently for the doors to open. He steps into the parking garage and again his phone is blowing up with another call.

Let's get this ass chewing over with.

He answers, and without even a hello, Sam straightaway tears into him. "What in the fuck is wrong with you? Why'd you invite Drew?"

Caleb doesn't answer, and the line is silent for a few moments.

"Answer me."

Caleb yanks the phone away from his ear and listens while Sam carries on scolding. Another long pause gives Caleb a chance to jump in. "Hey, chill out for like two seconds and let me say what I have to say."

"No. You have no clue how upset I am with you right now. I don't believe there's anything you can say to make any of this better," Sam says.

"Look, Drew reached out to me. He showed up at my office to offer his condolences and we ended up on the topic of moving on. I've spent too many years resenting him, avoiding him, and now we have a chance to make amends. You know, an opportunity for me to let go of all the resentment I've buried deep inside. Why can't you let me have this?" Caleb asks.

Sam scoffs. "You're old enough to do whatever you want, but mark my word, there's something off with him. I am skeptical about this."

"I can appreciate your concerns, but if we're being honest, I'm not convinced yet he doesn't have ulterior motives. My inner voice keeps reminding me to keep my guard up, but at the same time, I've known him since grade school. I can't . . . no, *we* can't turn our backs on him."

Caleb listens to his best friend drawing in deep breaths and exhaling purposely. Caleb keeps his mouth shut, hoping Sam is coming to his senses and gathering his emotions. He detects a break in the wrath, so he resumes expressing his point. "Also, we were *all* friends with him up until I told you we had a falling out in Toronto. You never asked for the full story—you automatically picked my side—"

Sam interrupts. "I chose your side because I trust you."

"Don't get me wrong, I'm thankful for the trust. But I lied to you about the details of the why. So you can't be mad at him without being mad at me," Caleb says. "I want everything to be okay, for my life to go back to normal. I'm so tired of the lies. I've already lost my husband—"

"But now you've lost your cheating, lying, felonious boyfriend too. All right, all right. I'll give him another chance—but . . ." Sam starts to say.

"No, we aren't doing any buts. I've lost enough people in my life, I don't want to lose any more. And I swear, Sam, if you cause a scene tonight, I'll never speak to you again."

Sam scoffs. "Fine. I'll be on my best behavior. Look, I need to get back to work. See you around six."

The call abruptly ends without as much as a good-bye. Caleb lowers the phone and heaves a sigh of relief. Caleb has never experienced Sam so pissed, but he understands why he is.

How do I make this better? I don't need this drama in my life right now.

FIFTEEN

February 17, 2017
Late Afternoon

THE **MERCEDES WHIPS INTO THE PARKING** lot of an unfamiliar grocery alongside the main road leading to Torbay. With an abundance of unfilled spaces to pick from, he chooses one closest to the door and throws the car in park. He cuts the engine and takes in the sight of his hardened face in the rearview mirror.

Damn, I need some sleep.

With the heated conversation with Sam still running through his mind, Caleb finds his behavior odd. *Why is Sam so angry?* Caleb wonders. *Better yet, why does he even care?*

Caleb can't answer the question he puts to himself. It's not like either of them did anything to him personally, so why is he so engrossed in rage?

The thoughts weigh heavy on his mind as he walks around to the trunk to grab a few canvas bags.

I'm a good person, and I don't deserve any of this.

He approaches the entrance to the store and the doors swipe open as he shuffles closer. His mind is so overwrought with emotions he doesn't realize the doors and continues walking forward in a daze. In autopilot mode he grabs a handbasket but stops in his tracks. The eeriness of the deserted store sends a shiver up his spine, which breaks the clutter in his mind.

For 3:40 in the afternoon, the store is a ghost town. And to make things more uncomfortable, there is a dark heaviness upon his back, the same tingly sensation you get when someone is staring at you. In a hasty move, he spins around, but no one is there.

He moves on, gathering the items he's scratched onto a scrap piece of paper. A bag of carrots, celery, a couple of onions. He continues weaving in and out of aisles of fresh vegetables and fruit, but the overwhelming sensation creeps up again and he picks up the pace.

This place is fucking creepy when it's empty.

Darting in and out of isles with backbreaking speed, he finishes his shopping list and finds the lone open register to checkout. He's emptying the contents onto the belt when a pleasant yet unfamiliar face greets him. "Mausey day, wha?"

Having been born and raised in Newfoundland, the local dialect is one he knows well, yet seldom uses. "Yeah, I sure wish spring would hurry up and get here."

"Don't I know it, sweetheart. I ain't see you here before. Where's you from?"

"St. John's, born and raised. But now I own a place on the outskirts of Torbay."

"Ah, a townie turned bayman, are ya?"

Caleb nods and flashes his first sincere smile in weeks.

"Torbay's a beautiful place," she says as she scans items across the scanner, "but have ya heard about the young American man who's gone missing up there? You know anything about dat?"

Caleb freezes, unsure how he wants to respond to her question.

Play dumb, play dumb. You'll never see this woman again.

"No, I hadn't. You know what happened?"

"Oh, well, there's an article in today's paper. The fella who wrote it says the police aren't sure yet, but they say he has a lover, ya know—a man he shacks up with." She whispers, like it's some taboo subject to discuss a gay couple.

Caleb's facial expression dulls as she finishes ringing up his items.

"Hey, mind ringing me up for a newspaper as well? I'd like to read more about this remarkable story," Caleb says.

"Sure thing, love. I tell ya, you know the loud-mouthed senior constable over at the RNC, the one who's always on the news."

Caleb nods his head in agreement.

"Well, she told the paper she thinks this fella's boyfriend is involved."

"You don't say. Well, for his sake, I hope they find him soon."

"Me too—stuff like this is bad for tourism."

Caleb steps back and frowns. He can't believe this woman. If his parents hadn't raised him proper, he'd surely scream and cuss her out. But he can't bring himself to cause a scene.

"Well, good day, love," Caleb says as he walks away, snatching a copy of the newspaper on his way out.

This woman doesn't even care about Gabriel. All she's worried about it tourism. What a bitch.

He reaches the front door and a burning sensation rises in his face. He's pissed, but not at the old woman. Poor sweet thing is ignorant but means well. No, he's pissed at Dawe and Barnes for going to the media and naming him as a person of interest, something he figured would subside with the information they had from the autopsy.

I guess I'm off the hook for Sebastian's murder.

He clicks a button, and the trunk opens. He drops the two bags inside, slams it closed, but keeps the newspaper close to his chest. He sits in the warm car, unfolds the newspaper, and gazes at the top story on the front page. Staring back at him in bold typeset is the headline. "American Man Missing from Torbay." Below in smaller italics, it reads: *"Local RNC constables suspect foul play."*

He scans the article and pauses when he finds the direct quote from Constable Dawe.

The RNC has questioned the man's partner, Caleb Winters, concerning the disappearance of Gabriel Parsons. While currently there is no evidence to suggest his direct involvement, we are not ruling him out as a possible suspect.

Caleb chucks the paper across the car and thumps his hands against the steering wheel. His anger is growing. His face has a hue of blood red. He's turns over the engine, but the article has him too upset to drive home, so he sits in the parking space, sporadically glancing at the newspaper he's scattered about the car.

She may as well flat-out brand me a murderer. How can I ever show my face around town again?

After ten minutes pass, Caleb has pulled himself together enough and he shifts the car into reverse and heads back out onto the road home.

***

WITH A QUICK TURN, THE FRONT door swings open and Caleb juggles the bags on his sprint for the kitchen. The short-lived drive home provides enough time to calm his nerves, yet the burnt fuse still smolders, and unbeknownst to anyone, even the slightest annoyance could trigger another flare-up.

He empties the contents of the bags, one by one, onto the counter and opens the cookbook propped next to the stove. If there is one thing in the universe to change his mood, it is cooking. He pulls out a couple of pans and swipes through his phone to find some perfect mood music to lift his spirits. It's 4:30 PM and he expects Drew to show up on his doorstep anytime.

He finds the perfect tune and continues lying the ingredients out methodically. The music starts, and he finds himself caught up in the song; still stuck in a bad place, he gently sways to the music. The music halts when a telephone call rudely interrupts his jam.

Damn.

He walks to the island and peeks at his phone. Susan's smiling face floods the screen.

"Hey, what's up?"

"Not much. How are you?"

"The same. Oh God, please don't tell me you're calling to cancel."

"No, no, of course not. But I am curious if you've talked with Sam?"

"You're kidding me, right? After I sent the text about Drew, you know his ass blew my phone up."

"How long ago?" He senses panic in her voice.

"I dunno, maybe an hour ago. Why? Something wrong?"

"I don't know. Dispatch called and said they've been unable to make radio contact with him and Nicole for the last half hour."

Caleb leans against the island. "Odd. Maybe they radioed in a break and dispatch missed it?"

"Nah, it's a slow day and she catches every little thing."

"Well, I'm worried. It's not like them to not reply. When'd you speak with him last?"

"Right after you sent out your text message. He was pretty pissed."

"Oh, you don't gotta tell me. I already suffered his fury."

"What should I do?"

"Does the ambulance service have people who handle situations like this?"

"Umm, the manager would, but he's worthless."

"Well, have you told him?"

"I did."

"Well, are they looking for them?"

"Not sure."

"All right, look, let's delay dinner and get out there to search for them."

She's quiet, but knowing her, Caleb realizes she's considering her options. "You wouldn't mind?"

"Nah. But Drew will be pulling up any minute, and I'm not going to send him home after driving all the way up here."

"Ugh. So, what you're saying is he's coming along?"

"I hope that's all right."

"I guess I'll survive," she begins and goes silent. "Can I be frank with you?"

"Since when do you ask?"

She sighs. "Well, like Sam, I'm not too ecstatic about Drew being back."

Caleb rolls his eyes. "Message received, loud and clear. Look, let's revisit this topic later, say, after we locate Sam and Nicole. Right now, I'm gonna go get ready. See you shortly." He hangs up without saying good-bye and releases the phone from his hand. It hits the island with a bang.

"Grrrr."

His aggravation with the entire situation is rearing its ugly head once more. His two best friends are making it seem as if he must choose a side, but it's a choice Caleb doesn't want, nor does he think it's something he must decide. On one hand, Sam and Susan have been there for him, no matter what is happening, since they were eight. But now there's the man who he secretly never stopped loving? How could he turn his back on him?

His phone chimes again with a text from Drew.

Five minutes away.

Caleb lets the phone fall without responding. He turns away, running his thick fingers through his soft, wavy hair. Caleb shakes his head and meanders toward the stairs. Lethargically, his feet stomp heavily against the treads. If he's about to spend his evening hunting the forests for Sam and Nicole, he needs something a little more comfortable than a suit and tie.

He pulls a navy-blue V-neck sweater over his head, and suddenly the chime from the doorbell echoes through the house. A quick glance in the mirror, and he rushes downstairs to find Drew waiting patiently on the porch in the unfriendly, murky elements.

"Hey. I was starting to worry," says Drew.

"What for?"

"Eh, no reason."

"Well, come and get out of the cold."

He gestures with his hand and Drew inches indoors, rotating his head from side to side, taking in the foyer with its soaring ceilings. This is his first time stepping foot into Caleb's home, and he uses a few seconds to take everything in.

Caleb smiles, mainly because he's happy to be starting fresh with Drew, but the little voice in his head begins filling his mind with doubt.

You're making a huge mistake. He's only going to break your heart again. Be careful.

But as he stares at Drew, Caleb quickly puts his doubting mind at ease when it becomes obvious the man feels nothing but grateful to be there.

"Caleb, this place is amazing. You've done extremely well for yourself."

"Thanks. Well, come in and get comfortable so I can break some unwelcoming news."

They walk into the living room and Drew turns to face Caleb. "What's up?"

"So, I don't want to alarm you, but—Sam and his partner Nicole have gone missing, and I told Susan we'd help her find them."

"Ah, shit—not good."

"And I don't want you to ruin your evening. I'm sure Susan and I can manage—"

Drew cuts off Caleb. "What evening? Sitting at home eating a frozen dinner alone. Nah, I think we should get out there and find them."

Caleb's attempt at getting out of spending an entire car ride with Susan and Drew in silence fails miserably. He'll have to suck it up and meet the inevitable tension head on.

Before Caleb can interject, Drew utters on. "Let's face it, though. The more eyes out there, the better, I suppose."

"True."

"He's been missing how long?"

"Maybe an hour, give or take. But it's not like Sam or Nicole to disappear or be off the grid this long."

"Wait? Are they on shift? Has the ambulance company been notified?"

"Yes and yes."

"And the ambulance company is out searching for them?" Drew asks.

"Susan says the manager is worthless, so I'm going to speculate they are not," Caleb replies.

"Hang on." Drew pulls out his phone.

Caleb stands by and watches Drew swipe his finger across the bright LED display.

What's going on?

Drew taps angrily against the screen, turns away from Caleb, and raises the oversized iPhone to his ear.

A few seconds elapse and whomever he's calling finally answers. "Hey, Robert. Drew Murphy here. Were you aware two of your medics are missing?"

A few head nods and filler words later, Drew speaks again. "Yeah, perhaps beneficial to get someone, anyone, out searching for them. Yeah, okay, sure . . . give me a call back with an update." He hangs up the phone and twirls around to face Caleb once more.

"I'm impressed."

"Eh, it's nothing. I'm friends with the manager, and he says he wasn't aware of anyone missing."

"Huh? Susan says she told him."

"Well, regardless, he's sending people out to search now."

Caleb relaxes, sensing his former best-friend-turned-lover-then-adversary is standing in his living room helping. "Well, thank you for agreeing to help. However, I hope you're not too upset this means dinner may be postponed."

"Eh, it's all good. Pack up some granola bars and water, and I'll be set. When did Susan say she'd be here?"

Caleb glances at his watch. "Any moment."

***

CALEB PULLS BACK THE CURTAINS AND sees Susan skid into the driveway. She's drumming her hands anxiously against the steering wheel. He observes for another few seconds until they hear three quick toots of the horn and Caleb's and Drew's eyes meet.

"Same ole Susan," Drew jokes.

"Yeah, she hasn't changed much," Caleb says. "Hey, do me a favor and try not to make this 'reunion' more awkward than it already will be."

Drew agrees.

The heavy door slams behind Caleb and they move along the pathway to the SUV. Caleb jumps in the front and Drew sits in the back. And before Caleb even closes the door, Susan tears out of the driveway. Her face gives a mixed story. On one hand, she looks scared shitless, but on the other, her rapid movements and demeanor say she's more annoyed than scared.

She's irked I brought him along.

The stillness of the car becomes stifling, and Caleb cracks the window before breaking the awkwardness. His hands are trembling, and for a split second, Caleb worries he's only going to do more harm than good. He lets the words fall out of his mouth anyhow. "Hey, you okay? I want you to know I'm worried about him."

Susan tips her head a bit. "Me too."

Caleb reaches across the center console. She releases her right hand from the steering wheel and squeezes Caleb's firmly before letting out a long sigh. With everything he's been through these past few years, the last thing he wants to see is his best friend going through the same stress he has. Her deer-in-headlights look breaks his heart.

Thirty minutes pass and the SUV zooms along the sparsely populated back roads of Newfoundland. The conditions are less than favorable for conducting this type of search, but even with as much ground as they've covered, there's no sign of the missing ambulance or its crew. Susan comes to a rolling stop at the intersection with the highway and hangs a right. Caleb is curious why they're heading away from Torbay.

"Shouldn't we be going the other way?" Caleb asks.

"I know he was here earlier," Susan says while passing a small, wooden green-painted sign posted alongside the road announcing they're entering Pouch Cove.

"Is he up this way often?"

"Sometimes."

Caleb hangs his head. "You know this is where Sebastian's remains were found."

A hush falls over the car, and Caleb feels Drew squeeze his shoulder. "You okay?" Drew asks.

"Yeah, we need to find them."

"Caleb, I'm so sorry to drag you out here. I didn't know who else to call. I didn't even think about the fact you have your own troubles."

"It's okay. With all the loss lately, it'll be nice to find them both unharmed. However, not to be too morbid, but do you think maybe we should check up there?"

"Where?" she asks.

"Old Pond. The place they found Sebastian."

"Worth a shot."

Caleb's eyes begin seeping, and he quickly wipes the lone tear away and puts on his brave face again. He's tired and leans his head against the icy glass window, hoping the shock will snap him back to the hardened soul he is.

Susan sees the sign that reads 'Old Pond,' pointing to the left, and without slowing down, she turns sharply. The wheels hit the gravel road and the SUV skids. Caleb starts Google maps, but by the time everything registers, the computerized voice is a bit late, and Susan hooks a hard right, nearly taking out a wooden fence.

"Nice save," Drew says encouragingly.

She's less than enthused to hear his voice and remains quiet. Her focus is solely on reaching the pond.

The SUV comes to a skidding halt where the pavement meets the dirt. Susan turns to Caleb for advice.

"Should we continue?"

"What do we have to lose? You got four-wheel drive, yeah?"

"Yeah."

"Okay, so best-case scenario, we don't find them there. Worst case, well—" Caleb starts, but then cuts himself off before saying something he'll regret.

She engages the four-wheel drive, releases her foot from the brake, and gingerly continues off the beaten path along the bumpy road. The SUV rounds a sharp curve, and as they crest the top of the hill, there it sits, the ambulance they've searched the last hour for. There are no homes out here, no humans in sight. The area is desolate apart from the ambulance parked with its hazard lights blinking.

Susan slams the car into park and rashly undoes her belt. Before Caleb realizes what's happening, he eyeballs Susan outside rushing toward the ambulance.

"We gotta stop her," Caleb cries. Caleb flings the door open at the exact time Drew does, each of them taking off after her through the deep, powdery snow.

Susan trips on something and Caleb rushes to pull her away. She's kicking and screaming, and it takes every ounce of strength inside him to get her back to the SUV.

Meanwhile, Drew studies the area, looking for any signs of foul play. But nothing apparent jumps out right away.

Drew turns around to gaze back at Caleb and Susan. "Let go of me," she hollers out.

Caleb grabs ahold of her with both hands and shakes her. "I need you to pull yourself together. You are not trained in handling evidence."

"But I have—"

"What, to see? Not going to happen. What I need you to do is get back inside and call for help."

Caleb knows firsthand some exonerated criminals who got off due to paramedics contaminating the crime scene. Now Susan has given up her fight and returns to a calm state.

"Get in," he instructs.

She sits in the passenger seat and shakes from the adrenaline coursing through her veins. Caleb stares at the ambulance and spots Drew tugging a pair of black leather gloves from his jacket.

"Can I trust you'll stay here?"

Susan gestures with an insignificant nod, and a tentative Caleb dashes to Drew's side.

"Anything?"

"I was about to pop open the back."

Caleb is edgy and fastens to Drew's side like a lost puppy.

"Um, Caleb, you might wanna step back in case a surprise awaits us."

Drew pulls open the door and jumps backward. Inside, they find the cabinets ransacked, and lying on the gurney is a black medic jacket covered in blood with the name "BISHOP" embossed above the left breast pocket.

"Doesn't look good for Nicole," Drew says.

Something dripping from the ceiling catches Caleb's eye, and he tilts his head backward to get a better look. Blood castoff, and a lot of it.

"Drew—back away."

The telltale signs of murder haven't even crossed Drew's mind yet. "Why? What's up?"

Caleb points up, and Drew follows with his eyes. He takes two steps back and falls onto the snow while Caleb slams the doors closed.

"There's so much blood."

"Yeah, I've never seen so much in person. But if I had to call this, I'd say we're looking to recover bodies instead of a rescuing them."

"Wait, wait—where's the blood trail. If someone murdered them, shouldn't there be more evidence?" Caleb asks.

"Who knows. It's been snowing heavily all day. Maybe the blood trail and footprints were covered up?"

"I think we'd still be able to see it regardless of the snow."

"Come on, Caleb, Forensics 101, you remember the class well."

"Yes, but I also remember no matter how good a criminal thinks they are, they are always going to leave a piece of themselves behind—the Locard exchange principle."

"I know the theory."

"Well, most of the time the principle applies, but we aren't dealing with common, thoughtless criminals. They are methodical, they leave nothing behind."

"I'm confused, we are talking about the same Sanderson who I sent to prison for ten years, aren't we?"

"We are."

"So, he's not as good as you think then. Everyone makes mistakes."

"Uh, you have no idea the types of people who work for him. Trust me, it's rare for them to make mistakes."

"Okay, let's say I do buy this crazy notion of Sanderson's involvement. If Nicole and Sam are dead, tell me this: Why isn't there any evidence outside of this rig to indicate anything happened?"

"Maybe his goons used plastic wrap or something," Caleb replies.

"Okay. So, you're thinking they're both dead?"

Caleb hangs his head in silence. "I don't know. Remember, we're lawyers, not criminalists. We had two forensics classes in law school, so I'd say we are far from experts."

"True."

Meanwhile, Susan watches powerlessly from the SUV. She studies the cumbersome movements of the two men, and without knowing what's said, their hand gestures and angry facial expressions force her to hop out and holler across the barren land.

"What's going on?" she yells.

Caleb hangs his head because he knows what he's about to tell her isn't the news she would be hoping for.

"Caleb . . . Drew . . . tell me," she screams.

"Have you called the constabulary?"

"They're on the way. What'd you find?"

Caleb trudges across the snow and stands with his arm resting on the door. "First, I need you to remain calm. Can you do that?"

She doesn't acknowledge his question.

"Look, I won't sugarcoat this: something sinister happened here."

"How bad?"

"Well, from what I've seen, things aren't looking good for Nicole."

Drew pulls Caleb aside.

"What should we do?" Caleb asks.

"We should wait in the car for the constables to arrive."

"They're at least forty minutes away. What if I'm wrong and they are in danger, or somewhere in the woods clinging to life?"

"What do you suggest?"

"I think we should fan out and search. But what do we do with her," Caleb says as he points at Susan. "Wait, where is she?"

"She was there a second ago."

While Drew and Caleb argued over what to do, Susan had rushed to the back of the ambulance to see for herself. When they finally arrive at the rear of the ambulance, she's already flung both rear doors open and stands in disbelief. Both hands clasped around her face.

"The fuck, Susan? What part of 'wait in the car' didn't you apprehend?" Caleb exclaims.

Drew stands aside while Caleb wrestles with her, trying his best to pull her away for a second time.

"Stop fighting me. I can't let you contaminate the scene," Drew hollers as he pulls out his phone to call Dawe himself.

Caleb manages to get a grasp on Susan and pushes her away from the scene. She falls back into the same spot Drew fell only moments earlier. She lays in the powder, her hands flailing, and a stream of tears wets her face.

Caleb crouches next to her, composing himself the best he can from hauling off and slapping some sense into her hysterical self. He reaches his breaking point and screams, "Susan, get a fucking grip!"

She stops and snaps back to reality. "I'm so sorry. I don't know what got into me."

"Come on, let's get you somewhere warm."

Caleb helps Susan to her feet, and they journey back to the SUV. This time, instead of putting her in the front passenger seat, he opens the rear door and engages the childproof lock. He'll do anything to not have a third round of fighting.

With a single swing, he slams the door closed and turns to stare at Drew, who paces back and forth a good ten feet away.

He's been on the phone awhile, I hope everything is okay.

Finally, Drew lowers the phone, slips it into his jacket, and rushes back to the SUV. He is speechless as he breezes by Caleb, opens the front passenger door, and lets loose on Susan.

"Why'd you lie about calling Dawe?"

Susan becomes hysterical again and ignores his outlandish accusation with fits of crying. Caleb overhears the exchange and grabs Drew from behind, swings him around, and shoves him against the body of the vehicle.

"Drew, what the hell?"

He brushes Caleb to the side and goes back in. "You said you called. Why'd you lie?"

"What are you talking about?" Caleb asks.

"Little Miss Goody-Two-Shoes lied. Neither Dawe nor anyone else at the RNC know anything about us being out here with a crime scene on our hands."

"Come on. Susan, tell him he's wrong."

Silence.

"Well, maybe their wires got crossed?"

"Doesn't matter. They're on their way here now," Drew says as Susan swings into a full-fledged breakdown. "Jesus Christ. You got anything to calm her?"

"No . . . do you?"

Drew pats his pockets. "Nope, I'm fresh out of Rohypnol."

"Not funny."

"Sorry. Humor is how I prevent going batshit crazy."

Caleb pulls Drew away from earshot. "Doesn't work for me. And besides, what is the point in grilling her like you are?"

"Why would she tell us she called when it's pretty clear she didn't? It doesn't add up, Caleb."

Caleb scowls and brushes off the comment. "You're paranoid. We're talking about Susan here—the same girl you referred to as Susie Q all through high school. You can't seriously believe she'd ever hurt anyone."

Drew scoffs. "People change. Trust me."

"Some, yes. Her, no. Tell you what, since you believe she's done something criminal, you babysit while I search around a bit."

Drew crosses his arms across his chest. "Have at it."

Caleb flips the hood of his jacket over his head and wanders away from the SUV in the twilight. He begins canvasing the area alongside the snow-covered road looking for any signs of foul play.

He takes in his surroundings: the snow-dusted pine trees, the untouched landscape. He tries to find peace, but the farther he walks, the more his thoughts impede his mission. They aren't even six hours into making amends, and he and Drew are squabbling like an old married couple. He tromps farther along the path, and suddenly the grimness of everything overcomes him.

This must be the last thing Sebastian saw before he died.

His efforts to hold back the flood of tears fails, but before he has the chance to shed a single tear, his eyes spots something shiny sticking out of the snow. He picks up speed, and when he reaches the spot, he crouches and examines the metal object: it's the keys to the ambulance.

And in this moment, the thought he thrusted to the back of his mind earlier returns to the foreground: Whoever murdered Sebastian and kidnapped Gabriel strikes again. One repeated name pops into his mind.

Sanderson.

SIXTEEN

February 17, 2017
Evening

AMONGST THE MURKINESS OF THE FOREST arise the twinkling blue and red strobes illuminating the wilderness surrounding Caleb, Drew, and Susan, who expect their arrival. When the three located the abandoned ambulance some forty minutes earlier, the sun had been dipping below the tree line. But now, as minutes pass, night falls quickly, and a dense fog moves in, reducing visibility. The two men linger outside the SUV. Caleb's body trembles from the harsh frigid air as the convoy of squad cars, ambulances, and one single unmarked police car at the tail end descend on the scene. He lets out a groan.

Drew advances, sympathetic to Caleb's soured relationship with the two constables, who are bound to be among the caravan.

Anything to get him away from keeping an eye on Susan, who remains confined to the backseat.

Drew is all-too familiar with which car they'll most likely be in, and he moves toward the unmarked vehicle.

Two doors fling open, and out scramble Constables Dawe and Barnes. Drew swoops in like a hawk, preventing them from getting any closer to Caleb until he's spoken with them first.

"Constable Dawe. Nice to finally meet in person. I've seen your face several times on TV," Drew says as he pulls his glove off and extends his hand.

"Ah, likewise. Nice to finally meet in person instead of through a screen," she replies.

"So, two medics are missing, you said, yeah?" Barnes asks.

"Right. Sam Butler and Nicole Bishop. Ambulance company lost contact with them about two hours ago. The three of us came out this way searching for them and stumbled across this," Drew says. He turns sideways and waves his hand side to side.

"You find something suspicious that gave you alarm to call?"

"You're kidding me, right?" Drew asks. "An ambulance, abandoned, it's hazard lights flashing in the middle of nowhere isn't suspicious enough for you? Wow, someone as untrained as me even knows something like this is a red flag."

She gives him a dirty look and brushes past to get the constables and cadets ready to begin a search of the wooded area beyond the ambulance.

"You haven't had the pleasure to meet her in person before, have you?" Barnes asks.

"Fortunately, no, I haven't. I've heard plenty about her, and seen her on the news, and each time I hear her name I cringe. How long's she been on the force?"

"Over ten years."

"Amazing our paths have never crossed in court before."

"Eh, well, we try to keep her off the stand. She's a loose cannon, and with her arrogance, let's say she doesn't garner any brownie points with the jurors."

"I can undoubtedly see why."

Barnes chuckles under his breath. "Enough about her. How's Mr. Winters?"

Drew's eyes turn toward Caleb who's dancing in place to keep his blood flowing. "He puts on a believable front, but I've known him forever. Inside he's undoubtedly breaking down."

"I relate to his suffering," Barnes says. The constable walks away and heads for the crowd.

"Hey, before you get started, can I tell you something?"

"Sure."

"Something seems off with Susan. For now, we've got her locked in the back, but I have a hunch she knows more than she's letting on."

Barnes's expression shifts. "How so?"

"She knew to come here, to this precise spot. How could she know?"

"Sounds notable, and I'll be sure to speak with her about it, but in all honesty, this is where we found Mr. Winters's husband. I'd have checked here first too."

"Well, at least find out what made her think to come here."

"I will, and thanks for the heads-up."

A couple constables tape off a perimeter around the ambulance while Dawe assembles the cadets to set off on a search-and-rescue mission in the solid woodlands beyond the abandoned rig. The temperature plummets with each fleeting moment, and Caleb can't decide if he should go search or wait in the car with Susan.

Drew approaches Caleb from behind and pulls him away.

"Hey, how are you holding up?"

"Meh. In shock. I want to get out there, to help find them. But if I do, who's going to stay here and watch Susan?"

"Well, it took some persuading, but Barnes will post a constable to keep an eye on her, so you can help."

"Yeah?"

He flaunts his alluring grin. "I mean, yeah, look at her; we can't leave her."

Caleb turns his head and stares at Susan with her head propped against the window. Caleb has never seen her in such a despondent state. She's almost unrecognizable to him.

A stocky constable approaches the SUV and posts himself outside the door. "That him?" Caleb asks.

"Yup."

"Jesus, he's wider than the door. She won't be getting away from him. Hey, you go get us a spot, and I'll catch up."

Drew pats Caleb on the back, and he quickly rushes toward the assembly area. The constable sees Caleb approaching and stands between him and the door.

"Hey, I'm no threat—I only want to check on my friend."

He steps aside, and Caleb reaches for the door handle.

"Susan, you okay?" he asks.

She's silent, but an angry look in her face speaks louder than words.

"I know you're pissed, but this is for your own good. This constable is going to stay with you while Drew and I go search for Sam and Nicole, okay?"

Again, she's reserved, but her face changes from livid to comforted.

He slaps his hand twice against the roof and treks across the snow. Caleb searches through the swarm of constables and cadets and spots Drew standing at the end of the parallel line.

They are all ready to search the area, they're only waiting on the final orders from Dawe. Caleb spots a place next to Drew, falls in line, and suddenly Dawe's obnoxious voice trumpets over the faint whispers.

"Listen up—you know the drill. Spread out, leave three meters between you and your neighbor, and if you come across something out of the ordinary, shout out," she begins. "If someone yells out, everyone stops until Barnes or myself investigate and give the all clear. Any questions?"

A hush falls over the cadets. Watching Dawe in action, it's clear this isn't her first search-and-rescue operation, and Caleb realizes their passiveness means they got the message loud and clear.

Drew inches closer. "You ready for this?"

Caleb shuts his eyes and grimaces. "Do I look ready? My best friend's missing, my boyfriend's missing, I planned my husband's funeral this morning—"

Drew cuts Caleb off and pats him on the back. "Hey, let's not get worked up—yet. Let's stay optimistic and hope for the best."

The corner of Caleb's eye crinkles. "I don't know, Drew, the volume of blood we found in the ambulance sends my hopefulness crashing."

Drew doesn't respond, and his silence forces Caleb to listen to the voices in his head.

This can't be real, I can't afford to lose anyone else in my life.

***

THEY'RE TEN MINUTES INTO THE SEARCH when a bellow slices through the sound of underbrush crunching beneath Caleb's feet. The shock sends his heart thumping harder and faster.

"Over here," the cadet shouts. The line stops, and Dawe hurries to poke around.

"They found something," Drew says.

Droplets of sweat roll laterally along Caleb's fingers inside the warm, wool-lined gloves. "Please don't let it be them . . . please," he begs.

He sees Dawe and Barnes staring at something dark on the ground. He's too far away from the action to catch what they are saying. The unknown makes him nervous, and he wants to move closer, but he's also keenly aware he should stay put.

Let the professionals handle this, Caleb.

She yells out. "Got another jacket. Can I get someone from forensics?"

This shocker smacks Caleb, and his heart drops. *Another jacket? Must be Sam's.*

The cadets stay still as two forensic investigators reach Dawe with a bulky paper bag. Another member of the forensics team begins snapping photos, and the flash illuminates the area. He sees the name clear as day stitched into the jacket: Butler.

He stoops and covers his mouth with his hands. "I better prepare myself to find something I don't want to find."

Forensics wraps up, and the line moves forward. They wander another fifteen minutes, and while sweeping an area with his flashlight, Caleb spots something shiny fluttering in the wind ten yards away. Without his contacts or glasses, his eyes aren't so reliable in these dark conditions. Still, it's odd, so he stops and whispers to Drew. "What is that?"

Drew shines his light in the direction Caleb has revealed. It takes a moment, and he moves a bit closer before gasping and hollering out, "Got something over here."

The search again stops, and Drew keeps Caleb distracted. "Hey, it's okay. Do me a favor, stay right there, all right, Caleb?"

"Why?"

Drew is still tight-lipped. "Just stay there, okay?"

Barnes runs over. "Whatcha got?"

Drew pokes his finger to a nearby tree, not uttering a single word. His hand trembles nonstop, but he's keeping his composure as to not alarm Caleb. Barnes dashes away, catching up with Dawe, and they prudently approach the area, their weapons drawn.

Barnes takes the lead and the glow from his flashlight illuminates the shadowy object: it's something, or someone, propped against a pine tree covered in a bloody plastic sheet, the type painters use.

Caleb gazes nervously on while Dawe unwraps the encasing. As quickly as she began, she equally retreats at the sight of whatever it is. She stands, looking before she speaks. "Got a body over here."

The CSIs descend on the scene, but Caleb decides to turn his face away. He can't bear it any longer. Drew senses Caleb's uneasiness with the situation and rests his hand upon his shoulder. Maybe the extra comfort will alleviate his restless condition.

His plan to calm him isn't working, and Drew watches as Caleb exhales and crouches to the ground, resting his elbows squarely against his knees. He wheezes for air, rearranges his wool cap in various positions on his head. He's doing anything he can to avert his attention. He intakes a bottomless mouthful of air, holds it for a few seconds, and exhales methodically. The tepid vapors escape from his lungs and manifest as steam as the particles strike the arctic air. He focuses on his breathing exercises, the one thing he clearly remembers from his years of therapy.

In one . . . two . . . three . . . four.

He continues in this squatted stance, and the only thing Drew does is stare at him expressionlessly. There aren't any words Drew can articulate to make the circumstances better. But as minutes tick by, he can't take the silence any longer and crouches next to him. As he thinks of something to say, words escape him again and instead he reaches out his hand and squeezes Caleb's.

Caleb's eyes shift toward Drew's, and for a split second the young prosecutor thinks his actions are comforting. But he's mistaken, and Caleb starts hyperventilating and swaying back and forth.

Caleb loses insight into what's going on around him, and all he wants to do is get a clench on his emotions and put them in check. Everything he'd become skilled at doing in these situations is failing, and seconds quickly turn into minutes. He coughs; his lungs ache from inhaling and exhaling at a brisk tempo. Abruptly, he lifts his head and tightens his grip on Drew's hand. "Where am I?"

Drew doesn't let go and yanks Caleb snugger. "I think you're having a panic attack. Are you okay?"

"I don't know," he sighs, "I remember trying to pull myself together and everything went black."

"It's okay. You're safe."

"Are they still over there?" Caleb asks.

"The ME is here checking the body."

Caleb lunges his body straight and twists to face the scene. The forensics team, Dawe, and the ME encircle the body, and Caleb involuntarily moves frontward in their direction. Part of him needs to see it up close, to know it's real, but there's a part of him that's terrified at witnessing the condition the body's been left in by the killer. Unconsciously he continues moving but stops five yards short.

Barnes catches the erratic movements from the corner of his eye and stops what he's doing and rushes over, putting both arms out.

"Whoa, Whoa, Mr. Winters, I can't permit you to come any closer."

Caleb doesn't move and tilts his head toward Barnes. "Okay, gotcha." Caleb pauses to catch his breath. "It's not Sam—is it? God, please tell me it's not Sam."

"Mr. Winters, please relax. We assume it's the body of Nicole Bishop, but I can't say until the ME identifies the body."

"Can I see her?"

"Eh, I think it's best if you stay here. Whoever did this was ruthless and left her disfigured. Not the last image I'd like to have of someone so close."

Caleb glances around Barnes's broad shoulders, struggling to see again, and with the area more illuminated, the first thing that catches his eyes is the brownish-red blood spatter covering the snowy ground.

He's squeamish at the sight of blood and he instead looks upward, but what greets him is no less nauseating. The wounds are extensive, and he closes his eyes twice on the chance he's hallucinating. He isn't.

Caleb gasps but instantly buries his face in his hands before attracting more attention to himself than he already has.

Drew finally darts to the rescue. "Hey, buddy . . . let them handle this. You and me, we still gotta find Sam, so I can't have you giving out on me yet."

Caleb retreats and concedes to Drew's appeal. Drew escorts him back to his spot in line and remains at his side, waiting for the search to resume.

Caleb's eyes are red, swollen, and it's obvious he's been crying. "I can't believe whoever did this left her out in the cold to die."

"You still think Sanderson is behind this?"

He sniffs, sucking back the runny mucus that dribbles. "What do you think?"

"Can I be real with you?"

"It's the only way you should be."

"Look, I know he's your client, but he's the type who'd do anything to keep his power."

Caleb hates admitting, but Drew's spot-on. Each new day brings fresh problems, and although he took an oath to represent Sanderson, those solemn string of words quickly lose their meaning.

I can no longer defend a madman who insists on destroying everything important to me.

"You're right. Tomorrow I'll pay him a visit and set things straight," Caleb says.

"I think you've done enough. Maybe you ought to let the constables do their job. If he is behind all of this, it'll all come out."

"Yeah, I suppose so, but clearly not quick enough for my friends."

Drew agrees. He can't help but consider if things would be different if Sanderson wasn't sitting in a seven-square-meter cell. Drew opens his mouth, but Dawe's rowdy voice interrupts his thought.

"All right, everyone, forensics has a handle here, but we still have one missing medic and a lot of ground to cover. I need everyone back in formation."

Again, the cadets mutely line up like the never took a break. Drew finds himself closer to Caleb while they struggle with the gradual slope in the terrain. For Caleb, the world is moving at a snail's pace. Everything he knows, everyone he loves, their fates are all unknown at this point.

God, I know I don't ask for your help often, but if you've trapped me in a nightmare, you can go ahead and wake me anytime.

Drew nudges Caleb in the arm. "You sure you are up for this? I mean, I don't know how I'd be if I came across the body of my best friend."

Complete silence ensues, not even a twitch to acknowledge he's understood Drew.

Drew's voice raises with more bass. "Caleb."

Caleb twists his head, annoyed. "I heard you. Can't I get a minute or two to think?"

"Sorry."

The silence carries on a few more seconds, but all the while, it's making Drew uncomfortable.

"Look, we can turn back and leave this up to Dawe, Barnes, and the cadets. You know they'll let us know what they find."

"We've come this far, and now I must do this. If those goons got to Sam, I need to see it with my own two eyes to believe it's true."

Drew has no comeback, and soon they begin moving forward in step with the cadets. The pace is quicker this round, and Caleb and Drew struggle to keep up with the hell-bent cadets.

Ten minutes pass without any indication they're on the right track, but as they crest a modest peak, everyone sees an intense, uncontrolled bonfire. Again, instead of focusing on preserving evidence, several cadets barrel off toward the billowing smoke, and Caleb goes with them.

"Hey, wait—" Drew shouts.

However, his pleas do nothing to stop Caleb, who is yards ahead of him and racing with an astounding swiftness. Not even Dawe can stop his momentum as he sprints beyond the constable and cadets.

For the second time, Caleb has gone rogue, and now Dawe is annoyed. She goes for her gun holster, whips her weapon out, and hollers. "Winters—stop! Now! I will shoot you and ask questions later."

He catches only one word, "shoot," and snaps out of whatever has possessed his body. He stops abruptly, and a mist of cloudy steam expels from his nose and mouth. He bends forward, fighting to get his breath.

Dawe catches up, spins him around, and before Caleb can even react, she tears into him. "What the hell? You can't run off like this. We may have a crime scene here," she huffs. "Someone, anyone, please restrain him for his own good."

Dawe shakes her head and grits her teeth while walking away. However, her disheveled mood fades and she composes herself. There's still a job to do, and she'll be damned if Caleb's stunt derails it.

She amasses three constables. "You three check the fire. Don't trample any evidence on your way," she says. "I'll be there momentarily after I deal with GI Winters."

The three young constables follow her orders and race downhill. Dawe circles, trying to collect her thoughts before traipsing uphill to speak with Caleb.

Atop the hill, two constables grasp Caleb's arms while Drew tries to plead with him. He's no longer resisting the detainment, but he sees, through the break between the constables, Dawe pacing back and forth downhill. The expression painted across her face is one of displeasure, but this is nothing new to him, as each time he sees her she has the same bitchy expression. He sees her heading his direction and tries to prepare something intelligent to remain in her good graces.

Once she's in range, Caleb exclaims, "Look, I'm sorry. I don't know what's happening in my head. I saw fire, and my gut instinct was, 'Sam's in trouble, and I gotta help.' I know it was wrong, and I'm sorry."

She stands before him, her nine-millimeter still gripped tightly in her right hand. Caleb scans the ground in shame.

Finally, she moans and speaks. "For a defense attorney, you know better than to rush a crime scene like you did. Worst, you show complete disregard for anyone's safety."

Caleb peers. "I know."

"Jesus, for all we know, there's a killer waiting there to ambush you." His head lowers again in disgrace.

"I'm an idiot—say it."

"You're not an idiot. Rather the opposite. You're brilliant. However, sometimes I have no idea why you let your emotions get the better of you."

Caleb narrows his eyes. "I wish I could explain it, but I can't."

"Well, this isn't the place for a therapy session. I get this is rough. We keep finding people you love, and you have to pretend to be a strong chap, but I know you, and I see all of this is tearing you apart inside."

Caleb smirks. He rubs his eyes but pulls them away quickly. He struggles to keep it together.

Dawe has a moment of sympathy. "Look, I know you're going through a lot, and I'm willing to let this little incident slide. But there's a catch."

He cocks his head to one side, "Go on . . ."

"You see these two constables? They'll escort you and Mr. Murphy back uphill. Once you arrive, you will wait until either Barnes or myself speak with you. Deal?"

Caleb's eyes shift side to side. "That's all?"

"Yup—we have a deal?"

"Deal."

She shouts, "Murphy, over here."

Drew has avoided coming close. The last thing he needs is to have constables agitated with him. He stands next to Caleb, trying his damnedest to keep distance between him and Dawe.

"I need you to take Mr. Winters back to the ambulance and wait," she restates her commands.

"Yeah, okay."

She sighs as Drew pats Caleb on the back. As they walk away, Drew leans in, "You're not helping your case with her any."

Caleb stops and throws his hands up. "All right, enough. I fucked up, I admit it—let's move on, shall we?"

They strain to ascend the snow-covered hill and do so in silence. Caleb snaps again at Drew, but after walking five yards his guilt sets in.

I'm such an asshole.

"I'm sorry. I realize you're only helping, but I'm being such a jerk."

"Oh, an apology? My, my, times really do change, huh?" he asks.

"Yeah, I suppose they do."

"It's all good. We both know you've always been slightly ill-tempered; however, I've never seen you under so much stress, and the side effects don't suit you."

"Nope."

"I did mean what I said earlier about wanting to fix what's broken, and part of my commitment is to see you get through this."

Caleb barely feels his feet any longer from standing on the cold earth for so long. Now all he wants is a warm place to repose while they await word from what the constables found at the bonfire.

***

THEY REUNITE WITH SUSAN, WHO REMAINS under police supervision. Caleb opens the front passenger door and plops on the cloth seat. He turns his head and finds Susan nibbling at her fingernails. She doesn't notice his stare, so Caleb clears his throat, and she stops and looks up.

"Did you find him?"

"We didn't."

The driver's-side door opens, and Drew sits, slamming the door closed to keep the cold at bay.

"Did you find *anything?*"

"His jacket." Drew pauses and Caleb takes over.

"Sadly, they found the body of a female who's been cut up pretty bad. I'm almost certain it's Nicole."

"Is she . . . dead?"

Caleb takes a long breath. "Yes, boo—she's dead."

"So, if you didn't find Sam, why are you here?"

Drew scoffs and glares disappointingly at Caleb. "You wanna field this question, Rambo?"

"Rambo? What's he talking about, Caleb? Oh, for fuck's sake, what'd you do now?"

Caleb's at a loss for words, so he does the only thing he can: breaks down. The tears flow heavier and harder than earlier, and through his watery eyes he stares at the most trustworthy and genuine persons he's known. He doesn't have the heart to pass the unwelcome news.

"There's a fire," he blurts out. Those words are all he manages, as he chokes on the rest.

Susan's sympathetic to Caleb, but she's also a panic-stricken wife whose husband is missing, and right now the only thing she needs is a straightforward answer to quell her overactive imagination. "Drew, as much as I hate you, you seem to have yourself together. So, give it to me straight."

Drew twists around and reaches his hand into the backseat, searching for hers. "We don't know yet. But after Dawe tore into Caleb for storming the fire, she sent us back here to wait. But, hey, we'll have answers soon. For now, let's wait here where it's warm, okay?"

Her head nods, and after watching Caleb sob for as long as she has, she too can't contain her emotions. With the entire car in tears,

Drew looks like an unconcerned asshole. But in his defense, it's been years since he last saw Sam. However, deep inside, Drew feels awful watching his ex-lover going through such turmoil.

"Everything's gonna be okay," Drew says.

Susan lashes out. "No, none of this will be okay."

"She's right. We've lost everyone who's ever meant anything to us. Life as we know it is over."

Twenty agonizing minutes pass and Drew sits detached while they sob on and off. He shuts his eyes. This is the longest he's ever remained this quiet, and all he wishes is for one of the constables to appear. He opens his eyes and ahead of him he sees Constable Barnes stepping out of the forest. "About time. Now, maybe he'll have an update so I can get the two of you home."

Caleb looks up to see Barnes closing in. He swallows hard and sucks back the stream of snot. "Doesn't look like he's bringing good news with him."

"No, it doesn't. You ready for this?" Drew turns toward Susan.

Her stare is vacant, and Drew gets no response to his question. Barnes shuffles around the front of the vehicle clutching two transparent plastic bags. Drew lowers the window and Barnes leans against the door. Blue latex gloves cover his hands.

"You got an update?"

"I wish I could think of a better way to break this, but we found another body among the ashes."

Susan gasps and covers her face.

"Is it Sam?" Caleb asks.

"The body's too severely burnt to make a positive identification. The ME will get a DNA sample during the postmortem, and we'll send it off."

"So, it's possible it isn't Sam?" Susan shouts.

"Mrs. Butler, given the circumstances, I won't feed you a line of crap. We found your husband's bloody jacket. The killer slaughtered Nicole. So, chances are likely it's him. I know it's not what you were hoping to hear, but I don't believe in giving false hope."

Caleb reaches his hand into the backseat, and she grips ahold tightly. Barnes tries to be as compassionate as possible. However, Drew reaches for the door handle; he must get some air.

"Constable Barnes, mind if we talk in private?"

"Yeah, sure. Will those two be okay?"

"They have each other. They'll be good for a few minutes."

Drew flings the driver's door open and steps out onto the crunchy snow. He's keenly aware there's something Barnes isn't saying, and he wants to get the details, for his own curiosity.

"What aren't you telling them?"

Barnes holds up the two evidence bags. One contains a bloodstained dagger and the other an ordinary white sheet of printer paper with words written in what looks like blood. "A likely murder weapon and something a tad more unusual."

"Did they use blood to write that letter?"

"Appears so. Now, whether it's human or not, that's for forensics to decide. But be sure to tell Mr. Winters I'm officially clearing him as a suspect in Gabriel's disappearance and the murder of his husband."

"Just like that? Whatever they wrote must be something pretty damning."

"All I'll say is whoever wrote it has claimed responsibility for all of this chaos—including Sebastian's murder."

"What? What's in that letter?"

"Okay, only an excerpt: 'I killed them, all of them. Trust no one in Torbay.' Creepy shit, huh?"

"Creepy is an understatement. I'm still confused how this clears Caleb."

"I've had my eye on him since his interrogation. I know he left his office at three o'clock today and stopped by the grocery on his way home."

"Okay, and . . . ?"

"The ME places time of death somewhere between three and four this afternoon, making it impossible Caleb was able to get all the way out here to kill anyone."

"Ah, up to speed now. But what about Susan? Should I worry she's involved or even the killer?"

"Too early to say, but after our conversation earlier I'd like to come by and interview her. Say, you think you can make sure she stays with Caleb tonight?"

"I can try. I'm not going to force her, though."

"Text me if she leaves. Otherwise, Dawe and I will stop by a little later," Barnes says, slipping a business card to Drew.

"Got it."

Drew extends his hand outward and shakes Barnes's hand. A devilish smirk graces his face as he watches Barnes retreat to the crime scene. He turns back toward the SUV and grips the handle. He shivers as he slides back into the driver's seat.

Caleb and Susan both appear numb, and instead of interrupting, Drew cranks over the engine and does a three-point turn out of the dead-end cul-de-sac.

An aloof Caleb senses they are moving and shakes himself awake. "We're leaving?"

"Barnes gave the go-ahead. We're heading back to your place, but Dawe wants to come by and speak with us. I guess they want some official statement."

"He didn't say anything else?"

"He said they found a possible murder weapon and a note written by the killer. His biggest concern was making sure you two stay put."

Susan's deafening sobs make Drew cringe.

"Will you stay?"

"Of course. But there's something else. He says he's clearing you as a suspect—officially."

"Really?"

"Yeah, really. Whoever wrote the note has taken responsibility for all the murders."

"Murders?"

"Barnes specified it in the plural. Sounds like whoever is responsible for this also murdered Sebastian. You're off the hook. I thought you'd be happier."

"None of this makes me 'happy.' Maybe now they'll focus on who's really responsible, though."

SEVENTEEN

February 17, 2017
Late Evening

C ALEB HANGS HIS JACKET AND KICKS off his shoes. The day hasn't gone how he expected, but what in his life lately has? Drew follows behind Susan and shuts the door behind him.

"You got her?"

"Yeah. Thanks."

Susan shuffles along the hardwood floor in a daze. She's barely coherent enough to know where she is. Caleb wraps his arm around her back and helps her ease onto the couch. She twitches from her stupor and turns her mascara-tarnished face to him.

"What am I going to do now?" she asks.

"Let's not get ahead of ourselves. Barnes says they'll stop by later, so there's still a chance it's not him."

She scoffs. "Who else could it be?"

He hesitates. *Valid point. Who else could it be? Think, Caleb, think.*

"I dunno. Maybe he found himself in a kill-or-be-killed situation. For all we know those remains are the killers."

Drew approaches the couch. "Don't sugarcoat things. You've done this our entire lives."

"No, I haven't."

"Keep telling yourself that," Drew replies. "I need a drink."

"Liquor cabinet's in the dining room. Help yourself."

Drew walks away, and Caleb focuses back on Susan. She's in no condition to be around when Dawe and Barnes arrive, and he remembers he left the bottle of Xanax sitting on the coffee table. He reaches for the bottle but sets it back before shouting to Drew. "Hey, can you bring me a bottle of water?"

"Yeah, hang on." Drew appears and sets the bottle of bourbon on the table and returns to the kitchen.

Caleb grabs Susan's hand. "I think you should stay with me tonight. I don't want you trying to make it home."

"I'll be fine. I can't impose on you."

"Impose? How are you imposing when I ask you to stay?"

She doesn't cave. "I think it'd be better to be alone. You've been so great, but I know you have your own troubles." She moves her eyes back and forth in the direction of the kitchen.

Caleb's never been demanding or overbearing with anyone his entire life, but this back and forth with Susan is driving him to turn a new leaf. He jumps to his feet, and his tone changes. "No, you are staying here. There's a killer out there, and neither of us even know if we're on their hit list? I've lost my husband, my boyfriend—"

She grabs ahold of his hand. "I know, we shouldn't argue about this right now. I'll stay, but I'm leaving first thing in the morning. Deal?"

"Fine."

Drew returns from the kitchen with a bottle of water and sets it in front of Caleb. Caleb smiles, and Drew smiles back. He reaches for the bottle again and pops off the top. He drops the pill into her hand. "Here, take one of these. Trust me, it'll help you sleep tonight."

She scrutinizes the oblong white tablet imprinted with numbers. "What's this?"

"Xanax."

She tosses the pill and it lands on the coffee table. "Why would I take this?"

"It'll help you sleep."

"I hate drugs. Where'd you get these from anyhow?"

"Um, your husband has a—ah, wait . . . you didn't know . . . did you?"

Her demeanor shifts. "What are you telling me? He's taking Xanax? That he's what, a drug addict? How long have you known about this?"

"I mean, I guess perfectly good people take Xanax for anxiety. No one said he was a drug addict. He gave me a pill the other day when I was a nervous wreck."

"I don't think masking your pain with medicine is the answer."

"You're right, but you have to get some sleep."

"I don't believe these are Sam's."

Caleb spins the bottle. "But they are. See, his name is here on the bottle."

She pauses, and her facial expression changes. "Thanks for the offer, but I'm not some drug addict like your boyfriend or anything."

Her once despondent condition all but a faded memory now, she rises from the couch and stomps away, leaving Caleb's head whirling with her out-of-character behavior.

In the dining room, Drew pulls out a chair, but as he gets comfortable, he overhears their heated conversation and gets up to investigate. He tiptoes along the wall with the glass of bourbon in his hand and stops to peer his head around the corner, seeing a visibly upset Caleb giving chase.

By the time Drew steps into the living room, Susan is midway up the stairs and Caleb stands on the landing. Drew attempts to take another step but sees Caleb's lips part so he stops and watches.

Caleb yells out. "No, no, you don't get to run away after a comment of this magnitude. The fuck is your problem?"

She shoots him a dirty look. "You heard me."

"After everything we've been through, and even in our agitated states, your comment is the lowest blow you could serve. Every one of us has our vices, secrets, and I don't know where you get off being so high and mighty like you're perfect."

"When it comes to Sam, I'll pass out judgment on whomever." She climbs two more steps and stops.

Drew realizes he must intervene, otherwise the two best friends will tear each other apart instead of being there for one another in their time of need. He appears in the brightness of the living room.

"Hey, hey, what in the hell is going on? You, little miss moody, get off those stairs and come here. And you, stay right there. Neither of you is going to bed angry. I don't care how long this takes, we're going to hash this out."

She leans against the railing. Her face is bright red, and it's taking longer for her to conjure up a comeback. The two men stare at her in an uncomfortable silence. After a delay, she opens her mouth, and instead of apologies, more vulgarities spew out instead. "Fuck off, the both of you. All I want to do right now is sleep and to be left in peace."

"Drew is making a valid argument, Susan. We're dealing with the same thing, so the least we can do is not fight about stuff."

"Look, I'm tired and I need some sleep. I've got a headache from hell and can't take anymore. Can we make up in the morning?"

Caleb looks at Drew, who speaks up. "Get some sleep. We'll see you in the morning."

Susan ascends into the darkness of the second floor. Caleb's face is beet red, but not out of anger, from the frustration of the situation. If this wasn't Susan, he'd already have walked away and washed his hands of them. But fortunately, he sympathizes with her state of mind—helplessness, despair, not knowing where your loved one is. Drew rests on the edge of the couch.

"You all right?"

"I'll be fine. The thing is, I'm not mad—how can I be when these were my exact feelings when Sebastian disappeared."

"But I'm sure you didn't lash out at anyone."

"No. I had nobody to lash out at. Sam and Susan have been my closest and dearest friends since I left law school, and all they did was help me through the loss. We never had anything like this happen."

"Well, something isn't right."

"How so?" Caleb asks as the doorbell chimes throughout the house.

"It's gotta be Dawe. Want me to get it?"

"Please."

He steps back through the dark dining room and into the foyer. The house is almost silent apart from the ticking sound escaping the grandfather clock. The door opens, and instead of the voice he expected, he hears the opposite: a man.

He stands and creeps toward the foyer. The closer he gets, he overhears Drew and the man speaking in a hush manner. He emerges from the shadows. "Everything all right?"

Barnes shifts his attention between Caleb and Drew, and frowns. "We need to talk."

***

CALEB LEADS THE WAY BACK. HE WORRIES Barnes isn't bringing good news. The constable's voice shakes, and he cracks his knuckles while stuttering. It's never promising to see a constable so nervous when they appear at your door.

"You look terrified—please, sit," Caleb says.

Barnes crosses his arms. "I won't be long."

"Okay, suit yourself."

Drew coughs. "You said you have news."

Barnes scans the room. "Where's Mrs. Butler?"

"Sleeping. It's the best place for her to be," Drew says.

"I was hoping to ask her a few questions."

"Tomorrow would be better. With the mood she's in, I don't think you'd get much information."

"Understood."

Drew nods. "You have some news?"

"Right. However, none of it is definite—it's more hypothetical—"

Caleb interrupts. "It's Sam, isn't it?"

"The ME determined height and bone structure are consistent with Sam. However, to speed up the identification process they're going to do a dental comparison along with sending off the DNA."

"I know damn well you didn't drive all the way here to repeat something you already told me an hour ago," Drew says. "So, out with it. Why are you really here?"

Barnes lowers his head. "I won't beat around the bush any longer. I do have more news. We located more evidence near the fire . . ." His voice trails off.

"What kind of evidence?"

"A permanent resident card."

Gabriel.

"Did you find anything else?"

"Um, a few baggies of a white substance, some drug paraphernalia, and Mr. Butler's wallet."

"It has to be Sam," Caleb says.

"Let's not get ahead of the evidence."

"And the permanent resident card? I assume it belongs to Gabriel?" Drew asks.

Barnes nods and Caleb falls onto the couch, his hopes of finding Gabriel alive growing bleaker with each passing day.

Caleb lifts his head. "I'm telling you, Sanderson, or someone working for him, is responsible. You squandered all your time attempting to pin everything on me, but look what it got you: more innocent people murdered."

Barnes is jumpy. It's evident he knows he took a few regrettable directives from Dawe. "You're right. Nonetheless, we can play the blame game later. Right now, I need to know anything and everything about Sanderson."

"What, exactly, do you need to know?"

"For starters, those guys who paid you a visit at the bar. Do you know them?"

"The Tucker brothers, Evan and Brett."

"Okay, and their main goal was to threaten you?"

"I think so. They said I'd end up like my husband, buried in the woods."

"Sounds pretty specific. After this happened, why didn't you come to us?"

"I know you're not serious. You know damn well why I didn't; she has a name, you know."

Barnes sighs and rolls his eyes. "You gotta let it go. I've made it clear I'd prefer you deal with me. Seem like a fair compromise?"

"Yeah, fair enough. Anyone is better than her."

"So other than the threat, did they say anything else?"

"No."

Barnes looks at Drew. "Mr. Murphy, surely you have your own opinion?"

"He's mixed up with some shady characters, this much I know. His cronies are loyal followers who'll do almost anything he asks."

Barnes shakes his head. "Even from behind bars he's still causing us headaches."

"I think it's time to bring these menaces in for questioning. I'm fairly certain the RNC has a thick file on every single one of them."

Barnes smirks. "I'm sure we do."

Caleb sits silently on the couch. His patience grows thinner as the questions continue in rapid succession.

Why are we covering this shit again? I answered these questions before when they interviewed me. Did I not make myself clear?

Caleb massages his temples. He's exhausted, and while his life crumbles around him, the only thing this newbie constable is doing is adding more kindling to an already roaring fire.

Caleb snaps out of his thought and catches Barnes staring at him. He plays it off like he's been paying attention the entire time.

"We're going to find the person responsible for this. Just give us time," Barnes says. "Anyhow, thanks for taking the time to talk. I'll let you get some rest and come by in the morning to pick up where we left off."

"Okay," Caleb says.

"Hopefully, Mrs. Butler feels a little better by then."

"Yeah, I hope so too. She has me worried."

Caleb shakes the constable's hand and escorts him back to the front door, leaving Drew propped against the couch. When they step into the foyer, Caleb taps Barnes on the shoulder.

"Barnes, there's something else I didn't want to mention in front of Drew."

"What's that?"

"I'm sure it's nothing serious, but a few times I got the impression someone had their eyes on me."

"Oh, maybe the undercover we've had following you around the past few days."

"Nah, not him. And a recommendation: if I spotted his ass a mile away, I'm sure others have too. Might want to hire people who are a bit more incognito."

Barnes chuckles.

"No, it's someone else. Perhaps your constable noticed something shady and hasn't reported it to you?"

"I'll call him on my drive back. But some friendly advice from me to you: ease up on the 'speak to my attorney' so we can figure this out together."

"I'll be cooperative. But I can't promise anything if you accuse me of crimes I didn't commit."

"I can promise you we're not looking at you as a suspect in either Sebastian's or Gabriel's disappearance anymore."

Caleb is hesitant to join forces with the same people who all but marked him a killer in the morning paper, but more than anything he wants to find out who's behind all of this. "Okay, I'll help under one condition: Dawe must contact the reporter who wrote the story and clear me publicly as a suspect."

"A realistic request. I'll speak with her."

"Perfect. See you in the morning, constable."

Barnes reaches into his pocket and grabs a business card. "Here, take my information and call if anything out of the ordinary happens. My cell number is on the back."

"Will do."

"And keep an eye on Mrs. Butler. She isn't in a good place, huh?"

"She's not."

Constable Barnes steps away and waddles carefully across the snow-covered porch toward the stairs. Caleb leans against the doorframe, ensuring Barnes arrives safely to the car. Barnes waves and lowers his thin-framed body into the seat.

Caleb closes the door and engages the deadbolt. After everything that's happened, the days of leaving the door unlocked are over. With a killer roaming the deserted streets of Torbay, he's not taking any chances.

Drew sits contentedly in one of the brown leather chairs angled toward the roaring fireplace. Caleb reenters the room and notices the decanter of bourbon and an empty lowball glass next to the vacant chair.

Drew senses Caleb's heavy footsteps pattering against the hardwood floor, approaching from behind, and he turns his head. "Hope you don't mind I started a fire."

"No problem. Pretty easy when all you do is flip a switch."

Drew smiles. "You look exhausted. Sit with me a while?"

"In a minute. I think I should check on Susan. She has me worried."

"All right, Mother Hubbard, but I'm sure she's fine. But go—I know you won't relax until you see for yourself."

"Remarkable how you're able to recall all my idiosyncrasies off the top of your head."

"I remember everything."

Caleb grins. "Hang tight."

He ascends to the second floor and creeps along the hallway toward the end of the hall. Beneath the door, a faint light escapes, but he expects to find her fast asleep. He lightly knocks and waits to for a reply.

Silence.

He cracks the door, with barely enough space to sneak a peek, and finds her lying on top of the covers, hugging a throw pillow.

He softly closes the door and returns along the pitch-black corridor. He feels on edge suddenly but can't figure out why and brushes it off. *No one's getting inside this house tonight.*

Stepping onto the landing, Caleb pauses, taking in the picturesque fire that flickers carelessly. Drew has poured a few ounces of bourbon into Caleb's glass and is already sipping on his second.

"Couldn't wait for me?"

Caleb's voice scares Drew and he turns around instantly. "Shit, don't sneak up on people."

Caleb walks around and plops into the empty seat. "I can't remember the last time I was this worn out."

"Finals week, 2005?"

"I was thinking something even more overwhelming…when Sebastian went missing was worse. I didn't sleep, eat, nothing for days. My entire life was a mess."

"You still miss him, huh?"

"More than you'll ever know." He takes a sip. "Anyway, enough about the past, we need to focus on now and figure out who's got it out for me."

Drew swirls the bourbon around and glances up. "Agree. But before we get into the nitty-gritty of Sanderson, I have something I have to get off my chest."

Caleb's left eyebrow raises.

"I've carried around a lot of guilt since Toronto."

"Guilt of what?"

"Breaking your heart. When Sebastian disappeared, it dawned on me . . . maybe if I—"

"If you what? Stayed with me? You can't think our breakup caused any of this."

"Maybe if back then I was brave enough, you know, to profess my love for you, we'd have lived happily ever after and none of this would be happening."

"Who's to say we were destined to be together? Besides, after all these years, you can't still have feelings for me. That'd be crazy." Caleb laughs under his breath.

Drew freezes up, not a single word falls from his mouth. He looks fiercely into Caleb's eyes before gulping another mouthful of bourbon from the glass he clasps firmly.

Caleb tries to tie the fragments together—the awkwardness, the silence—and he realizes why Drew wants to let bygones be bygones. His muscles tense, his palms grow clammy, and with a quivering lip he blurts out, "Wait, you *are* still in love with me."

Drew dodges Caleb's stare and replies with one simple, forthright word. "Yes."

Caleb's head drops, and an uneasiness pumps through his veins. He's uncertain if he ought to be livid or receptive with Drew's undeclared admission. Caleb draws an intense gasp before raising his head and doesn't filter the words that spew out.

"You know what? You're right. If you'd stayed with me, I'd never have met Sebastian or Gabriel. We'd most likely never have returned to St. John's, and no one would be dead."

Drew's taken aback. While he didn't expect Caleb to reciprocate his desires, the comeback he gets isn't what he expected either. He lifts from the chair, his brows drawn together.

"I said sorry because I feel bad, not because I *truly* am responsible any of this. But wow, you, I never thought you'd say something so brutal." Drew lunges forward. Only inches separate them.

Caleb steps backward. "What, you wanna hit me? Go ahead, take your best shot."

Drew throws up his hands. "You'd like that, huh?"

"Better question is would *you* like it?"

Drew lunges again and Caleb shuts his eyes.

He's really gonna do it.

However, what he gets is far worse than a beating. Caleb senses Drew's balmy palms press forcefully against his cheeks and those same hands pull his face closer. He feels Drew's warm breath hit his face, and the warmth of his ex's lips connect with his. Caleb's eyes flutter open, and after the initial shock wears off, he shoves him away.

"What the ever-living hell?" Caleb wipes the dampness from his lips.

"I'm sorry, I don't know what came over me. I wanted to feel that tingly sensation, like I used to."

Caleb breaths heavy and grabs his bourbon to wash away the saltiness of the kiss. "We can't do this. I've never wanted anything more in my life, but we can't."

Drew hangs his head in humiliation, says nothing, and sulks away like a child who's been reprimand. Caleb shakes his head, scoffs, but restrains himself from giving chase. Drew disappears into the dark foyer, and finally the guilt kicks in and Caleb gives chase.

"Hey, wait up," he begins. "Look, don't leave angry. Neither of us wants that. It's—you can't come here and kiss me."

"I'm sorry."

"Don't be sorry. It's not cool to reappear and within the first day drop the news you're still in love with me."

"I know. I should have kept my feelings to myself."

Drew lays the guilt trip on thick, and in typical fashion, Caleb gives in. "This is the stuff Constable Dawe will use to add more ammo to her arsenal—to say I murdered Sebastian and Gabriel to be with you."

"But they cleared you as a suspect."

"That may be, but honestly, I don't believe them."

Drew sighs.

"Andrew, you are aware I made funeral arrangements for Sebastian, my boyfriend and best-friend are missing, and we found

Nicole disfigured and killed. And to top it off, you sit in my living room and confess your love for me. You see how this might be overwhelming for one person to handle?"

"You're right. Shit, I have the worst timing."

Caleb scoffs under his breath. "Yup."

Drew lifts his head. Sadness clouds his striking features.

"But let's make one thing clear: I want you in my life. I need time to readapt to the 'new normal.' One step at a time."

Drew affirms.

"Good. Now, what'd ya say we finish our drinks? I can use the company—makes it seem a little less lonely."

Drew forces a smile. "Sure, I can stay a while longer, and I promise I'll keep my hands *and* lips to myself."

Caleb pats him on the back and Drew hangs his jacket again.

"But after this drink, I should head home before it gets too late."

They return to the fireplace and finish the drink, and the awkwardness slowly fades. While he sits chatting and watching the fire twinkle, one crazy notion rests in Caleb's mind: *Did Dawe set this up?*

EIGHTEEN

February 18, 2017
Early Morning

T HE WEE HOURS OF THE MORNING are quiet, too quiet, and the stillness of the house bothers Caleb. His eyes shoot open, as they have every hour. He yanks the duvet cover closer to his body and rolls onto his side, struggling to fall back to sleep. So much races through his mind: the altercation with Susan, Gabriel missing, Sebastian's remains, and now Drew resurfacing. He reaches across the nightstand and twists the clock toward him. 3:59 AM. He sighs before closing his eyes and rolling onto his back.

You're overreacting to all of this. Get some sleep.

He tries his damnedest to quash the racing thoughts in his head, but nothing he does works. Minutes pass by and the stillness of the house jostles to life with a single gunshot cutting the stifling air.

Without giving his own safety any thought, he springs from the bed and races for the bedroom door. He flings it open but finds nothing but a dark hallway. He places one foot outside the door and suddenly a masked intruder zooms by in such a rush that he or she overlooks Caleb standing in the doorframe.

Caleb bellows, "Hey, you, stop."

The booming voice alarms the intruder, and Caleb watches the figure spin around while hustling away, but they miss a step and slam against the wall, sending a picture crashing to the floor. Everything happens so quick, and when Caleb realizes he's not dreaming, a bright flash of exploding gunpowder lights the hall. Caleb has no time to react, but the bullet ricochets off the doorframe, missing him by a few inches.

He composes himself enough to slam the door closed. His shaky hand twists the lock, and when he's confident the door is locked, he backs away and falls backward over a shoe he lazily left in the middle of the floor. He flies across the floor, never taking his eyes off the door.

I'm gonna die. I don't want to die yet.

He crawls to the bed and watches another bullet penetrate the solid wood door. He wriggles his legs underneath the bed, but stops to grab his cell phone before pulling the rest of his body under.

He jiggles the phone and the screen comes to life. He struggles to hold his thumbprint against the home button, but it unlocks.

"Hey, Siri—dial 911," he frantically yells.

The phone rings but the shakiness worsens.

Come on . . . come on.

A male voice answers the line. "911, what is your emergency?"

Caleb whispers, "There's an intruder in my home, and they've fired two shots at me."

"Is your address 89 Moore's Street in Torbay?"

"Yes, that's me. Please, hurry and send help."

"An ambulance and constables are on the way, sir, please remain on the line. Are you or anybody in the house injured?"

"I'm okay. The bullets missed me," he begins, but his voice cracks. "Bu-uh, I have a friend staying in my guest room, but I don't know her condition. I need to check on her."

"Has the suspect left the premises?"

"I'm, uh, I don't know. This can't be happening to me. This has to be a nightmare—wake up, Caleb, come on."

"Sir, I assure you you're not asleep. Are you able to remain on the line with me until help arrives?"

"I can't, I'm sorry . . . I gotta check on her. Just tell them to hurry."

Caleb's body is half beneath the bed, and his other half sticks out with the phone clenched in his hand. Every fiber of his being tells him to go check on Susan, but he's paralyzed with fear.

What if the intruder is lurking outside the bedroom door, ready at the twist of the doorknob to blow my brains out?

It's not a risk he's willing to take, and instead, he drags his body farther beneath the bed for protection. He swipes up through his contacts and stops on the one name he can't believe he's calling: Drew. The phone rings four times and goes to voicemail.

"Fuck," Caleb whispers.

He instantly redials, and after the second ring, a disorientated voice answers. "Caleb? Are you okay?"

"I didn't want to call you, but right now I have nowhere else to turn. I've got a slight situation. How fast can you be here?"

His mystified tone changes right away. "Twenty minutes. Why? What's going on?"

"Short version: someone broke in, shots were fired, and now I fear for my life under my bed."

"Are you hurt?"

"I'm fine . . . stop wasting time and get here."

There's no hesitation and a fully alert Drew replies, "On my way."

The line goes silent and Caleb drops the phone on the shaggy rug to wait nervously for help. He slows his breathing, listening for any signs of movement in the house. Thirty seconds pass, and everything is quiet, like before the unwelcoming jolt from bed. The wailing of the wind is all he takes notice of now.

Minutes tick by and the eerie stillness perseveres. His heart palpitates in his chest, and the pressure from it bumps in his ear. All he wants is the constabulary or Drew to show up so he has some protection. With all the mayhem surrounding him on the outside, coming home is the one place where he could drown out the world and be safe. But now even his sanctuary isn't impenetrable. And knowing this insinuates that a nasty situation is only about to get worse.

The muffled echo of sirens pierces through the whistling gale. He swallows hard. His anxiety flares up, and he's giving it his all to not get too thrilled help is close.

Just a few more minutes and I'll be safe. Just hold on. You got this.

Over the years Caleb has grown comfortable talking himself from a ledge when tricky situations enter his life. His strength to hit them head on endures, but the last thing he expected was to come face-to-face with an armed intruder—in his home, of all places.

He retrieves his iPhone, and the home screen wallpaper of him and Gabriel in Key West illuminates the darkness underneath the bed. Fifteen minutes have passed since his 911 call, and the sirens grow louder. An unexpected thud against the bedroom door unnerves him. He turns off the screen and closes his eyes.

It can't be help this fast. Stay put and don't move.

The thumping continues, and after a minute of hearing the doorknob rock back and forth, several pairs of legs charge the room. They mumble, but when he overhears the police radio blaring full blast, he knows it's safe and cries out. "Under here."

A muscular constable kneels and raises the bed skirt. "You're safe now."

Caleb wriggles out and the constable helps him to his feet. He smooths out his shirt and glances up to find three constables standing in front of him with another guarding the door.

Caleb plops on the edge of the bed and the same constable kneels. Caleb recognizes him from someplace but can't place where. "Are they gone?"

"We're sweeping the house, but so far no signs of an intruder when we arrived."

There's no blubbering, no alarm in Caleb's voice—fear sucked up all his energy. He inhales and exhales slowly, trying to relax, but then he remembers Susan. He jumps to his feet and rushes for the door, but the broad-shouldered constable blocks his exit.

"Hey, hey, where's the fire? Stay in here until we clear the house."

"My friend, she's down the hallway. Someone, please, check on her."

The muscular constable speaks. "You two, go." They rush from the room. "Caleb, please come back and sit."

He wants to argue but gives in knowing it won't do any good. The constable guarding the door escorts Caleb back to the edge of the bed and sits while the other two constables disappear into the darkness of the hallway with only their flashlights to guide the way.

"How do you know my name?"

"From dispatch. I'm Constable Hathaway. You have any idea who did this?"

"I have a good suspicion. Can you do me a favor?"

"Sure."

"Can you get Constable Barnes out here?"

The constable nods comfortingly and walks far enough away to radio dispatch. Caleb leans forward, placing both of his hands over his face, drowning out the conversation Hathaway has, but soon comes an epiphany: *This break-in was never about killing me. They wanted Susan. Sanderson is trying to mess with my head.*

Hathaway returns. "All right, they'll get ahold of him, and they'll send him out," he begins, all the while staring at Caleb. "Wait, where do I know you from? Are you the guy whose husband went missing a few years back?"

Caleb glances up, and his eyes lock with Hathaway. "Yeah."

240 AMONG THE ASHES

"Man, I can't imagine how difficult these past few weeks have been for you. I'm sorry you've had to go through all this shit."

"Thanks," Caleb replies, turning his head away.

"You know, two years ago when I was a cadet, I went out every day looking for your husband. I always hoped we'd find him."

Caleb turns to face the constable and forces a smile. "I appreciate that, constable. I wish things turned out differently." Caleb hangs his head.

"Me too."

They wait silently until an imposing baritone voice shouts from down the hall, "Miller, get over here."

The constable standing guard at the door looks at Hathaway and Caleb. "Be right back."

He rushes from the room, leaving Hathaway unsure of what to do. Caleb looks at him. "If you need to go, it's okay. I'll wait right here."

"You sure?"

"Yeah, if something's wrong, you're more valuable to them instead of babysitting me."

"I'll be back. Don't leave this room."

Caleb sits on the edge of the bed wearing only a white V-neck shirt and plaid pyjama bottoms. A flock of constables and two medics zoom past his bedroom so naturally he quickly rushes to the door to get a closer look. Detecting that no one's focus is on him, he creeps into the hallway and tiptoes toward the guest room. The pungent smell of iron fills the air, and even though the odor makes him queasy, he endeavors closer, being as silent as possible to not draw any attention.

The guest room is only a few yards ahead of him, and he's close enough to overhear the chatter between the constables but can't make out their exact words. From the anxiety in their tone, he knows something's wrong. He takes another step closer, which gives him a view inside. His favorite photo of the Toronto skyline he had blown up and framed catches his eye, but he sees it covered in blood spatter. In a state of shock, he gasps for air, and instead of retreating, he takes another step forward.

Caleb presses his luck a little too long, and finally it happens— the floorboard beneath his feet squeaks loud enough to bring the chatter to a halt. The four constables and two medics turn their heads and see a shell-shocked Caleb approaching.

Hathaway shouts. "I thought I asked you to stay in the room. You can't be here. It's now a crime scene, and we can't have you tainting it."

The constable's approachable nature shifts harshly and Caleb skulks away because he knows he's the reason why.

"No, nope, this can't be real. It can't be. I must be trapped in some twisted nightmare."

Wake up, wake up.

"I, I need to che—"

"Nope, this way," Hathaway says while closing in.

"But . . ." Caleb tries everything to get a word in.

"If this person means anything to you, this isn't how I'd want my last memories of them to be.

He places his hefty hand against Caleb's chest, forcefully pushing him farther down the hallway. He turns and shouts to the other constables, "Carry on, I'll be back shortly."

Once out of the view of the others, Hathaway pulls him by the arm and jerks him along the unlit hall and down the staircase and tosses him against the couch.

Caleb doesn't try to free himself from the man's tight grip—he's at least five inches taller and forty pounds heavier—even though his hysteria steadily increases until it reaches a melodramatic climax. In a panic-stricken voice, Caleb asks, "What's wrong with Susan? Why can't I see her? No, this is unacceptable, you're going to let me in there, and I won't take no for an answer."

Now standing in front of the fireplace, Hathaway grows annoyed with a distraught Caleb and decides he must do something to get him under control. He clenches him with both hands and shakes him while gritting his teeth and breathing heavily.

"Hey, Caleb, listen for a second. Can you do that?"

Caleb stiffens, the flow of tears pauses temporarily. "What?"

"She's gone. There's nothing you can do now for her. Come, let's sit in the kitchen and wait for Constable Barnes."

He sucks back his tears and wipes his hand underneath both eyes. "Don't have a choice, do I?"

Just as they begin to move, Drew runs into the house flapping a white envelope in his hand.

"Caleb," Drew shouts as he races across the living room. Hathaway steps between Drew and Caleb.

"Whoa, whoa, hold up—you are?"

"Drew Murphy, the Crown prosecutor, and a friend of his," he says, pointing his finger at Caleb.

Hathaway turns around. "You know this guy?"

Caleb nods. "Okay, well, he's all yours."

"Thanks," Drew brushes past Hathaway and wraps his arm around Caleb's shoulder. "Don't worry, I can take it from here. I'm sure you have more pressing matters to deal with."

Hathaway steps out of the way as Drew escorts Caleb into the kitchen. He turns his head and mouths to the constable, "Stay here."

Caleb's upset, and Drew keeps him moving. Hathaway shouts from the living room, "Don't touch anything."

"Not my first crime scene, constable."

They are alone, and Drew pulls out a barstool for Caleb. "Are you okay?"

"Physically, but emotionally, that's another story."

"Where's Susan?"

Caleb shakes his head side to side. "I don't know because they wouldn't let me check on her, but I think she's dead."

"Fuck. I'll be back."

"Okay, maybe Hathaway will talk to you."

"Worth a shot. All right, I'll be in the living room if you need me."

Drew walks out of the kitchen, the envelope still firmly in his grip, and finds Hathaway waiting by the fireplace.

Drew extends his hand. "Sorry, constable, my friend's been through a lot lately."

"It's all good. My heart goes out to him. So, what can I help you with?"

"Is it true? Is she dead?"

Hathaway nods.

"Shit. And to think I thought she committed those murders last night. Guess I'll need to come up with a new theory now."

"Wait, you think she murdered those medics last night?"

"I did, yeah. Why?"

Hathaway leans in and whispers, "Everyone knows who's behind this, but no one can convince Dawe to look into it."

Drew bites his lower lip. "That's all about to change."

***

CALEB SITS NERVOUSLY IN THE KITCHEN while Drew and the constable chat in the living room. The house remains dim. If it weren't for the moonlight penetrating through the large picture window, he'd be sitting in pitch blackness.

Caleb places his feet on the floor and walks over to the picture window. It's dim; however, there is a slight glow from the front porch lights. He stares off, and something moving catches his attention. He looks closer, and he makes out the shadowy outline of a person, their face obscured by a black mask and a hoodie covering their head. Caleb retreats but keeps his eyes on the figure, who motions with their fingers across their throat.

Caleb yells out, "Drew, I need you."

Hathaway and Drew rush into the kitchen, and Caleb's stare fixates outside the window.

"What's up? Whatcha looking at?"

Caleb turns toward Drew and back out the window, but the hooded figure has vanished. "They were right there."

"Who was?"

"The intruder, and they made a threat."

"Just now? Someone was outside in the yard?"

He nods.

Hathaway takes off outside and searches for any indication someone was there. Soon Caleb sees the beam of his flashlight searching around the front yard, and he focuses on a fresh set of footprints left in the snow. It isn't long before he follows them out of sight. Drew returns to the kitchen, holding the envelope in his hand.

Caleb feels his presence and turns.

"I was right, she's dead—isn't she?"

Drew gives it to him straight. "I'm not going to lie; she's gone."

The words sink in, and an unemotional Caleb clears his throat. "So, this is how it's going to be: I'm going to lose everything."

"Don't say that. We'll catch them."

"Everyone I know is going to die. And for what? Because I lost some stupid fucking case."

Drew holds up the envelope. "Not to change the subject, but I found this on your windshield."

Caleb looks at the plain white envelope, his name scrawled across it like the last two packages left. "I can't bear to read this one. You open it."

Caleb steps away from the window and back to the barstool. Whatever the newest message is, he knows he should sit before Drew utters the first word.

Drew tears along the side of the envelope carefully and inside finds a typed, nondescript letter. "Read it aloud?"

He nods and leans forward in the chair.

Drew starts. "I told you to be careful who you trust, but you aren't listening. Do I have your attention yet, or does another person in your life need to die?"

Caleb falls forward, his elbows land on the granite counter top. "Something doesn't add up. Why does Sanderson give two fucks who I trust? Do you think I'm wrong and he's not behind this?"

"If not him, who else could it be?"

"I have no clue, but my list of suspects is shrinking. I didn't mention this to you before, but they left a package for me the other day."

"What kind of package?"

"A DVD."

"I'm gonna need more info."

"It was a video of Sebastian and Gabriel—they were . . ." Caleb stops, unable to even put into words what he saw.

"They were what? Come on, spit it out."

"Sebastian cheated on me . . . with Gabriel. They were having an affair."

The admission stuns Drew. "What? When?"

"The date on the video was three weeks before Sebastian went missing. I handed it over to Barnes, and of course Dawe alleged I murdered over their affair."

"But you didn't know until the other day an affair was even going on, right?"

"Right. I thought my marriage with Sebastian and relationship with Gabriel were both solid until the other day. I guess in life, not everything is what it appears to be."

Drew hovers and lays his hand against Caleb's back. "I know you. You're strong and we're going to get this son of a bitch."

"I know."

As Caleb closes his mouth, Barnes rushes into the kitchen.

"Caleb, holy shit. Are you okay?"

"Shaken up, but I'm not hurt."

"We need to get you someplace safe. Hathaway says the killer came back?"

"Yeah, which is confusing. It's like one minute I think they're going to kill me, but they leave notes as if they're on my side."

"Note? They left another one?"

Drew picks up the envelope and letter off the kitchen island and holds it in the air. Barnes pulls a pair of fresh latex gloves from his pocket. "Who all touched the envelope?"

"Me," Drew says.

Caleb raises his hand.

"I'll get this to forensics. Hopefully, any biological evidence hasn't been compromised." Barnes pulls out a plastic evidence bag and seals it.

Caleb sighs. "I had to know what was inside."

"Let's get you out of here and someplace safe. Mr. Murphy, can you drive him to headquarters and wait for me?"

Caleb jumps up from his seat. "I'm not leaving."

"Um—this isn't up for debate, counsellor," Barnes replies.

"Yeah, I'll take him."

Drew grasps Caleb's forearm and leads him toward the door. However, Caleb still attempts to argue his way into staying.

"But—"

Drew interjects. "Are you crazy? You're not safe here. I don't want this psychopath coming back to finish you off."

"I can take care of myself."

"Oh really? If you're so brave, why'd you need me here?"

Silence.

"It's obvious you can't. I'll wait with you so you won't be bored, okay?"

Caleb nods. "Fine. If you both think it's what's best."

Barnes chimes in. "We do. I'll see you shortly."

Drew follows Caleb into the living room, and they spot the crew from the ME's office struggling with an old stretcher on the staircase. Caleb sees the black, zipped-up body bag and turns his head.

Drew reaches for Caleb's jacket. "Eh, let's go."

Caleb slips on his jacket and takes one final look around. He can never fathom returning here ever again.

NINETEEN

February 18, 2017
Midmorning

C**ALEB CLUTCHES THE VENTI CUP OF** dark-roast coffee Drew fetched from Starbucks around the corner. For a Saturday morning, the RNC Headquarters is a frenzied mess with people of all ages dashing in and out of the packed lobby, but thankfully for Caleb, he's tucked far away from the hustle and bustle in a tiny interrogation room.

The ex-lovers haven't spoken but a scarce sentence here and there to one another in the past two hours. The cramped conditions aren't ideal, and after the shocking event from earlier, the atmosphere remains uneasy and heavy. Caleb's trembling hasn't ceased, and his mind repeats the entire evening and early morning, and he finds himself asking the same question over and over: *How could I let this happen?*

His brain won't shut off, but he wishes he held some magic, top-secret power to make it. At the forefront is Susan and pondering why she needed to meet an untimely end. Sadly, he finds himself in a vicious circle, gyrating from one place to another and landing on the same name that has been at the tip of his tongue for the past eleven days: Timothy Sanderson.

Barnes called an hour earlier to update Caleb on their progress. "Still processing the house, waiting for forensics to finish up. Be there soon."

At no time during the quick ninety-second conversation did Barnes make any mention of Susan, or whether they found the intruder—nothing. Just the same scripted statement and small talk he always made when they spoke.

They're coming for me next.

A fear swells within Caleb at the idea. The newest letter, which he handed off to the constables hours earlier, only fueled his repeated cries of guiltlessness in any of the disappearances and murders. He expects that with Barnes personating an alpha investigator now, hopefully the investigation will shift, sending them toward new, undiscovered suspects. Even with that said, a new problematic situation develops: how to bring Oliver into this mess without getting an earful.

Maybe a quick call to give a heads-up should suffice.

Caleb stands, and Drew reaches out, grasping his forearm. "Hey, where ya going?"

"Oh, I—" he pauses. "I need to give Olli a call, you know, bring him up to speed."

Drew loosens his grip. "Ah, okay. That's perhaps a wise idea."

Caleb leaves the room and trots along the long corridor. He steps out into a calmer lobby and passes by the reception desk.

"I'm going to step outside for a minute to make a call."

She looks up at his familiar face. "Sure thing, Mr. Winters."

He presses against the door and out into the sub-zero air. Having grown up in the cold, each passing year, he yearns for warmer weather.

He shivers and swipes across the screen of his phone, searching for Olli's number in his contact list. Their exchange takes less than three minutes and ends with Olli giving Caleb a play-by-play of what he's going to do.

"I'm heading your way," Olli replies and abruptly hangs up.

Caleb glares at the black display reflecting his image back at him, and a sarcastic laugh falls from his mouth. He looks around, and unexpectedly a strong gust of wind blows by, stinging his face and neck. A shiver travels down his spine, and he pulls his jacket closer to his chest before turning to face those all-too-recognizable doors. He's doing his best to keep his shit together, so no one sees how weak he is.

He noisily blows out and pulls the handle of the door, swinging it toward him. The young receptionist sits on a phone call but notices him as he passes and buzzes him in. It's back to those dreaded four bland walls, which is agonizing for Caleb. It's like he's a prisoner of his own making.

As he strolls the sterile hallway, he pictures how he hoped his life would have turned out, instead of what it has become. He stops mid-stroll and closes his eyes. With a deep breath, he reminisces back to college, the days when life was less complicated. With Drew's reentrance, he realizes ever since the day he walked out of the apartment on Beverly Street, everything in his life had been out of his control: love life, finances, work. You name it, he managed to screw it up while making everything look perfect.

This isn't how things should be.

Caleb opens his eyes and continues toward the room. He approaches and finds the door slightly ajar, as he left it. With a light push, the creaky door slowly opens. Drew sits, fumbling with his cell phone, oblivious to the fact Caleb is back. Caleb clears his throat and Drew glances up from whatever has him so fixated.

"Everything okay?" Drew asks.

"Eh, well, you know how Oliver is. He insists on dropping everything to race over here."

Drew rolls his eyes.

"Seriously? I think you're safe with me. Tell ya what, let me call big brother and tell him he's wasting his time coming over here to rescue you."

"You guys can fight over who gets custody of me when he shows up."

Caleb returns to the uncomfortable plastic chair his ass has occupied all morning and crosses his arms across his chest. Drew flashes him another coy smile and returns to his phone. Two minutes pass and the unpleasant awareness of Caleb's stabbing stare firmly engrossed on him makes him a little tense. He knows

Caleb is testing his patience but nonetheless keeps his concentration on his upcoming calendar. Caleb tightens his lips, conjuring up some witty thing to say, but nothing comes, so they sit in silence for a few moments.

The nervousness overwhelms Drew, who can't endure the stare any longer, and he clicks a button, shutting off his phone's screen. "So, since I can't seem to get any work done, why don't you and I recap what we know."

"Okay."

"All this chaos began the morning you received a call from Dawe telling you they found remains up near Pouch Cove?"

Caleb looks away. "Yeah."

"Okay. So, the same day, you end up losing the Sanderson case to my arrogant ass."

"You said it, not me."

Drew remains professional. "What can I say? I'm merciless. But let's focus here."

Caleb nods. "Anyway, as you pointed out, proudly, I lost the case, so Olli and I went to a bar. We sit, order our drinks from this handsome barkeep, and wouldn't you know it, in waltz two of Sanderson's goons."

"I'm sure it was fairly unnerving? Let me guess, they didn't stop in to talk about the weather. So, what'd they want?"

"What are you now, a prosecutor *and* a constable?"

At last, a grin gleams from Drew's face. "Maybe. Look, I'm not the enemy here. I'm your friend, and to be perfectly honest, I'm a little agitated with the fact I'm only finding out about this encounter. You want to find out who did this, right?"

"Of course I want to know."

"Good, because so do I. All right, so, these thugs pay you a visit, threaten you, and the next day Gabriel vanishes?"

"That about sums it up."

Drew nods and steals a pause in the conversation to gather his theories. "So, Gabriel disappears. Next, we find Nicole and Sam, both dead."

"You were there."

"I was. Then not even six hours later, someone breaks into your house, murders Susan, and tries to kill you in the process. Am I up to speed?"

"Yeah, but is this bus going to stop soon?"

"I sure hope so. You weren't legal counsel for Sanderson back when Sebastian disappeared, were you?"

"No, he wasn't a client until last year—why?"

Drew has a mystified expression on his face. "So, I suppose my problem with all of this is this: If you didn't know Sanderson back then, why in hell would he murder Sebastian? It doesn't make any sense to me."

Caleb takes a moment to consider Drew's remark. *He's right. Could it be Sanderson isn't the one behind this? But then again, who's to say he isn't?*

"Even so, I think we shouldn't rule Sanderson out. He and I may not have been acquainted, but it doesn't mean Sebastian didn't find himself into some shady shit. Let's face it, he was banging Gabriel and he does have a history of drug abuse."

Drew sits up, his attention now grabbed. "What are you talking about? The way you painted Sebastian, he was the poster boy of a perfect husband and someone you'd never worry about. Sounds like there's still a lot I don't know."

"Well, for once in my life, I'm not going to paint a perfect picture. In fact, Sebastian wasn't the perfect husband I made him out to be. But back then I was clueless to everything. Sebastian was my entire world, and there wasn't anything he could do wrong. Then Gabriel came along, and again, I turned the other cheek to his problems."

Drew looks sorry he asked. "Look, I didn't mean to insinuate—"

"Yeah, you did, but it's okay. Knowing what I know now, it's not an insinuation—it's facts."

Drew sighs.

"I tried my hardest to make myself believe everything was perfect with Gabriel, you know, like maybe for once in my life I had everything figured out. But I'm not naïve. I was fully aware Gabriel was using behind my back since day one."

"Why'd you tolerate any of it? You're too good a person to be wrapped up in that shit."

Caleb ignores the remark and continues. "But when it came to Sebastian, the affair, the drugs, I'd never believed in a million years any of it was true."

"But it's all true . . . isn't it?"

"Yeah. I don't get it. Why would he cheat on me?"

"I wish I could give you an answer, but I can't. But wait, you don't find it odd—"

Caleb cuts him off. "I already know what you're gonna say: Don't I find it odd Gabriel and I ended up together?"

"You must be a mind reader or something. That's exactly what I was gonna say."

"When it happened, I didn't think anything of it."

"But now?"

"After seeing the tape, yeah, I have more questions than answers."

Drew's eyes water up. It's clear he still has an emotional attachment to Caleb, but grief consumes him and he's unaware of how deep those feelings go.

Changing the subject, Drew lightly touches his eye and shrugs it off. "Sorry, had something in my eye. All right, so there are two questions that we have yet to answer: First, so what if Gabriel was using drugs, or the two of them were having an affair. Why would any of it matter to Sanderson? Secondly, even if it did matter, why would he want them killed for it?"

Caleb deliberates long and hard about the questions Drew puts to him. Unfortunately, everything makes perfect sense in his head: If it's not Sanderson, who else has it out for him? Still, he's hellbent on continuing the Sanderson angle. It's too much of a coincidence that the day after he's threatened, Gabriel turns up missing.

"You of all people know Sanderson runs the drug trade not only here but pretty much everywhere in Newfoundland. If it's seedy, he's got his grubby paws all up in it."

Drew nods and watches as Caleb's lips continue moving.

"He's the kind of man who'd off someone first and ask questions later."

"I hate to state the obvious here, but hear me out."

"Sure."

"Is it possible Gabriel is the one behind all of this? What I mean is, he was having an affair with your husband, using drugs, and for all we know he could have been secretly working for Sanderson on the down low."

Caleb is about to open his mouth to give some silly remark on why it can't be Gabriel, but he's interrupted by Barnes, who storms in. His face is flush. Caleb and Drew stare at each other in silence while Barnes wipes away the beads of sweat that cling to his thick hairline. Barnes notices their obtuse looks, cracks a grin, and clears his throat. Their attention now focuses solely on the constable.

"Everything all right in here?"

In sync, their heads turn once again, and all the two men can do is stare at one another, until finally Drew replies. "Just trying to figure this whole thing out."

"Aren't we all. Dawe and I have instructed a few constables to begin fetching Sanderson's known associates. But I'd like to get your statement about the events that took place this morning, Mr. Winters. You think you're up for it?"

Caleb sits, his hands resting against his abdomen. The sensation of fear exudes from his body, but he musters up a "Yeah."

Barnes pulls the chair across the floor and parks catty-corner from Drew and directly across from a cool and collected Caleb. The notepad he always writes in drops against the table and he taps his jacket for a pen.

Caleb is at ease and less intimidated than the last time he sat face-to-face with Barnes. No video camera, no Dawe giving him the third degree.

"How was the mood around the house after I left last night? Did anything seem out of the ordinary? Did you place or receive any calls?" Barnes asks.

Caleb thinks for a moment and recollects every memorable event from last evening in his mind. Everything's fuzzy, and over the past few hours, he's tried to pull the fragmented pieces together. He takes a deep breath. "The only thing out of the ordinary was Susan's behavior. I polished off my nightcap around midnight, and by 12:30 AM I was upstairs."

"So, you didn't place or receive any calls?"

"None," Caleb hesitates, "unless—"

"Unless . . . what?"

"Unless you know something I don't."

Barnes shrugs and grimaces. "It's not a trick question. Either you did or you didn't."

"The only phone calls I placed were when I awoke to the sound of a gunshot. I don't think any calls came in, but then again, I didn't check."

"Okay. And how about you, Mr. Murphy, what time did you leave?"

"I stayed with Caleb until around midnight. Like he said, we finished up a nightcap. The evening was rough, and I didn't want to leave him there until I was certain the craziness subsided."

"And you didn't notice anything strange outside the home when you left?"

"No. The neighborhood had an eerie calmness about it."

"And did you place or receive any calls after midnight?"

"No calls, but I did send Caleb a text to let him know I made it home safely."

Barnes's head hangs while he concentrates on the white-lined paper he's scribbling notes on. He's writing so quickly Caleb can't make out anything he's written. Barnes jabs the pen hard as he places a period at the end of his final sentence.

"I'm gonna level with you, Mr. Winters. I don't believe you were involved in the disappearance of your husband or Mr. Parsons. However, I'm beginning to favor Dawe's side when it comes to Sanderson. I've looked at the evidence, and I can't find any connection to Sebastian or Sanderson from two years ago."

"You're wrong, ya know."

"Mr. Winters, Dawe and I have been at this for a long time. If she's convinced, you of all people know there is no way in hell she's going to change her mind without some compelling evidence."

Caleb shakes his head.

"Yeah, well, when you two conduct those interviews, you'll uncover something."

Barnes scrunches up his face. He wants to speak, but the door pivots open, and standing on the other side are Oliver and Constable Dawe. Oliver gives Constable Barnes a dirty look, but Dawe stands next to him with a lopsided grin. She seems at ease knowing she's again managed to piss someone off.

***

THE MOOD IN THE ROOM CHANGES instantly. Once relaxed, Caleb now cringes and folds his arms across his chest. He can't stomach to look directly at Dawe. While she stands firmly in the doorway, Oliver rushes to the table and positions himself next to Caleb.

Dawe finally speaks. "Mr. Winters, first, I have something I must say."

His eyes widen, his mouth salivates harder, and his curiosity peaks. He leans forward, uncrossing his arms and planting his elbows on the table. "I'm listening."

"I'm sorry. I'm sorry for all the harassment I've made you endure over the years. I truly thought you murdered Sebastian. But after everything that's happened these past two weeks, I now realize I was wrong. So, please accept my sincere apologies."

Caleb's eyes light up and he grins. Finally, the moment he's waited over two years for has arrived. Those two simple words are all he's wanted to receive. Yet, as he stares at her, the validation he expects isn't there.

She's only saying it to save face later.

"Thank you, Constable Dawe. Well, now that we got that out of the way, do you all think we can figure out who this madman is?"

Her brow raises, and she flips her curly, fire-red hair. There's an expression of disapproval on her face from his outlandish comment, but on the other hand, she has a new respect for him. "I don't believe Sanderson's behind any of this, but you do. We'll investigate this perspective. But be ready—if we find no evidence to link him or his crew to anything, we'll have to jump back to square one."

"Understood. And while I realize you don't believe it, there's something in my gut, and it tells me he's trying to ruin my life from behind bars. But, whatever you uncover, I'll accept the results."

Oliver waits patiently for Dawe to wrap up her apology so he can speak with Caleb in private. Even though Dawe makes it known she doesn't deem Caleb a suspect any longer, he's worked with the constabulary plenty to know they sometimes use manipulation. It's something Oliver won't take a gamble on.

A chiming sound dings from Dawe's inner blazer pocket and she pulls out her iPhone. She scans the screen from top to bottom twice and turns to Barnes. "They're here. You ready?"

Barnes smiles and walks through the door with Dawe. Before stepping away, he peers inside the room to see Oliver sit in the seat across from Caleb. "We'll let you know how things go. For now, if you guys can sit tight a little longer."

"Wait, when can we leave? I'll make sure he stays safe," Drew says.

Barnes turns and replies, "Soon, I promise."

They both shake their heads, and Barnes smiles, closing the door behind him.

Oliver delays cracking the door to check for eavesdroppers. He looks left, then right, and finds the hallway deserted. He softly latches the door closed and returns to the table.

The corner of Oliver's eyes crinkle and a tiny vein in his neck pulsates. And Caleb knows this look all too well. It's the look Oliver has before unleashing holy hell. "Have you two lost what's left of your fucking minds? Neither of you could call to tell me what happened?"

Caleb snaps back. "Okay, first, crazy man, calm down. You're lucky I called at all. I didn't want to, but I trust you and I thought you should know."

"You should always call me, Caleb. I'm your friend and attorney."

"Whoa. Whoa. When someone kills your best friend execution style, takes a shot at you, and your life flashes before your eyes, I presume your business partner's main concern shouldn't be, 'Why didn't I call you sooner?'"

Oliver's at a loss for words. But instead of taking a few moments to de-escalate the situation and think of the right thing to say, he goes off half-cocked and blurts out, "Yet you weren't in too much shock to call *this* guy."

Caleb leans in closer to Oliver. His elbows scoot forward across the table, his teeth grind together like a rabid dog. "*This* guy came to mind first because he was there with me when I needed him. This same guy spent over two hours last night searching in the sub-zero temperatures while you were at home undoubtedly having cocktails with your wife. So, excuse me for not thinking of *you* first, especially when I could count on *this* guy to help."

Oliver stands, plants his hands atop the table, and leans forward. Their eyes lock. All the while, Drew sits uncomfortable, wondering if he's about to break up a fight. Caleb's face grows redder, and he jumps up and follows suit. He leans across the table until only inches separate them. After thirty seconds of silence, but a lot of heavy breathing, Oliver speaks. "Fine. I know when I'm not needed."

Caleb withdraws and steps away from the table. "Grow the fuck up, Oliver. How old are you? Ten?"

"Why'd you call if you didn't need me?"

"I called because you're my attorney and I'm sitting in an interrogation room. I called because I've lost my husband, my boyfriend, and now my two best friends. You and Drew, you're all I have left. So, sit your ass down, get over your ego, and let's work on figuring this out together."

Indifferently, Oliver slothfully falls back into the plastic chair. He knows that when the scolding tone comes out of Caleb's mouth, it's best to do what Caleb says. "All right, you got my attention. I'm listening."

Caleb eases up and leans back in the chair. He thinks for a few seconds about what he should say next to decrease the tension from a situation that spiraled out of control. There are many things Caleb has never been good at in life, and one of them is apologizing, especially if he knows he's in the right. This time proves no different.

They bounce names of potential suspects out, but Oliver's fragile ego is growing more pissed from Caleb not apologizing. His mind goes astray, and his anger reaches a climax.

"I never pictured we'd ever end up at this point," Oliver says as his eyes curtly scan between Caleb and Drew.

"What d'ya mean?"

"I've known you for over ten years, and in those years, you've never once raised your voice to me. You've been an asshole too many times, and so many times I let it go. Not this time. No.

Here's what I'm gonna do: I'm gonna pretend like this entire conversation never happened."

"You're being a baby again."

"No, Caleb, you're the one acting like a baby. I get it, you're strained, and the unknown is causing you to lose your mind."

"I'm well in touch with my faculties, thank you," Caleb says.

"Okay, Mr. 'I got it all figured out.' I'll ask once more: Do you need me or not?"

Caleb takes a moment to think it over. On the one hand, the constables are now focusing on other suspects, which means there isn't a need for him to have an attorney present. However, on the other hand, Oliver's his law partner. He debates whether telling him to sod off would be out of line.

The silence in the room makes him more anxious than he already was, and he finally utters, "I promise I'm fine. I know you have things to do at home, and I'm sure Drew will ensure they don't get out of hand with me."

Oliver's face shifts and he graciously bows his head and stands. "Yes, I'm sure he'll take diligent care of you. See ya 'round."

A look of jealousy radiates before he heads for the door. He moves slowly, taking his time doing so. Oliver hopes Caleb's Catholic guilt will kick in and he'll change his mind. But he reaches the door, and not a word. In the blink of an eye, he leaves and doesn't turn back.

Drew's speechless. Caleb turns his head and scoffs. "I did what's right—right?"

Drew loosens his posture. "I hope so. Because after what I saw, I'm pretty sure you'll be looking for a new law partner."

"Nah, I'm sure everything will be fine."

Caleb projects the confidence, but things are quite different in his head.

I'm a fucking idiot. When will I ever learn to keep my big mouth shut?

TWENTY

February 18, 2017
Midmorning

DAWE STANDS OPPOSITE A ONE-WAY MIRROR glaring in on a unkempt, long-haired biker dressed in a black leather jacket and matching leather chaps. She's entranced with his behaviors, and even as he digs his fingernails into the open sores dotting his face, she can't turn away. It's clear to any competent investigator, such as herself, he's detoxing from crystal meth, or something even more potent. She watches him cringe in pain before Barnes walks in, interrupting her enjoyment. "All set?"

"I'll take him, you take the other one."

She knocks once against the door before bursting in without waiting for a reply. She steps to the empty chair crosswise from the suspect. She towers over the disheveled man, who hasn't even taken notice she's appeared. She's poker-faced and with one long tug, the metal legs of the chair scrape piercingly across the tile floor. The man shakes to and his eyes squeeze together in pain from the shrilling sound. She sits, and the man nods off again into a trance.

Drug addicts are her favorite bunch to interrogate, so without wasting time she bangs her hand loudly against the metal table and the man comes to again. With the flick of a wrist, she unfastens a binder holding a few reports and several large crime scene photos. She neatly stacks the reports and photos into a pile and picks up the first photo—the burnt body from last evening. She holds it in her hand and stares for a moment and disgustedly tosses it across the table where it slides in front of the strung-out biker.

"What's this?"

"What's it looks like to you, Mr. Sampson?"

"Looks like a crispy dead dude." He slides the photo across the table out of his view. "Why you show me this?"

"I wanna know how this dead crispy dude ended up like this."

He shakes his head. "How would I know? Never seen this feller before in my life."

"How do you know? You can't even make out his face."

The man stares.

"I didn't ask if you knew him. I asked how he ended up like this."

"I don't know. I know I didn't burn nobody up."

She flings over the second photo, this one a close-up of Susan's bloodied face. He takes a quick peek before gaging and spinning his head away. "Nope, don't know her neither."

"Let me ask you this: You work for Sanderson. What exactly do you do for him?"

"Who's Sanderson?" he says as another photo comes flying across the table.

"Oh, you know—you're telling me this isn't you with Timothy Sanderson from two years ago?" she asks with a scowl on her face.

"Okay, let me look again. Yeah, I thought you meant someone else. I don't do anything special for him. Did some work on his bike a while back. But isn't he gone off to prison?"

"Yeah, best place for him to be."

"So why am I here?"

She's annoyed. "I wanna know if you slaughtered these two people." She holds the photos up again, shoving them in his face.

"And I said I don't know 'em. How can you murder someone you don't know?"

"Happens every day."

"I ain't ever heard of nothing like that before. Look, can I go?"

"Not so fast, slick. If you didn't kill them, maybe you've overheard some gossip about Sanderson ordering a hit on them?"

The forthright question disrupts the drug-induced stupor he's spent most of the interview in. "Wait, what? A hit? We're not the mob."

"You heard me right. Did Sanderson order a hit on these two?"

"Jesus Christ, lady. Dude might have his hands in a lot of shit, but one thing he's not is a murderer."

"Ah, okay, so I guess he draws the line at rape and kidnapping, eh?"

The man slouches in the chair silently brushing off her outlandish accusation. "Look, sweetheart, I got places to go, people to see, and things to do. I know you can't hold me against my will if I ain't done nothing wrong."

"Ah, we got a lawyer here. Tell me, where'd you get your law degree from?"

"I ain't got no damn degree, but I know my rights, and you can't hold me here."

"Yeah, in fact, I can. Now answer my questions honestly and I won't steal the next twenty-four hours from you while you sit in a holding cell."

"What else you need to know?"

"If you weren't too high, do you remember where you were this morning, say around four?"

"At home, asleep. Well, I was until your people burst through my front door and hauled me in here."

She taps her pen against the table. "Wow, for someone who we abruptly awoke this morning, you sure do seem pretty jittery. You sure you aren't on something?"

His eyes widen. "I ain't no druggie."

"Coulda fooled me."

"It's people like me get a little nervous when we're sitting in a police station, ya know."

"I wouldn't know anything about how it feels, sorry. What about yesterday between two and four. Where were you? Still in bed?"

He thinks, taking his time, and conjures up an answer. "Over at Vinny's bar. You know it, the place where people like me hang out from time to time."

She forcefully exhales, hangs her head, and drums her freshly manicured fingers across the top of the table. "Yeah, I know the place. We all do."

"Well, head over there and check out my story with the bartender. Fella's name is Viper. I was there until the sun set."

"This Viper got a *real* name?"

"Just know him by Viper."

She scribbles the name in all capital letters in her notepad and folds the cover closed. "Thanks. You're free to go, but don't leave town in case I need to see you again."

The man stands, flings his worn-out black leather jacket around his stocky body, and rushes for the exit.

The door closes with a loud thud, and she collects the photos she's sprawled out on the table. "One down, six to go."

***

BARNES FINISHES UP WITH SOMEONE AS equally squirrely. He asks his final question, and after listening to the half-ass answer, he rubs his fingers firmly against his temples before escorting the rat-tailed man to the hallway. Barnes positions himself in the doorframe, already tired after only one interview. With his forearm propped against the jam of the door, he watches the man stagger his drunken self along the corridor.

He snickers under his breath and squeezes his eyes closed. The sour stench of booze still tickles his nose hairs, and standing in the corridor gives him some much-needed fresh air. He inhales deeply, trying to expunge the lingering stink that clings to him.

He opens his eyes and lifts his head to see Dawe leaning against the wall a few meters down the hall. Her famous scowl greets him, and he cracks a half smile. She doesn't flinch or return his greeting. Instead, she crosses her arms over her chest and cocks her left foot out. His smile droops into a frown, and all he can do is shrug before moving toward her.

"How'd your interview go?" he asks.

She points to the man clinging to the wall, straining to find the exit. "Complete waste of time. What about with Don Juan there?"

"Him. Psh, he don't know shit. I don't even know if he knows he's on Earth right now."

The witticism makes Dawe laugh quietly.

"Who's next?"

"Brett and Evan Tucker. I think we need to tag team these two," Barnes says.

"I think you're right. If we're going to make headway in this case, we should focus our energy on these two. These other fools are so low on the totem pole I doubt they know anything of value."

"Agree."

They walk side by side toward the lobby. As any good gentlemen would do, Barnes opens the door and allows Dawe to pass through first. Congregated in one corner of the atrium sit the three remaining men they want to question. One person is still a no-show: Brett Tucker.

The constables approach Evan Tucker, who sits amidst several junkies who doze in and out of consciousness. Tucker scans the floor until suddenly he's interrupted by two pairs of black shoes standing inches from him. He raises his head and Dawe flashes him a fake smile.

"Evan Tucker?"

"Yeah. You are?"

"Constables Dawe and Barnes. Wanna come with us?"

"A'right." He grunts softly but follows alongside Dawe as asked.

They return to the room Barnes left. The tart smell of the previous suspect still loiters in the air.

"Have a seat," Barnes insists, pulling out the chair for him.

"A'right."

The man sits, his eyelids droop. "Before I say anything, why am I here?"

Neither of the constables says anything. Instead, they stare at him hoping his paranoia kicks in and gets the better of him. The table begins to slightly vibrate, and Dawe sees his body jerking. The intimidation is working faster than she hoped.

She clears her throat and reaches for a glass of water. "Need anything?"

"Yeah, an answer to my question."

"Right. How about this: Why do *you* think you're here?"

He clears his throat. "No clue. I've been a good boy."

She laughs at his biting wittiness. "Yeah, okay, sure you have. Are you acquainted with Caleb Winters?"

"Sure, I know Caleb. He works for a big, fancy law firm. What about him?"

"Buzz is you threatened him a few weeks back in a bar on George Street. Is this true?"

He grins. "There weren't no threats. I paid him a friendly visit on behalf of my friend and asked him, respectfully, to have a word with the judge lady, you know, get her to review the verdict. Nothing more." Tucker's body stops jerking and he relaxes.

Dawe smirks. She won't be letting him off too easy. There's still plenty of tricks she hasn't even reached yet. Barnes pipes in.

"We were kind of expecting you and your brother to be here."

"Haven't seen him."

"Strange. I thought the two of you traveled together like a pack of nuns."

"Nah, not always."

"Where is he?"

"He left for an ice-fishing trip couple days ago. He's out on some lake with no cell service."

"Must be nice. You know which lake he's visiting?" Barnes asks.

"Three Arm Pond, about twenty-five clicks outside town."

Barnes notates the information as Dawe opens a beige folder. She hopes whatever it holds will be the break they've been seeking.

"Perfect, we'll send some constables out there to speak with him shortly. So, where were we?" Dawe asks.

"This is your show. You tell me."

"Ah, yes, you know this guy?" She flings a photo across the table.

It's the same photo of the burnt body Dawe used with her last suspect. The picture now stares at Evan Tucker. She watches his expression, his body language as he quickly gives it a casual glance and pushes it away. "The fuck is this?"

"It's the area's latest homicide victim. You know him?"

"Seriously? No, I don't know no burnt-up body. This unlucky soul got a name?"

"Does the name Sam Butler ring a bell?"

His eyes slip to the right while he reflects on the name. Dawe watches him carefully, but not giving away her ulterior motives of why she's scrutinizing his every move. She sees his eyebrows draw upward and the corner of his mouth twitches slightly, but he looks straight into her eyes. "Don't know nobody named Sam."

Busted.

"Okay, how about this lady?" The second photo, of Susan Butler, flies across the table.

He looks down, not even taking a second to look at the photo before pushing it away. "Nope."

Dawe leans against the top of the table. "I'm not the smartest person in the world. Hell, I barely graduated high school, but I've been doing this job a really long time. And you know what I've learned in all those years?"

"Don't really care, but I'm sure you're gonna tell me anyway."

"I've learned how to tell when people aren't honest. And right now, your skittish behavior tells me *you do* know Susan Butler."

"I said I don't know the bitch. Never seen her, never even heard her name. You ready to tell me what all this is about?"

She glances at Barnes who has a sly grin on his face. "Might as well tell him."

"Tell me what? And why you ask me about Caleb then show me these bodies? Is he dead?"

She continues the silent treatment. Watching him squirm in his seat not knowing gives her real pleasure. Tucker's eyes widen, and he slams his fists against the table. "Is he dead?"

Dawe's pouty mouth gapes open in disbelief. At last, she gives in and answers him. "No, Mr. Tucker, he's not. But these two people were his best friends, and after your comments the other day, and I quote, 'Fix it, or you'll end up like your husband—buried in the woods,' did I get the wording right, Noah?"

Barnes nods. "See, with a comment this detailed, even an imbecile can see why we'd drag your ass in for questioning."

"Look, I didn't mean for it to come across threatening. But I didn't hurt no one—I swear."

"Oh, you didn't? Well, what about this guy?" Dawe flings out a color photocopy of Gabriel's permanent resident identification card.

"I've seen him around. What about him?"

"Where have you seen him 'around'?" Barnes asks.

Tucker bites at his fingernails and can barely restrain himself to his seat. If he answers the question, he risks implicating himself in something illegal. However, if he doesn't answer it's giving the constables more ammo to use against him.

"I'll ask again: Where have you seen him before? And don't make me ask again," Dawe says.

He tries to speak, but he stammers over his words. Dawe sits patiently, leaning in closer because she senses what he's about to unleash may be the break she's looking for. He finally stops stuttering, takes a deep breath, and speaks. "I'm not saying shit until I get immunity—in writing."

"Well, it's your lucky day. It so happens our Crown prosecutor is here. So, tell ya what, make yourself comfortable while I grab him."

Tucker presses his back against the chair while Dawe stands and exits. He takes a deep breath, and Barnes's razor-sharp eyes fixate on him.

"Whatever you have to say better be damn good and get us somewhere."

Evan grins. "Trust me, it is.

TWENTY-ONE

February 18, 2017
Early Afternoon

CALEB SITS NODDING OFF. THE FULL extent of what has happened hasn't hit him yet. Suddenly, the door flies open, and he jostles to. Casually, Drew looks up from his almost-dead iPhone and analyzes the out-of-character expression on Dawe's face. Something's different; there's a flicker of optimism twinkling in her eyes.

"Everything all right?"

"Eh, can I borrow you a minute?"

"Yeah, Caleb, I'll be back."

Caleb nods, and Drew walks into the hall with Dawe. "What's up?"

"I think we may have the break we're looking for. Evan Tucker knows something, but right when I thought he was going to spill it, he demanded an immunity marker."

"I hardly ever issue those, let alone an expedited one. What kind of information do you think he has?"

"Not sure, but when I pressed him for more information on how he knows Gabriel Parsons, he got really nervous. So, whatever he knows must be pretty damn good."

"Really? Gabriel?"

"Yeah, my gut tells me something isn't right, and I really need to know what it is. So, you gonna get me the marker or not?"

Drew taps his foot while he assesses his options. Offering a suspect an immunity marker gives the suspect a huge incentive to be honest, which typically provides prosecutors with valuable underground information. On the flip side, prosecutors run the risk of allowing someone who's committed a serious felony to walk free and clear.

"Tell you what. I want to hear from him before I agree. However, there is a catch: if I do this for you, I want something in return."

"And what's that?"

"I sign the paperwork, and you leave Caleb in my care for the weekend."

She doesn't even hesitate to think but instead blurts out, "Deal."

Walking the few yards along the hallway together, Dawe steps in front of Drew and opens the door. Barnes still stares at Evan

Tucker, but his concentration breaks when the door squeaks open. He turns and smiles at Drew, who's now in full work mode and doesn't return the gesture. He approaches Evan and extends his hand.

"Mr. Tucker, I'm Andrew Murphy, the Crown prosecutor. I've been informed you may have potentially incriminating evidence regarding Gabriel Parsons?"

Tucker acknowledges with a quick shake of his head. "Yes, sir. But I ain't sayin' nothing further until I know I won't be charged as a coconspirator."

Drew steps back and props himself against the wall, crossing his right leg over his left. "Tell you what. You're asking for a lot. Before I agree to approve an immunity marker, give me a brief overview of what sort of information we're talking about. Sound fair?"

Again, he nods but is still hesitant to spill what he knows. "This is bigger than Sanderson ever was to you. And the person you call Gabriel Parsons is smack dab in the middle of it all."

Tucker points at the photo of Gabriel in the permanent resident identification, which lays in front of him on the table.

Drew stands erect. "What do you mean 'person you call'? Is he not who he claims to be?"

"He's the fella who dates Caleb, right?"

Drew nods.

"Yeah, he's not who any of you think he is. If you give me what I need, I'll tell you everything you need."

"Thanks, Mr. Tucker. Dawe, Barnes, you mind if I speak to you in private?"

The constables nod in agreement.

"We'll be right back."

They follow Drew into the hallway and Barnes closes the door. Drew paces while they stare in silence.

"Boy, you all struck gold finding this guy. And he's so eager to give up the information."

"Yeah, perhaps he's a little too eager."

"Tell you what. It'll take me about an hour to write up the paperwork, but I need you two to locate a lawyer or public defender for him. The faster all this happens, the quicker you can wrap up your case, and poor Caleb can try to get back to his life."

"I think we can all agree," Barnes says.

"Well, let's get to work and find out this deep, dark secret regarding Gabriel Parsons," Dawe says.

The constables return to their office to locate a public defender while Drew returns to the interrogation room where he left Caleb alone. In the two earlier instances where he granted immunity to a defendant, the cases fell apart. But the information Tucker seems to have far outweighs the disappointment of the previous cases.

He stands at the door, mentally preparing to face Caleb. His shaky hand twists the knob and quietly he enters the room. Slouching forward in the chair, Caleb rests his head on the table. He doesn't move when the pressure in the room changes, or even when the clacking of Drew's shoes against the floor grows louder. It's not until Drew taps him on the shoulder that he lifts his head.

"Everything okay? I didn't wake you, did I?" Drew asks.

"Might have. Have you found out anything, like when can we get the hell out of here? I'm getting pretty drained by this room."

"We'll be outta here soon. I have to draw up some paperwork, but once it's done, you'll be spending the weekend at my place."

Caleb sighs. "I wanna go home."

"I had to promise Dawe if they let us leave I'd keep you safe until everything gets figured out."

"What kind of paperwork?"

"An immunity maker. Looks like Evan Tucker is ready to spill what he knows."

"That speed freak has information?"

"Might be what we need to figure out what's going on. Promise we won't be here much longer."

"Wait . . . when can I go back to my house? I have to get a change of clothes."

Confused, Drew pulls out a chair and sits next to Caleb, staring into his eyes. "Um, I'm aware you haven't processed everything, but your house is a crime scene."

"Yeah, I haven't lost my mind. But forensics should be wrapped up by now."

"Yeah, I don't think so. Someone broke into your house, murdered your best friend, and tried to kill you."

Caleb appears dazed.

"You sure you're okay? Your house will be a hive of police activity for a couple days, minimum."

Caleb frowns at the thought of not being able to return home anytime soon—worse still, maybe never.

"Right, I should make a hotel reservation, eh?"

"H-e-l-l-o, Caleb," Drew shouts and snaps his fingers, "I'm bringing you to my place. And before you even try to negotiate your way out of this, you can't: it's the only option if you want Dawe to release you from police custody."

Caleb deliberates how to manipulate his way out of this arrangement, but skimming Drew's face, he rolls his head away and doesn't try. "Okay," he utters instead.

Astounded at the easiness of convincing him, Drew reaches and touches his hand. "Okay. I'll be down the hall doing this paperwork. Give me an hour, okay?"

Caleb signals with a trivial bob of his head and then rests it back on the table.

***

AN HOUR PASSES, AND AT LAST a public defender arrives at headquarters to act as legal counsel for Evan Tucker. The immunity marker has sat in front of Dawe for the past ten minutes, but with it being a Saturday morning, things in this sleepy town move a bit slower. The constables introduce themselves, but the fresh-out-of-law-school defense attorney already recognizes them and the circumstances.

"Don't worry, constables, I spoke with Mr. Murphy who filled me in on everything. The immunity marker is valid so the only reason I'm here is to make sure he receives fair treatment and you release him at the end of the proffer."

"Well, remind me later to thank Mr. Murphy for making this process go smooth. Shall we get going?"

He smiles at Evan Tucker. Dawe presses record on the video camera and begins the interview.

"My name is Constable Gretchen Dawe, and present with me today are Constable Noah Barnes, Barrister Peter Simpson, public defender, and Evan Tucker. This interview is taking place at the Royal Newfoundland Constabulary Headquarters located in St. John's. Today's date is Saturday, February 18, 2017, and the time is 1:09 PM," she begins. "Mr. Tucker is here to give a proffer regarding illegal activities about which he has information. Mr. Tucker has received an immunity marker, granted by the Crown prosecutor, Andrew Murphy, so any information in which he incriminates himself in he is free from arrest and prosecution. Are you ready to begin?"

"Yes," Tucker says as he turns his attention away from his public defender and back on the constable.

The young man pats him on the back. "Just tell them everything you know."

Tucker begins confessing, "I am acquainted with this man." He picks up the photo of Gabriel and aims it at the camera.

"And how is it you two are acquainted?" Barnes asks.

Tucker rubs his bony fingers across his forehead and wipes the perspiration that has accumulated on his sunken face. "First thing we should get straight is his real name isn't Gabriel Parsons. I've only heard people refer to him as Miguel. Never got a last name, though."

"Okay. So what sort of illegal stuff are you and this Miguel mixed up in?"

"He fronts like he owns a database management company, but really, he's a deep-rooted drug cartel leader from Miami."

Dawe chimes in. "And how did you learn this information?"

"Because I work for him."

"I thought you worked for Sanderson?"

"Used to. As you know, Sanderson pretty much owns, well owned, the drug smuggling 'round these parts, but when Miguel showed up with his boss, Sanderson set up a meeting with them."

"And?"

"And they worked out an arrangement for Miguel to take over but let Sanderson take a cut of the profits. Sanderson wanted to remove himself as far as possible, yet still get a cut."

"And since Sanderson was your boss when this handover took place, you suddenly had no choice but to work for Miguel?" Dawe asks.

"Right, but that's not what's important here. What's important is, and honestly it's the strangest thing I can tell you, the lawyer fella he dates, well, he's using him as a cover."

"I don't understand," Barnes replies.

"Dude's not gay. In fact, he has a girlfriend on the side he sneaks off with from time to time."

Barnes and Dawe look at each other, both in complete shock at the revelation. "Wait a minute, wait a minute. I'm confused. Miguel has been living with a man, having sex with a man, pretending to be a gay man for the last eighteen months? And this is the same guy who had an affair with Caleb's husband. Yet you're telling us he's not gay? Do we look like we were born yesterday?"

"No, that's not what I think. All I know is what I've seen and overheard. And I'm telling you, with 100 percent honesty, he has a girlfriend. Who the hell knows, maybe he's bi or something. Lord knows I couldn't sleep with a man. But you don't get it—this guy is so hardcore he's willing to do anything to keep his secret life, well, secret."

"I don't know if I can believe this," Barnes says as he laughs.

"Well, it obviously worked. None of you even suspected the boyfriend of a prominent, law-abiding citizen of running a drug ring in town, did ya?"

Dawe flounces back in her chair and sighs. "So, this girlfriend, she got a name?"

"I dunno her name. All I know is she's some paramedic chick who lives outside Torbay."

"Have you ever seen this girlfriend?"

"Yeah."

Dawe pulls out a photo the forensic techs took of the mutilated body of Nicole Bishop and tosses it across the table. "Is this her?"

He picks up the photo and studies it for a few seconds and sets it back on the table. "Yup, that's her. Obviously, you've met her. I'm telling you, someone is trying to clean up loose ends. If anyone finds out I'm here telling you all this, chances are pretty good I'll be next."

Dawe grabs the photo back from Tucker and slips it back into the folder. "Then you should know why all of these people are dead, since you work for the guy."

"Look, I don't know anything about any murders. But if you ask me, I wouldn't put it past Miguel to have ordered them all taken out. Dude is fucking crazy," Tucker says as he inserts the tip of his index finger into his mouth and begins chomping away at his nails.

Barnes interjects, "So, you think this guy killed all these people and staged his disappearance to throw us off track?" He flips the picture back on the table and jabs several times with his finger at Miguel's picture.

"Yeah, exactly, that's what I'm telling you. It wasn't me. The only thing I was ever involved in with this guy was selling some coke and heroin. That's it."

Dawe stands and gives Barnes a look. She presses pause on the camcorder. "Um, excuse us for a minute. Noah, can we speak outside?"

Barnes scoots out his chair, adjusts his shirt, and disappears out the door with Dawe.

"This is some serious shit. You think it's possible this Miguel could be behind all of this?"

"I mean, why would this guy go through all these hoops for immunity if he's going to waste our time. I think it's in our best interest to consider this guy to be authentic. And like it or not, it's time to consider the reality this Miguel is a murderer and used his disappearance to throw the responsibility onto Caleb."

"This guy is damn good, if that's the case. He seduces Caleb's husband, kills him, and waits a few months before moving in on a heartbroken Caleb, who has no fucking clue any of this is happening."

"Well, before we go back in there, we should call Caleb and warn him to be careful if this guy returns."

Dawe nods in agreement as they walk along the hallway toward the where they left Drew and Caleb. She reaches the door and opens it to find the room empty.

"Where are they?" Barnes asks.

"Damn. I told Murphy they could leave once I got the signature on the immunity marker. I didn't know this junkie was going to unleash something this entangled."

"Better get him on the phone and let him know."

Dawe pulls out her cell phone and finds his name. She presses the phone against her ear as Barnes begins pacing.

"This is bad—like really bad."

"No shit," she replies as the call redirects to voicemail. "Fuck. No answer."

"Get Murphy on the phone."

She hangs up and tries him—voicemail.

"Both phones, straight to voicemail."

"Well, Gretchen, my advice: we better find them before our new prime suspect does."

TWENTY-TWO

February 18, 2017
Early Evening

T HE SUN BEGINS TO SET, AND Caleb stares out the window of the coffee shop. The sun slowly fades behind a handful of mid-rise buildings downtown, and he clutches an oversized ceramic mug of green tea tightly with both hands. The warmth of the water eases his nerves, but it's still noticeable his hands are unsteady.

Drew stands a few feet away at the counter, paying for another soy vanilla latte, his third for the evening. Caleb lets his eyes wander across the uncrowded room, but soon he returns his attention to Drew but bashfully turns his head away. He pretends he's been watching the crowds of people passing by in their party clothes, all these twentysomething somebodies are maybe heading downtown for an entertaining evening out.

"Hey, you sure you don't want a refill?" Drew asks, sneaking up on Caleb who is daydreaming out the window.

Caleb jumps. "Nah, I'm good for now. Thanks, though."

Caleb's responses are increasingly curt, and Drew realizes everything that's happened has finally caught up with him psychologically, so he backs off to give him space.

Drew's phone rings for the twentieth time, this call from the same number he's seen each time flash across his screen. "Ugh, I'm gonna go take this call. Must be damn important for them to keep calling."

Caleb doesn't reply and instead glances back out the window. Drew walks to the exit and steps outside into the cold.

"Drew Murphy," he answers.

"Thank God. I've been trying to call you all day."

"Who is this?"

"Constable Dawe. Listen, we have a situation."

"What now? By the way, we're both fine."

"Good to know. I think we've been looking at everything wrong."

"How so?"

"Caleb's boyfriend isn't who we think he is."

"Huh?"

"His real name is Miguel Escobar, a notorious drug dealer from Miami."

Drew tensely laughs. "This can't be true. I mean, I've never met the guy, but I can't see Caleb falling for someone like him. No, you guys made a mistake."

"Trust me, it's true. Spoke with the major crimes unit with the Miami-Dade Police. They've sent over two mugshots, and if it's not him, he's got a doppelgänger."

Drew is in shock and collapses against the cold brick façade of the coffeehouse. "None of this makes sense. What am I supposed to do now? Are we in danger?"

"Maybe best if we set up some police protection. It's my belief this guy isn't missing unwillingly. I'm pretty sure he vanished on his own."

"Okay, let's get an unmarked car in front of my place for the weekend, or at least until you catch this guy."

"If you think that's best, consider it done. Also, I've reached out to the Mounties, and they'll be working with us going forward in this case."

"Smart move. Listen, thanks for the heads-up, I should get back to Caleb."

Drew listens as she gives him a few more bits of advice, and he nods, hangs up, and walks back through the door into the warmth of the coffee shop.

He's blown away by what he's learned, and slowly walking back to the table, several things he still can't wrap his head around run through his mind.

How do I tell Caleb that Gabriel's a fraud?

Drew wrestles back and forth, thinking of reasons why it's not the right time to tell Caleb.

I can't be the person who tells him. Nope. This guy made Caleb's life better, and now if I tell him he'll always remember me as the guy who destroyed it.

Drew approaches the table with his mind made up: he'll keep Caleb safe, but without dishing out the nitty-gritty details surrounding the case. He already blames himself for everything. Always telling himself if he'd come out back in Toronto, they'd still be together, and none of this would be happening.

I'm an idiot.

Drew pulls out the chair, which sits cockeyed underneath the table. It's heavy and he gives it a yank. The metal legs score the floor, the sound echoing through the sparse dining space like fingernails scraping a chalkboard. Caleb cringes at the noise.

"Argh, that is the worst noise in the world."

"Yeah, sorry, didn't realize it would be so loud."

"It's okay. So, what'd Dawe have to say?"

"How'd you know it was her? I didn't even know."

"Figures they'd call to check up on us. Was it even important?"

Drew sits still. He doesn't want to lie to him, but he also doesn't want to freak him out. "Well, she did have a reason for calling."

"And the reason is?"

"I'm worried about telling you because, well, I'm not sure how you'll react."

Caleb slouches in the gray velvet upholstered chair. "What did she tell you?"

"Okay, Evan Tucker gave them some information." He pauses. "Gabriel's a drug dealer from Miami, and they think he's responsible for all the murders, including Sebastian."

Caleb tries hard not to laugh at the outlandish accusation. "Gabriel, a drug dealer? No, really, tell me what she said."

"I'm telling you the truth. His name isn't Gabriel Parsons either. It's Miguel Escobar."

Fear engulfs Caleb's face. "No, none of this can be true."

"She's going to provide us with police protection until they find him. I'm so sorry to be the one to break this to you."

Caleb sits silent in shock, but it doesn't last long. Caleb glances at Drew's iPhone, which begins to vibrate across the table.

"Your phone's ringing."

"Ugh. Probably Dawe again," he says, looking at the screen.

Rebecca Mueller

Why's my assistant calling? Then it hits Drew. *Fuck, I'm late.*

He picks up the phone and answers it. "Oh my God, I'm so sorry, I've had so much going on, and I forgot you need a ride to the airport."

Drew listens to an earful (possibly a mixture of guilt and swear words), and for a moment Caleb is humored watching him scramble to smooth things over.

"All right, yeah, okay. I said I'm sorry. Look, give me ten minutes, and I'll swing by to pick you up?"

His head bobs from side to side. "Yeah, okay, see you in ten."

He hangs up and sighs frustratingly.

"Glad to see I'm not the only one who forgets things. Everything okay?"

"No, I'm a moron. I forgot I promised to drop my assistant, Rebecca, at the airport for her flight. I guess we should get going."

"I think I'll hang here while you go. You'll only be gone, what, an hour max?"

"I dunno, Caleb. I don't think it's wise for you to stay here alone."

"It's fine. I mean, who's gonna come and murder me in a coffee shop in front of all these people." He looks around the nearly deserted café. "Besides, I got the rental car out front if I need to make a quick getaway."

"Please, don't joke at a time like this. Look, I'll be back in forty-five minutes, so hang tight. Oh, and if you need more tea, it's on me," Drew says, throwing a ten onto the table.

"Big spender. Okay, drive safe."

Drew looks back but feels uncertain about leaving him in the mental state he is or following through with a promise he made a week ago, before everything got out of control.

Drew walks past the window, motioning with his fingers: four and five. Caleb slyly grins and waves him on. Drew slides behind the steering wheel and pulls out of the parking space along Gower Street and drives off into the darkness.

***

Caleb sits alone at the table and remembers he has no clothes for the weekend.

He picks up his phone, which he's had switched off since leaving the constabulary, and powers it on. He sets the phone back on the table and waits for it to boot up. He sips on his tea, and after a few moments, his phone begins dinging, and all his missed calls and texts flood in.

He sifts through the missed calls and sees twelve of them are from Dawe. He ignores them, knowing Drew already spoke with her not even ten minutes ago.

Must have been urgent.

He moves on to his text messages instead. Four of them stand out right away: Gabriel Parsons.

He looks around the café suspiciously before opening the messages.

We need to talk.

Can you meet me at the house?

Why are you ignoring me? I'll be at the house around seven thirty.

Come alone.

He drops the phone, and his once-quelled tensions flare up once more. His legs bounce beneath the table, and his fingertips thump rapidly against the reclaimed wood tabletop.

I must see him. I'm the only one who can get the real story.

Just as he's about to stand, the lone barista makes her rounds through the dining area, passing by his table to check on him.

"Everything okay over here?"

Caleb smiles. "Everything's good. But, hey, do you mind if I get another green tea? I might be here for a while."

"Yeah, of course. I'll be right back."

He reaches for the ten on the table, but she's scurried away too fast. "How much do I owe you?"

"This one's on me," she yells across the room.

"Thanks. Oh, on second thought, you think you can make my tea to go?"

She nods, and he waits, fumbling with his phone. He hasn't decided yet if he should let Drew know his plan to return to the house or not. He isn't even sure it's wise to mention Gabriel reached out.

Maybe it's a setup. Perhaps he's an innocent man on the run. Drew's been nothing but extra charming, so I should let him know exactly what I'm doing, in case something goes wrong.

The barista is gone less than two minutes when she returns with his tea. Service like this is sporadic, and Caleb wants to make sure the young woman gets what she deserves. He pulls out a two-dollar coin from his pocket and drops it into the palm of her hand.

"For you. Thanks for everything," he says, and she shyly smiles. "Awe, thanks, much appreciated."

He takes a sip of the scalding-hot tea, flinches, and unlocks his phone to pound out a quick text to Drew.

I need clothes. I spoke with Dawe, and she says they cleared the house a few hours ago. I'll be fine.

He takes a couple of sips of the tea and stands, grabbing his jacket from the back of the chair, and he heads for the exit. He makes it to the rental car, which he parked a few spaces ahead of the spot Drew vacated only moments earlier.

He throws his phone into the cup holder, cranks the engine, and pulls out of the spot as a reply from Drew comes in.

Oh, hell no. Stay there, and we'll go together when I get back. DO NOT go in that house alone.

With one eye on the road, Caleb gazes with his other to read the message. He scoffs before voice-texting a reply.

"It's not a big deal. I'll be in and out in under five. I'll meet you at your place once I'm done."

He now gives his decision a second thought. "Maybe he's holding back information on Gabriel, and he *does* know more than he's telling me. Am I making the right decision?" he asks himself aloud.

But his stubborn side surpasses his common sense. "Eh, fuck it. I'm a big boy. I'll fire off another text when I'm halfway there, good reason not to turn back."

He thrusts the gear shift into third and speeds down the street. He'll be at the house in time to meet up with Gabriel by seven thirty.

***

A FEW KILOMETERS ON THE OTHER side of town, Drew waits in front of Rebecca's house drumming his fingers against the leather steering wheel of his black BMW 5 Series. He hasn't concluded if Caleb's serious about driving out to Torbay or if he's playing some cruel joke. However, he knows the old Caleb, the one who frequently ignored any advice given and did his own thing.

He's halfway to Torbay by now.

Rebecca steps onto her front porch with a midsize suitcase and two shoulder bags, which she struggles with on the top step.

Drew flings open his door and races up the walkway to help her. "Hey, don't kill yourself."

"Thanks. Sorry to bother you with this. I know you have a lot of other stuff going on. How's Caleb holding up?"

"The best he can. And don't worry, it's fine. I promised you I'd take you, and I always keep my promises."

"So why isn't Caleb with you? You know it would have been all right to bring him."

"He said he was fine waiting in the coffee shop. But now I'm worried because I left him."

"Why? Everything okay?"

"He's talking crazy. He sent me a text saying he was going to drive back to his house to get clothes."

"Wait . . . what? Why would he go back there alone?"

"Because he never listens to anything anybody tells him, that's why," Drew says, slamming the trunk closed.

They both climb in and Drew peels out on a mission to get back to Caleb as quickly as he can. The car is traveling along Portugal Cove Road heading toward the airport when a traffic light changes from yellow to red. The car skids to a stop and suddenly the phone rings.

Unknown Caller

It rings a second time and Drew debates answering. However, after the third ring, he picks up and puts the call on speaker.

"Hello."

The caller's voice is disguised. "Hello, Andrew."

"Who's this?"

The silence on the line is intimidating, given the situation.

"Look, I'm not in the mood for games today. Who is this?"

"I think you know who *this* is."

"Miguel? Dude, you better turn in your ass."

"This isn't Miguel. He's gone and won't be coming back anytime soon."

"Gone? What do you mean, 'gone'?"

"Far away from here. But you or Caleb won't have to worry about him anymore. Right now, I think you should be more worried about me and what I have planned."

Rebecca gestures for him to pull over into the gas station parking lot, and once the light changes he does. "I know you're calling because there's something you want, so let's not waste each other's time."

"You're right, there is something I want. Stay away from Caleb—"

Drew interrupts. "Never gonna happen. Ever. And for you, whoever you are, how about you stay the hell away from him. He's stronger than you think."

The caller laughs wildly and instantly his tone switches. "Yeah, don't see it happening. Listen, you're only making things worse for yourself *and* him. Do what I say, otherwise I can't promise a happy outcome for either of you."

Rebecca sits nervously in the passenger seat listening to the exchange on the car's audio system. Rebecca has been around in the legal world long enough and has a few constables on speed dial. She secretly pulls out her phone and shoots off a text to the most trusted guy at the RNC she knows.

Caleb Winters is in trouble. Can you get people out to his residence in Torbay?

The close-knit legal community all know what's going on, and Rebecca is confident the straightforward text will convey loud and clear with the constable. Meanwhile, Drew grows more worried as he counts the seconds along with the killer's breath.

After waiting long enough for a response Drew clears his throat. "You still there?"

The voice comes back. "I'm warning you once more: stay away from Caleb."

"And what if I don't?"

"Then you'll pay. He belongs to m—"

"No, asshole, he doesn't belong to anyone. I swear on all that's holy, if anything happens to him, I'll—"

"You'll what? Hurt me? Punish me?"

"Yeah, exactly. You'll wish you never messed with me. I don't have time for these games."

"Don't worry, no one's playing games. I'll be seeing you sooner than you think."

The line suddenly goes dead, and he and Rebecca exchange a horrifying glance. Neither of them speaks, but she can see the determination in Drew's eyes. He must save Caleb from whatever situation he's gotten himself into.

She doesn't need to speak, all she does is nod. "I'll catch a flight out tomorrow. Right now, we must save Caleb."

With a quick jerk of the steering wheel, the car skids across the wet asphalt. Rebecca grabs ahold of the handle as the tires squeal loudly and the stench of burning rubber permeates into the car. Drew hollers over the ruckus and tosses his cell phone to Rebecca. "Text Caleb and find out where he is?"

"There are two missed text messages. Let's see. Caleb texted eight minutes ago and said: 'I decided I'm a big boy and can take care of myself, I'm heading to the house. I promise I won't be in there more than five minutes.'"

"Okay, what does his second message say?" Drew asks.

"Um, hold up. The second one isn't from Caleb."

"Well, who's it from? Dawe?"

"Not Dawe, it's from your *new* friend."

"Well, read it."

"Nothing to read. It's a photo of Caleb sitting in a car." She turns the screen so Drew can see.

He twists his head several times, trying to keep his eyes on the dark back road they're traveling on and to see if the picture is legit.

"Yup, that's the rental car we picked up," he says, punching the accelerator to the floor. The forward motion pulls them tighter against the seats.

"Uh, where did he take this picture?"

"Caleb's driveway."

"Shit."

Drew scoffs, part sarcastic but part realistic. "Yeah, shit is right."

TWENTY-THREE

February 18, 2017
Evening

ALEB KILLS THE HEADLIGHTS OF THE rental car and
pulls into the driveway of his darkened home. It's
unnervingly still, and the hairs on his arms stand on end as
he opens the driver's-side door. He steps out onto the
asphalt driveway and flips the hood of his hoodie over his
head. Clinging to a pillar of the front porch, a torn piece of yellow
crime scene tape flapping in the stiff gale is the only remnant of
anything sinister happening there.

Maybe I should have waited for Drew. This place is fucking creepy.

The floor of the porch creaks beneath his feet, cutting through
the otherwise silent surroundings. He pats the outer pockets of his
jacket, hunting for his house keys. He curls his fingers around the

clump of metal and pulls the jangly mass out. He squints, seeking to find the right key in the dimness of the moonlight. The shrieking ringtone of his cell startles the ever-living shit out of him, and he drops the keys onto the wooden porch.

"Damn."

He pulls out the phone and answers without looking at the screen. "Yeah?"

A familiar voice asks, "Where are you?"

"Drew. I told you, I'm at my house, but it's okay, I'm almost done. Geez, you worry too much."

"Don't go—" the call drops suddenly.

"Drew? Hello?" he asks before pulling the phone away from his ear.

No Service

"Not good," he mumbles.

Bending over, Caleb snatches the keys from the weathered wood porch and slips the cell phone back into his pocket. His hands shake, and the pressure of the blood coursing through his veins grows overpowering. A lump in his throat forces him to swallow hard.

He inserts the key, and with a single twist, the door unlocks, and he presses against the door with his shoulder, pushing it slightly ajar. Like a sealed tomb, a gust of air escapes the house and the strong smell of iron blasts his face. The pungent smell sends a chill racing up his spine as he retreats. He takes a deep breath and crosses over the threshold, all while trying to repress his overactive adrenaline.

Once inside, he finds the house pitch black, and his mind drifts back to only hours earlier, lying in his bed, and then the booming sound of the gunshot jogs him back to reality and he moves deeper inside the house. He runs his hand along the wall in search of the light switch. He clicks it, but nothing happens.

Damn.

He reaches back into his pocket and pulls out his phone. With the flick of his finger, he swipes up and taps the flashlight app. The room illuminates, and Caleb moves forward. The only thing the voice in his head can do now is provide encouragement.

The faster I get this over with, the quicker I can get out of here.

With the phone in one hand, he uses the free one to shut the front door. He steps cautiously through the foyer, working his way to the staircase. He isn't sure where Gabriel is, or what he wants, but he's paranoid and hyperattentive to his surroundings with each step he takes. His heart pounds harder with each step, and he feels the thump in his ear. He steps into the living room and again tries the lights: nothing.

He calls out to the empty house. "Gabriel, I'm here. You can stop playing games and tell me what you want."

But only silence greets him in return. He tries not to overdramatize and tells himself: *Maybe the wind knocked out power to the neighborhood.*

Caleb stops in the middle of the living room and does a 360, shining the tiny LED light from his phone around the room, searching for anybody hidden, waiting in the shadows. But not a soul awaits him. He takes in a deep breath, looking around the room. It's different now. There's no way to express his emotions other than saying that the house that at one time was full of life, now sits empty and devoid of those happy moments.

Caleb reaches the coffee table, which on a normal day would be immaculate; however, tonight it's nothing more than a thin coat of black fingerprint powder swirl marks.

He shakes his head and strides to the staircase. He waits at the landing and listens for any signs of life. The silence surrounding him is deafening, and the empty house has him feeling insignificant. Even though everything is quiet, his hands grow clammy, his saliva dries up, and he does everything possible to psych himself up to return to the same room where he nearly lost his life hours earlier.

He grasps the handrail and pulls himself forward, slowly. He knows the longer he dillydallies, the longer he'll be scared and it's more likely the killer could return at any moment. He picks up his momentum, and once he reaches the second floor he stares at his half-ajar bedroom door.

Did the RNC forensics team leave the door open like that, or someone else?

He recognizes he's doing it again—allowing his mind to play him into thinking things changed. Everything did. After all, a murder happened a few feet from where he stands.

He stands outside the bedroom and calls out once again in a hushed voice. Nothing. He shines the light against the door and sees the bullet hole that penetrated and missed him. He waits a moment longer for a reply, but the uncomfortable quietness persists. He holds out his iPhone, and as his right shoulder brushes

against the door, the hinges creak. He jumps but manages to take
two steps forward.

Looks clear to me.

Another two steps.

Man, my legs feel like jelly.

He clears the door and remains still. Straight ahead of him is his
rumpled bed and the same ball of clothes he left on the floor.
Caleb gets a faint whiff of kerosene in the air, but figures
someone's scent from either forensics or the ME's office brought
the smell indoors. With nothing more to fear, Caleb relaxes a bit
and darts for the closet to gather some belongings.

Guess he's a no-show.

He's barely four feet inside when the door slams behind him.
The crashing sound of a glass picture frame falling from the wall
distracts him, and before he knows it, two strong hands shove him
forward. His phone tumbles from his hand and flies across the
room and disappears somewhere near his nightstand. He lands on
the bed face first, but quickly rolls over to stare straight ahead.

He's staring into blackness but senses movement in the room.
There's a heaviness upon him; the same sensation that washed over
him in the grocery store. Someone's in there, but he has yet to see
them. A dim spark soon gives way to a dim light. His eyes begin to
adjust, and after a few seconds Caleb scans the dimly lit room. But
there's still no sight of whoever is in there with him.

Everything changes when the figure steps out of the shadows
and into the light. The masked attacker hovers at the foot of the
bed, staring piercingly through two crudely cut eye holes. Caleb
looks past them and sees his only escape route impeded. It's

unclear if the attacker is a man or a woman, but whoever it is stands over six feet tall and their all-black getup is something straight out of a horror movie.

His eyes shift toward a reflective object in their left hand: a machete. Caleb's efforts to cry out fail. He's so paralyzed with fear his vocal cords close. He scoots backward across the bed, putting enough space between him and the psychopath, but it's fruitless. Every time he scurries away, the attacker only moves closer.

At last, Caleb lets out a whimpering sound but only because he's running out of the space, and the oppressive fight-or-flight sensation clouds his common sense. He's alert and jumps from the bed to overtake the killer, but soon he finds himself back on the bed.

Caleb cries out, "Gabriel, why are you doing this? It's me: Caleb." There's no acknowledgement, so he cries out again, "I'm warning you: stay back."

However, his urgent plea goes unheeded.

Whoever's behind the mask continues moving toward him. With each step they take, their grip on the machete gets tighter. Caleb never once believed people when they said their whole life flashed before their eyes when in near-death situations. But after today, his opinion changes.

He squeezes his eyes tightly closed. Tears of fear free-fall, and the only choice he has left is to accept reality: *This is how I'm going to die.*

"Please, God, I'm not ready to die yet."

Caleb feels the heat radiating from the mysterious stranger's body and his eyes quickly open. His eyes swell to the point of overflowing, and he doesn't see the figure anymore. All his concentration focuses on the edge of the machete, which is less than a foot away. This is it. This is how his short life will end.

He watches as the assailant lifts the weapon into the air, and the sense of death shrouds everything.

Do something . . . anything . . .

The blade is still hovering over him, and he's seconds away from the blade slashing and hacking him into God only knows how many pieces when something inside his head cries out.

Look into their eyes.

Through the blackened mask, he notices for the first time the emotionless, piercing sea-blue eyes staring at him, and Caleb can't believe it. He recognizes these eyes, but they aren't those of whom he expected. And worse, he can't fathom why they're in his bedroom trying to murder him.

He shouts out.

"Sam, stop!"

Is it really him? How can this be? He's dead.

The machete lowers, and the intruder pulls the hood away from their head and peels away the mask, uncovering the attacker's identity. Caleb's jaw drops, and he rubs his eyes several times to be sure who he sees standing before him.

"Hello, Caleb."

"Wha—this can't be happening."

Sam drops the mask to the floor. "Not who you were expecting, huh?"

"Where's Gabriel? Why are you here? You're dead."

"Yeah, everyone thinks I'm dead, and if you don't mind, I'd like for everyone to keep thinking so."

TWENTY-FOUR

February 18, 2017
Late Evening

"**B**UT WHY? WHY WOULD YOU WANT** people to think you're dead?"

"Because—I'm in way over my head, and there isn't anything I can do to fix the mistakes I've made. We don't have much time. Let's get as far away from here as possible and create a fresh life."

Sam reaches out his hand, but Caleb doesn't. "I'm not going anywhere with you until you tell me what's going on. First, why does everyone think it's your charred body lying in the morgue, and more importantly, why are you trying to kill me?"

Caleb feels the linen headboard against the scruff of his neck, and when he turns his head, he realizes he's run out of space. He slides his knees against his chest and wraps his arms around them. He does whatever he can to stop his body from shaking.

Sam sighs, lowers the machete, and finds a spot on the bed that is far enough from Caleb to put him at ease. "Where do I even begin?"

"I've always found the best place to begin is at the beginning."

Sam massages his right temple with his free thumb. "Okay, but first, I have something I gotta say."

Caleb doesn't speak. How can he when he's too petrified to do or say anything. His eyes skim the room hoping to catch a glimpse of the bright light emitting from his iPhone.

After a few passes, he pinpoints its possible location next to his nightstand or under the bed. Either way, it's close enough to clutch.

Just wait, don't make any sudden moves.

"I'm listening."

Sam turns toward Caleb. His lower jaw trembles, his eyes are watery, and it's clear whatever he has to say is tough. "I love you."

Slightly scoffing, Caleb replies, "Hey, I love you too. You're like one of my best friends in the entire world. I'm here for you, but first, I need you to ditch the blade before I can help you."

"No, I need it."

"Why do you need it? Just drop it and let's talk. Obviously, something's bothering you, and I want to help."

Sam sits in silence, the machete resting across his legs. "You don't get it, do you?"

"Get what? Sam, please, I've had a rough day, and I'm not in the mood for games."

Sam leans in closer. The scent of burnt pine wood twitches Caleb's nose.

"I'm *in* love with you," Sam mutters.

Caleb exhales. He's still oblivious to what Sam truly means. "You're in love with me? Are we talking 'love you like a brother' or 'love you like I want to see you naked'?"

"Love. You know, the kind where I come home and ask you how your day was. The same kind where I sneak up behind you in the kitchen and wrap my arms around you. That kind of love."

Confusion becomes frustration. "This makes no sense to me. You can't be in love with me. For starters, you're straight. Secondly, your wife's been dead less than twenty-four hours. Do you even know she's dead?"

Sam remains silent.

"Wait . . . you do know she's dead because you . . . you killed her."

Sam lowers his head. "I shoulda killed the bitch years ago. If only I had, I wouldn't have needed to do all the things I did."

"What things?"

Sam goes silent again and scoots away from Caleb.

Caleb puts the pieces together. "You're the one who tried to snuff me out after you murdered Susan?"

His head stays drooped. "Yeah."

"And Nicole? Did you have anything to do with her?"

He nods.

"Why? What did any of these people ever do to you?"

He stands up and grips the machete closer. "You are so fucking oblivious. These 'so-called friends' cheat on you, lie to your face, and gossip, and all the while they smile in your face."

Caleb nervously shakes his head. "You're jumping around, let's jump to the beginning."

Sam leaps from the bed, and things go from calm to erratic again. Each step Sam takes, Caleb fears he might snap at any moment. He doesn't want to upset Sam, but he also wants to know the truth about everything.

After pacing, Sam turns around. "From the beginning?"

"Yes, the beginning. When did all of this start?"

Sam collects his emotions and returns to the edge of the bed.

"Back in early 2015, around the time Sebastian began cheating on you with Gabriel."

Caleb perks up. "How'd you know about the affair? I didn't even know about it."

"You had us over one evening for dinner. I remember Sebastian excused himself from the table and snuck off outside to make a phone call. Something wasn't on the up-and-up, so I pretended I forgot something in the truck—"

"I remember this night."

"I stepped outside and eavesdropped. He was making plans with someone on the phone."

"So, what, you decided not to tell me any of this?"

"Doubt you'd have believed me. Anyhow, he tells the person you'd be away at a conference in Vancouver all week, and it was the perfect time to come by."

"Yeah, I remember the conference in Vancouver. I came back one day early."

Sam ignores Caleb's interruptions and presses forward with his story. "Well, the morning you left, I waited for Sebastian to slink off to meet up with Gabriel. I used the spare key you gave me and went upstairs and installed a wireless camera in your bedroom. I'm sorry, I didn't want to do it, but I had no choice. It was for your own good."

"So, you spied on me?"

"No. No. That's not it. I wasn't spying on you. I wanted to catch Sebastian in the act, so if it ever came to it I'd have proof and maybe you'd leave him, and I could have swooped in. I was only trying to help."

Caleb shakes his head, biting his lower lip, as he typically does when he's either angry or nervous. "No, your intentions weren't to help. You wanted Sebastian out of the picture so you could have me for your own."

"And clearly, we see things didn't turn out the way they should," Sam mutters under his breath.

"Things turned out exactly the way I wanted them to. So, you decide to leave a damn DVD on my doorstep instead of being a man and telling me face-to-face?"

Silence again.

"No, you thought I'd be so devastated I'd come running to you for comfort."

Sam nods. "For once, I wanted to be your knight in shining armor."

"Why? Why'd you wait three years after the fact?"

"You deserve to know what they did to you. How their lies nearly destroyed your life."

Caleb swallows hard. "What difference does it make now? Sebastian's dead, Gabriel's missing, and here I sit held against my will."

"Don't be mad at me. The people you should be mad at I took care of . . . for you."

"I'm not mad," Caleb says, wiping away a tear from his eye.

Sam slams his hand against the top of the three-tier dresser. "Get angry . . . I know you have it in you."

"I'm too brokenhearted to be mad."

Sam stares blankly at him.

"There, are you happy? The always 'put-together' Caleb finally buckles. Is this what you wanted all along?"

"Never. I don't want to see you sad. I wanna see you happy."

Caleb scoffs. "And you think telling me my entire life has been a joke makes me happy?"

"Your life hasn't been a joke. You've made some bad choices, though."

"Yeah, okay. Seeing as we are this far in, let's continue. Tell me what you did to Sebastian. I mean, after all, you killed him, right?"

"I did. I lured him out to Pouch Cove, said I had evidence of their affair."

"Ah, blackmail—real sexy, Sam."

"My initial intent wasn't to hurt him, but you know Sebastian; never did what anyone said. If he'd only listened, if he'd left, I wouldn't have had to stab him."

"I had no premeditation to do it, it . . . it just happened. Something in me overtook my rational thoughts, and the next thing I remember there was blood everywhere and his body lie there sprawled across the snow. I tried to give him CPR, I did everything I could—but he was gone."

Caleb's tears flow heavier now. "Why Nicole?"

"She had to die, and you know why."

"Enlighten me."

Sam realizes Caleb doesn't know who Nicole really is. "Ah, those constables didn't tell you, did they?"

Caleb's patience is growing thinner with the childish games. All he wants is details, and the man who holds them rambles on like a lunatic. "Sam, enough of this back and forth. This is what I'm gonna do: I'm gonna shut up, and you tell me everything."

He sighs. "Fine. Your knight in shining armor, the man who swept you off your feet, the same one who masquerades about calling himself Gabriel, is really Miguel Escobar—a ruthless drug cartel guy from Miami."

Caleb laughs. "Drew already told me all about him."

"Ah, but it seems he failed to let you in on a secret. Nicole was Miguel's girlfriend."

"Girlfriend? What are you talking about? Trust me, he's gay."

"Yeah, not quite. Along with the fake name, he also had an entire fake life. And guess who falls right in the middle of it all? That's right—you."

Caleb folds his arms across his chest and stands. "Why should I believe anything you say? For someone who isn't gay, he sure the hell coulda fooled me."

Sam slams his balled-up fist against the dresser, and Caleb returns to his docile position on the bed. Sam grunts, "You're so damn stubborn. I'm telling you the truth: he's not gay. Never has been. Never will be. He's been bumping boots with Nicole since he arrived in Newfoundland."

Caleb is now too afraid to find time to cry, but inside his heart breaks even more. The man he confided in, gave his heart to, in the end, turns out to be nothing more than a con artist. And worst of all, the friend he's known since childhood appears to have known about this the entire time and never said a word.

He doesn't waver. Instead, he keeps his head held high and withstands the pressure Sam puts on him. "So, Nicole was Gabriel's girlfriend—and?"

"Thank you. You finally get what I'm saying."

"And she had to die for it?"

"She had to go."

"Okay, fine, I don't think she needed to die for it, but whatever, there's still one question you haven't answered: Why all of this now?"

"The night you told us about how Sanderson sent the Tucker brothers to threaten you, I recognized I had the ideal person to pin everything on. Pretty good stunt, huh?"

"Yeah, duped me."

"I sat there for a few days and planned everything out, even how to tie it all to Sanderson. It kept you and the constabulary at bay long enough to finish almost everything I set out to do."

"You're sick."

"Guilty. You still haven't thanked me for taking care of your problems."

"Why would I thank you for killing everyone I know?"

Sam slams his hand against the ruffled sheets. "You're such an ungrateful bastard. You should be on your knees thanking me. They all wronged you, Caleb. I'm sorry, but they had to pay the price."

Caleb reaches his breaking point with all this nonsense. At last, the tears he wasn't sure would fall finally do, and his anger slowly begins to build. A minute later, he unleashes his aggravation on Sam.

"Fine. Some people did some shit behind my back, but if I'd ever found out, my bags would have been packed and I'd have booked a one-way ticket back to Toronto."

"You'd have stayed. I would have made sure."

"I'm even more pissed at you for lying to me and now using some bullshit excuse for murdering everyone."

"I do love you."

Caleb shakes his head in disbelief and wipes away his tears. "If you really love me, you'd have told me you loved me, not killed everyone so I had no one to turn to."

Caleb's tears slow, and Sam continues spouting off gibberish, which Caleb ignores because no matter what Sam says, it won't bring anyone back.

Caleb lets out a nervous laugh after sitting in silence, processing everything, and finally he's caught up except for where Gabriel is and why Sam murdered his wife. Although, Caleb has formed a solid theory as to why she died.

"You think this is funny? I killed four, no wait, five people to be with you."

Caleb stops laughing and hugs his legs even tighter now. Sam moves around in an erratic fashion, and he clinches the machete closer to his side as he rambles on and on, making entirely no sense.

I gotta get my phone.

That's Caleb's new mission. He keeps a close eye on Sam, but he's tuned him out as he resumes pontificating about God only knows what, and Caleb scoots painstakingly slowly to his side of the bed.

He sees his phone. It's only five feet away. He glances in Sam's direction; he's turned away. Caleb gingerly reaches out his left arm and braces his body weight against the nightstand.

With his thin fingers only inches away, Sam unexpectedly twists and catches him diving for it. However, to Caleb's surprise, Sam doesn't rush toward him. Instead, he stands across the room with a mute facial expression.

"It's not worth it. The phone won't work." Sam pulls out a small black box from his pocket, shaking it in the air. "Gotta love how small they make these cell phone jammers these days."

Defeat washes over Caleb, and he hoists himself up and regresses to his submissive spot on the bed. "Explains why I lost my signal at the front door."

Sam nods and smirks. "I mean, I can't have you trying to summon help or anything. Besides, I expect your whore of an ex to smash in the front door any minute to come save you."

"He doesn't even know where I am, and besides, he's not a whore."

"Oh, you truly believe he doesn't know where you are? That's cute."

"I didn't tell him I was coming here."

"Oh, trust me, he knows exactly where you are. See, I texted a photo of you sitting in your rental car right before you walked in. And we've already had a nice chat."

"He has nothing to do with this. Leave him out of it."

"I can't wrap my head around what you ever saw in him. Must have been purely sexual."

"No, you don't get to assume or judge our relationship. At the time, we were head over heels in love, but shit happens. Besides, what makes you think you and I'd have been any better?"

"You're getting mad at me again. Why? Don't you see, I did all of this to be together. You don't want to be with me?"

Caleb buries his head in his knees, and he realizes there are only three ways out of this room: in a body bag, someone comes to his rescue, or he must make Sam believe he's on his side and con his way out.

I'm not leaving here in a body bag, so here goes nothing.

With Sam's back turned, Caleb blurts out. "Wait, I do love you."

Sam stops pacing. He isn't sure what he heard. "What'd you say?"

"I said I love you."

"Don't say it unless you mean it."

"I mean it."

Secretly though, Caleb's insides are slithering at the lies he's orating merely to extend his time on Earth a little longer. He stares at the shell of a man he's known since he can remember, and yet he can't decipher what's going through his whacked-out head. What would drive him beyond recognition?

Even with Caleb's knack for the theatrical, this situation teeters outside the realm of his comfort zone. Sam creepily parks next to him, scooting closer, and reaches out his hand, resting it on Caleb's knee.

With every fiber of his being, Caleb reaches his hand out and allows it to land on top of Sam's. He can't show his disgust. He must do whatever it takes to convince Sam he's in love with him, otherwise he's a goner. His fingers scratch along his brawny hands before he moves them against his upper thigh. He caresses softly against his black cargo pants, and his pinkie finger taps something hard inside the side pocket.

Holy hell, he's brought a gun!

He keeps this tidbit of info to himself and carries on as if everything is okay.

"So, you'll run off with me? I hope you know everything I did, it was all for you."

Caleb grins. "It's okay . . . let's not rehash this again. But if you killed them for wronging me, why didn't you kill Drew? I mean, you know he hurt me a long time ago too."

He leans in and murmurs in a psychotic tone. "Up until a week ago, I had no idea you two were ever a thing."

"Ah, right, I kept it a secret for a good reason. It was all a mistake."

"You won't ever have to think of him again. I did try to kill him a few times, but his damn entourage never leaves his side. That'll change soon."

Reading between the lines, Caleb cries out. "Listen, if you let him live, the two of us, we can go, get away from here, and never look back."

Sam ponders his suggestion, but after thirty seconds, he becomes thirstier for blood and revenge. "No. He must die like the rest."

Caleb's mouth drops, and he tries to telepathically convey a forewarning to Drew, even though he knows this is an utter waste of his time.

Drew, if you can read my thoughts, don't come here—don't.

TWENTY-FIVE

February 18, 2017
Late Evening

REW AND REBECCA PARK DOWNHILL AND Drew cuts
the engine. The wind wails, and the fresh coating of snow
drifts carefree amidst the air. Drew's hands are sweaty, his
mouth is dry, and he peers at Rebecca who sits tensely.

Drew reaches for the door handle. "If I'm not back in
five minutes, call Dawe and let her know to pick up the pace."

Rebecca's hands shake. "I already let Constable Walsh know
what we're up to," she says. "I think we should wait for help. I'm
sure they're not far."

"I can't. Caleb's in danger. I know it."

Rebecca reaches across, and her hand grips his forearm. "Wait."

"Rebecca, my mind's made up. I have to save him."

She shakes her head side to side, reaches for the glovebox, and removes a SIG Sauer nine-mil. She pulls back the slide and slams the cold steel into Drew's hand. "If you're going, you'll want this."

"How'd you know I had this?"

"Drew, we all know you have this in your glovebox."

It's in this moment the seriousness of the situation sinks in. He's owned the weapon for over five years, but never in his life did he ever think he'd have to use it. Rebecca relaxes her grip and jerks her hand away. Drew opens the door.

"Five minutes," he repeats.

She stays silent but bobs her head, giving her blessing.

He stands in the cold, scanning the area for anything suspicious, but everything is clear. He clutches the gun, and with a bump, he closes the car door with his hip. He works up the nerve, and once he's certain no one is lying in wait, he dashes toward the house.

Even though all is quiet on the outside, what awaits him inside is more on his mind. The thought of it drives his heart to beat faster, harder, with every stride he takes.

If I don't try, the last time I saw him will be the last time.

He glances back at the car through the blowing snow: he's made it around a hundred feet. He's still close enough to see Rebecca's head hanging, her shoulders bent forward, and he second-guesses his erratic intention.

Maybe she's right; I should wait.

His hesitation persists a few seconds before he refocuses on the task: save Caleb. He quickly turns away and feels his legs moving again.

How did I let this happen? Neither of our lives were supposed to turn out this way.

Minutes pass and he finds himself on the front porch. Around him the area is quiet, so quiet the hairs on his arms stand on end. He smashes his back against the cedar shingle siding and counts in his head.

One, Two, Three . . .

With the nine-mil in one hand, he turns the flashlight on and holds it above the gun. His hands tremble, and he takes a few deep breathes, working the nerve to go in. A bright white steam fills the air in front of his face.

A light tap against the door and it squeaks open. He rushes into the foyer, twisting and turning, searching high and low for any shadows in the corners.

Nothing. Not a soul in sight.

He moves alongside the wall, tiptoeing. Each passing second his only goal is to make it out alive. He shuffles quicker and finds himself flanked between the foyer and living room. The flashlight beam darts from corner to corner, scanning every minute cranny until Drew exhausts all thinkable hiding spots.

No one.

He restarts his movement along the long load-bearing wall until up ahead he sees a gap in the wall. Stopping, he takes a few seconds to get his heavy breathing under control and do whatever he must to get control over his nerves.

There's no counting in his head this time. Instead, he swings his body around and stands where he can see the entire kitchen and living room. He swings the flashlight side to side, but Drew finds the same lifelessness there too.

A soft thud echoes through the house, and Drew jerks around to check where the sound came from. He holds his breath while swinging the gun nervously back and forth. He anticipates someone jumping out and attacking him, but after a few seconds pass, no one appears. Then it dawns on him where the sound came from: *They're upstairs.*

His heart races faster and he stealthily shuffles across the hardwood floorboards. At the bottom of the stairs he waits, allowing his eyes to adjust to the dimness, but also giving himself time to devise a plan. He scans upward and can see a dim light spilling from underneath the door closest to the upstairs landing.

Found him.

Drew presses his back tightly against the wall and hikes into unknown surroundings. There's a dead calm surrounding the house, and he can't help but fear maybe he's too late to save Caleb.

He reaches the halfway point, the crown of his head now level with the second-story floorboards, and he shifts to the opposing side of the stairs, his back now pressed against the wooden railing.

He takes a couple more steps, now moving faster. The nine-mil in his hands shakes as he mumbles a small prayer to himself before trudging into the do-or-die situation ahead of him. He reaches the landing on the second floor, and before he's even ready, the underlit door flings open forcefully, and a mysterious broad figure fills the frame of the door.

Drew's disorganized. His eyes finally adjust, and he sees that the person standing before him isn't the person he thought. The entire time speeding to Torbay, he thought he'd be face-to-face with Gabriel; however, when he sees Sam holding a gun and aiming it toward him, Drew tries to retreat, but the bright muzzle flash and pop send him diving for cover.

One shot, and two shots. Each of them miss him, but only by a mere foot. The bullets richochet against the wall and Drew has no choice now but to fight back. He points the gun, squeezes his eyes closed, and pulls the trigger several times. The bullets expel in rapid succession, and even with his eyes closed the sound of agony tells him he's struck his target. Drew can't open his eyes. He's paralyzed with fear. A loud thud rumbles the floor and the gunfire ceases.

He expects wailing, but he gets the opposite. No crying, no screaming, only silence. Oddly, this isn't precisely how he envisioned killing somebody, but the sound the body made when it slammed against the ground held all the characteristics he'd grown desensitized to by all the years spent watching horror movies.

His eyes flutter open, and he sees, with a little help from the lantern inside the room, Sam's unresponsive body sprawled across the narrow hallway. He moves closer, his gun pointing toward his mark. With a quick glance he spots the two entry wounds, one in the arm, the other in the chest. A stream of blood pools onto the untreated wood floor, and even before Drew has fully grasped what's happened, Caleb flees through the door and rushes to safety behind Drew.

With tears gushing from his eyes, Caleb can't move. He leans against Drew's back and clutches him.

"Caleb, get the hell out of here . . . now," he hollers.

Caleb wavers. He doesn't want to leave Drew there alone.

"Go. I'm right behind you."

Caleb obeys and misses steps on purpose, anything to get away. Sam's lifeless body isn't moving, and Drew steps closer to get a glimpse of what remains of a man he once admired and respected more than anyone he'd ever known. Sam's pliable fingers still grip the gun and Drew pulls it away and tosses it aside. Drew takes a few calming breaths and presses two fingers against Sam's neck to check for a pulse.

Nothing.

Certain he's deceased, Drew descends the stairs and runs like hell for the front door. Anxiously waiting in the foyer, he finds Caleb biting his fingernails and dancing in circles.

"Keep moving! Get the hell out of here."

***

REBECCA SITS IN THE CAR, NIPPING at her glossy nails. Seven minutes pass, and she nervously wonders whether she should call for help like Drew asked, or give it a few minutes more. Four gunshots pierce the otherwise quiet night, and without hesitation, she flings open the car door and hurries toward the house. Mid-jog she fetches her cell phone and scrolls through her contacts while sprinting faster than she ever has in her life. She presses the phone against her ear, and before it rings a second time, Constable Walsh answers.

"We're almost there. Is everything all right?"

"No. I allowed Drew to convince me to let him go inside, and now there's been four gunshots. How close are you?"

"Four, maybe five minutes."

"Not close enough. I gotta get in there and save Drew."

"Rebecca . . . do not, under any circumstances, go in there."

She breaks her speed. "Okay, okay—I'll wait outside. Please hurry."

Walsh huffs. "I thought I was crystal clear in my text to wait outside for help."

She comes to a halt. "Well, Jonathan, there's what you say and what Drew does. You can't stop the boy."

"True. All right, hang tight."

Rebecca hangs up and paces at the end of the driveway. She's freezing, and after a minute of waiting, no one emerges from the house and dread fills her mind.

They're dead.

After she completes another circle, she spots Caleb leap from the porch into the driveway, and three seconds later Drew follows.

"Keep running. Don't stop until I tell you it's safe."

He runs past Rebecca and downhill, putting as much distance between him and the house as he can. He doesn't even turn his head back to see where Drew or Rebecca are.

After running almost two hundred feet, Caleb's lungs give out and he bends forward trying to catch his breath. His legs give out and he falls face first onto the slushy pavement and vomits. The fight-or-flight mode reaches its climax, and as Caleb is on all fours gasping for air, he feels the adrenaline coursing through his veins subside.

Drew falls to the ground and pulls Caleb close to him. He grabs ahold of his face and stares in his deep blue eyes and pulls his hand inside his hoodie and wipes away the bitter bile that clings to the corners of his mouth.

"I'm sorry. I'm sorry for leaving you alone in the coffee shop. You fucking scared me to death. I thought you came here and Gabriel was going to take you from me."

Caleb is in such a state of shock he can't construct words. Instead, he buries his face against Drew's chest and bawls. Drew pulls him tighter as Rebecca finally catches up, crouches to the ground, and wraps her arms around them both.

"You have no idea how glad I am to see the two of you," she cries out.

The sound of sirens from the convoy of police and rescue vehicles washes out the sound of tears falling, and Caleb pulls his head away from Drew and stares blankly ahead.

"Please, tell me it's over, Drew."

"Hey, we're alive and safe, and whatever else happens, know we're gonna be all right."

"Exactly. We're not gonna let anything happen to you," Rebecca says.

Before they realize, a dozen squad cars, two fire trucks, and two ambulances pull up shy of where they squat. Dawe and Barnes get to them first, but Drew gets defensive when Dawe moves to grab Caleb.

"No," Drew hollers.

"Let him go so we can get him aid."

Drew let's go and Dawe rushes Caleb away to a waiting ambulance. Meanwhile, Barnes ushers Drew and Rebecca behind the driver's door of the unmarked police cruiser.

While she's swept away, Rebecca cries out, "I think he's still in there."

The SWAT team marches onward, none of them turning back to acknowledge her remark. Caleb overhears her and double-checks over his shoulder in time to see the police barge through his front door. He's barely keeping it together. He spins his head forward, and nothing Dawe utters to him registers in his fractured mind.

Two medics await their arrival, with one helping Caleb into the back of the ambulance while the other fetches a tan blanket and wraps it around his shoulders.

"Are you hurt?"

"I'm okay," Caleb musters.

Dawe sits beside him and holds his hand. "I'm so, so sorry I let this happen. When you're up for it, I'll need to get your statement."

Caleb nods.

"Miguel Escobar won't ever see his freedom again."

Caleb realizes she really thinks his good-for-nothing-drug-dealing boyfriend is responsible. He wants to set the record straight but finds himself interrupted by the medics.

"I need to check your blood pressure. Try to relax," he says.

Caleb closes his eyes and breathes in a slow breath and exhales equally as measured.

Thirty seconds pass and the man tears at the Velcro cuff. "Eh, a bit high. One fifty over ninety."

Dawe intently looks at him. "Your blood pressure would be high too if someone tried to murder you, wouldn't it?"

"Look, lady, I'm here to help," he replies while stepping away with his hands up.

Caleb finally has the moment he needs to relay the information before they go hunting for the wrong person.

"It wasn't Miguel."

She cocks her head. "Who's in the house?"

"Sam."

"You're telling me Sam Butler, your best friend, tried to murder you?"

Caleb hangs his head.

"So, none of this had to do with Sanderson after all?"

"Oh, he had a hand in some of it, but the killings—no."

Sensing Dawe has calmed her attitude, the medic returns and sits across from Caleb. "Do you need anything to take the edge off a bit?"

Caleb nods.

"Okay."

Caleb buttons his sleeve after the medic finishes up. He watches the scruffy-faced man toss the spent syringe into the biohazard box, and out of nowhere a thunderous eruption trembles the earth. Caleb ditches the blanket on the gurney and leaps from the ambulance to the street below. He darts around disoriented constables and parked vehicles, and when he finds a clearing, he looks up to find a massive inferno engulfing the second story of his home.

"What the—" Dawe says while rushing away.

Caleb stops in utter terror. The color empties from his face, his mouth gawks unguarded, and he doesn't even notice the constables disperse for cover. He can't comprehend any of it. The home he constructed, the home he formed good and bad memories in—all of it incinerating before his eyes.

A soft touch against his back breaks his focus, and with a slight turn sideways, a cozy voice speaks. "Caleb, please, for once in your life let someone take care of you. This medic needs to finish checking you over, okay?"

Without expressing a lone sound, he returns with Drew and sits on the bumper of the ambulance. Drew scoots next to him, reaches out his hand, and holds it while the medic continues the examination.

He modestly glances over at the man who once stole his heart, and later broke it. All the years of hate, pain, and love flood his mind and Caleb realizes Drew, even amongst the chaos, is showing him who he genuinely is.

"It's really over now—isn't it?" Caleb asks, wiping away the tears that stain his face.

"Don't worry right now. You're alive, safe, and no one is going to ever hurt you again. That's all that matters now."

"Did they find him?"

"I don't know. Either way, he'll never be able to touch you again."

Caleb rests his head against Drew's shoulder and his eyelids begin to droop. Finally, the medicine kicks in and all his stress slips away. "I'm too tired to think right now. I'm gonna rest a few minutes, okay?"

"Just rest," Drew says as his head falls atop Caleb's.

***

AN HOUR PASSES AND EVERYONE STANDS at the end of the driveway staring in shock at the ashes of Caleb's life. The drugs wore off only minutes earlier, and an emotionally numb Caleb crouches near the ground between Drew and Rebecca, staring at the muted orange glare of popping embers twinkling in the pitch blackness.

The fire inspector and forensics supervisor approach them, and Dawe steps away, but not before turning her head to say, "Be right back." She shakes the fire inspector's hand. "Tell me you've found him."

"No, ma'am. We've found no remains in the house."

She turns her attention to the forensics supervisor. "People don't disappear. Is it possible he survived and fled the scene before we arrived?"

"Given his medical knowledge, anything's possible. But I'd expect to have found a trail of blood leading away."

"And did you?"

He shakes his head. "Nothing. No blood, no footprints. But the debris and fire department have compromised the scene."

"So, it's conceivable he escaped."

The supervisor nods. "We'll let you know what we find. For now, I'd say let's treat it like he's on the run."

"Noted. Inspector, do we know yet what caused the explosion?"

"I'll bet money it was a pipe bomb of some sort. The guys are still searching."

Dawe nods. "I seriously doubt this much destruction is from one pipe bomb. Three or four, maybe, but surely not from one."

"You'll have my full report first thing Monday morning," he says, peering around Dawe's shoulders at Caleb. "Um, ma'am, there's no need to stick around here."

Dawe looks back at Drew, Caleb, and Rebecca, who impatiently wait to learn something, anything, to give them closure on such a tumultuous situation. Dawe extends her hand toward the fire inspector and he returns the gesture. Dawe walks away from the two men.

Drew pulls Dawe aside. "So, did they find him?"

Dawe whispers. "No, he says the house is empty. Are you entirely sure you shot him, and he was dead?"

"I'm more than 100 percent sure. I struck him twice; once in the arm and the other in the chest. I even checked for a pulse before running out. Sam Butler was dead when I left."

Caleb clutches the blanket around his upper body and inches closer to eavesdrop on their conversation. He overhears four words, which send a shiver up his spine: "The house is empty." When he begins to think it's over, he realizes it isn't. How can the psychopath who murdered nearly everybody he trusts still roam the community a free man?

His emotions begin to flare up, and his impassive, numb demeanor soon shifts to angry. "How am I supposed to heal? Huh? How do I move on if I have to look over my shoulder every five seconds?"

Caleb stomps away to escape dealing with reality, and Drew calls out, "Caleb, hold up."

Barnes blocks Drew's path to give chase. "No, wait. Give the man a chance to grieve."

Drew hates watching his friend in pain, but with Constable Barnes blocking his escape, he finally withdraws.

Dawe shakes her head and turns to Barnes. "Not the news he wanted to hear."

"Yeah, not the news *any* of us wanted. You should check on him, Gretchen."

"Right." She steps away and races toward the rocky overlook where she finds Caleb sitting on a boulder, his knees pulled against his chest.

"Hey," she says and sits next to him.

Caleb sobs uncontrollably and Dawe doesn't interrupt. After years of handling losing a husband, and now a boyfriend and friends, Dawe realizes in all the time she hounded him, she never allowed him to come to terms with any of it. She sighs, rests her hand against his back, and they sit in silence listening to the waves crash against the shoreline below.

One minute becomes ten, and eventually Caleb looks over through his gloss-covered eyes and wipes his face. "Thank you for sitting with me."

"Yeah. But we should get you somewhere a little safer—and warmer."

Caleb agrees.

"You want another minute?"

He stands. "I'm ready."

Dawe grabs Caleb's hand, and he hoists himself from the boulder. Walking along the street, he scans his neighborhood and sees the destruction left behind. He turns to Dawe. "No purpose standing around here, staring at the leftovers of my former life."

"We're going to catch him, you know. He thinks he's smart. Well, we're smarter."

Caleb pulls the blanket tighter around his neck and sees Drew and Rebecca racing toward him. "I hope you're right."

Dawe continues walking as Drew wraps his arms around Caleb's neck and Rebecca steps aside. "I promise I'm never going to let anything bad happen to you ever again."

"I know you won't. Things will never be the same, huh?"

Drew nods. "Things will be vastly different now. I promise you."

Barnes interrupts the tender moment. "Mr. Winters, let's get you to the hospital."

"Better safe than sorry."

Caleb climbs into the ambulance while Rebecca and Drew wait outside. Barnes gives Dawe a glance and she nods. "You should go with him."

"I think there's someone more important who should go," Barnes says, turning his attention toward Drew.

Dawe, for once, cracks a grin. "On second thought, Mr. Murphy, I'm confident you can handle things."

"Me? You sure?"

"It's obvious you'll be better company than either of us."

Drew grins, hoists himself into the back of the ambulance, and sits across from Caleb on the bench.

"We'll meet you at the hospital in the morning to get your statement," Dawe says. "For now, rest."

Caleb lays his head back, and Barnes slams the rear doors closed. The medic secures Caleb and soon the sirens wail as the rig moves slowly from the scene.

Caleb stares out the back, watching the three grow smaller until eventually they are out of sight. Caleb rolls his head sideways. "Thanks."

"What for?"

"For risking your own life to save my crazy ass. What was I even thinking coming here?"

"For starters, you're stubborn. Just relax and we'll chat more once you've rested and the doctors give you the all clear."

Caleb coyly half-smiles and closes his eyes for the rest of the journey to St. John's.

TWO MONTHS LATER

THE HAUNTING EVENTS OF THE EIGHTEENTH of February remain rooted in Caleb's mind. The fact he lived without a scratch is nothing short of a miracle, or at least he tells himself that every day. Through the recent changes—from losing people, his house, and everything he owns—the emotional scars would take longer to mend than replacing the inessential belongings that only bring him torment.

After an intense two-week manhunt, the constabulary came across the frozen body of Miguel Escobar, hidden in the woods adjacent to Blast Hole Ponds. The report states that when they found him he had seventeen stab wounds, his hands were bound around a tree with plastic ties, and shoved deep in the back of his throat was a gauze bandage. A grotesque ending for an equally dreadful man.

After extinguishing the final embers, Dawe, Barnes, and a full team of forensic investigators combed through the ashes, hoping to find Sam's body to wrap up their case; however, the team came up empty. Sam Butler was not among the remains of the house.

With Sam's whereabouts unknown, Caleb's left with a troubled sense of not knowing when the psychopath (who he once disclosed his deepest, darkest secrets to) might reemerge. Caleb has kept a low profile these past few months but is growing tired of looking over his shoulder every few feet. He knows the constabulary is still on the hunt for Sam, and it gives him a sense of comfort, but he really wants to put it all behind him and move forward with his life.

Caleb stares out the window onto a treelined street. How he misses the serene backdrop of the mighty Atlantic, which he'd grown comfortable with after spending so many years in Torbay.

He smiles as he stares at the neighborhood children playing, laughing, with no care in the world. The sight brings back memories of when he was their age. He laughs softly and walks away toward the corner where seven more ashy boxes await his attention. He picks up another box—the fifth box he's sifted through—and runs the box cutter across the taped seal.

He pulls the final flap open, and sitting on top of some old clothes, certificates of achievement, and college gear, he finds a framed photo of him and Drew, standing outside their old apartment on Beverly Street. They're both beaming from ear to ear; the camera lens caught their lighthearted outlook on that day.

Caleb stands and steps over to the new red armchair he received only yesterday. Never taking his eyes off the picture frame, he sits, running his hand across the glass to wipe away the dust and cobwebs that cling to it.

Caleb tries to hold back his smile, but his willpower crumbles, and before he realizes, he's shedding tears of happiness all while smiling. *I may have lost a lot, but at least I'll have some memories to hold on to.*

A soft knock sidetracks his concentration from the happy moment. He sets the frame softly on the coffee table and cries out. "Coming."

Looking through the peephole, he finds the same face he'd spent the past few minutes staring at. He unlocks the door and allows it to swing open.

"Hey, was wondering when you'd show."

"I'm not late—am I?"

Caleb laughs. "We're not on a deadline, ya know. Come in."

Drew moves through the door and unzips his embroidered gray hoodie marked with a large "T" and a maple leaf. He scans the room. "Looks like you're settling into your new digs all right. You like it so far?"

"It's growing on me."

"Well, after living in the sticks so long, it'll take time to adjust."

"Yeah, but living in the city does come with a few bonuses: I'm closer to work, I'm driving less, and it brings a sense of relief living so close to people."

"You missed one: I'm two blocks away. I mean, it does sweeten the deal a little."

"There is that. So, I've meant to ask, how are you handling things since you came out? Is the weight lifted?"

"I psyched myself into thinking it would be some big to-do, but everyone I've told has taken it pretty well. I got a lot of "oh, I already knew" but there were a few people shocked when I told them."

"And have you made a decision about what we talked about last week?"

Drew nods. "I have—kind of why I came by."

"And . . . ?"

"And, let's do it."

"Are you serious?"

"Dead. I already turned in my resignation this morning."

Caleb's face lights up. "Wait, you did it?"

"Of course. Why wouldn't I want to open a law firm with you? Besides, as a former Crown prosecutor, I know all the inside tricks of the trade. Together, we'll be an unstoppable force."

"You have no idea how happy I am right now. Given everything I've been through these past three months, if you'd asked me a year ago if I ever saw this day happening, I'd have laughed in your face. But look at us now."

Drew walks over and sits on the new couch. "Yup, look at us." Drew pats the empty cushion next to him. "Have a seat . . . I have more news, but you should sit."

The jovial mood in the room changes. "More news? I hope it's good." Caleb meanders over and sits, leaving a few inches between them.

"I've got both: good and bad. Which one you want first?"

"Bad. Always open with bad and end on a high note."

"All right, well, I saw Barnes yesterday, and they got the whole story regarding Miguel Escobar."

Caleb's curiosity now peaks. "And . . . what did it say?"

"First of all, let me say, I don't know how he flew under the radar for so long. I'm surprised you're still alive."

"What d'ya mean?"

"He was wanted in the United States by the DEA for smuggling drugs and violations under the RICO Act, and he was also suspected in the murders of nine people—three in Florida and six in Columbia."

Caleb's speechless. The man he shared his home and bed with for a year and a half hid his surreptitious life so well, at no point did he ever imagine any of this.

Drew continues. "But it gets worse. The Royal Mounted Police are investigating whether someone on the inside at immigration pushed his paperwork through."

"I don't even know what to say."

"There's more. You ready?"

"Rip off the bandage already."

"Barnes came across some CCTV footage that he believes is the exact moment when Sebastian and Miguel met."

"When? Where?"

"Outside a dance club on George Street in October of 2014."

"Sebastian was clubbing?"

"Well, on this night he was."

Caleb rolls his eyes. "Well, enough about Miguel. He's dead, and I've washed my hands of the entire thing. We got bigger issues, such as have they found Sam?"

"Nope. It's like he utterly disappeared off the radar. I still think he died in the explosion and they haven't found him because there isn't anything left to find."

"Eh, that conclusion seems too simple for such a fucked-up sage. Nah, I'm telling you, he got away, and he's out there, passing the time until he feels the heat is off. Trust me, he'll reappear on his terms and try to seize what he feels is rightfully his: me."

"Let's hope not."

"That all for bad news?"

"Yup."

"So, what's the good news?"

Drew pulls out a white envelope and hands it over.

"What's this?"

"Open it and find out."

Caleb tears the envelope open and inside finds a single sheet of paper with the RNC letterhead printed at the top.

Dear Caleb,

I wanted to take a moment and express our deepest sympathies to you for all you have endured over the past three years.

As you know, admitting you're wrong is never the simplest, but I'm going to do it anyway. I'm sorry for everything I put you through, and I hope one day you'll find it in your heart to forgive me.

Barnes and I continue to hunt for Sam Butler and when we find him, trust me, he'll receive the punishment he deserves. If there's anything you need, I'm a phone call away.

Sincerely,
Gretchen Dawe

Caleb folds up the letter. "This is the best thing anyone could have given me, you know, considering everything I've been through these past few years. So, thanks for making this happen."

"Huh? Oh, don't look at me, I had nothing to do with it. She did this all on her own."

"Well, regardless, if I haven't told you enough, I'm so glad to have you back in my life. No more secrets, no more fighting from here on out. I only want complete honesty. I can't promise it'll work, but let's take what life gives us one day at a time."

"I couldn't have said it better."

"So, I guess this means we can go out, huh?"

"Ha . . . we'll see. Still a lot to do around here."

A few seconds later the metal from the mail slot clanks, and Caleb turns his attention in time to watch a single envelope drop to the floor. He cautiously walks over to the door.

He examines the envelope—blank with no indication it went through the post. An adhesive flap, nothing written on the front—it all seems suspicious, but he tears along the side and carefully removes the letter.

A single bold-typeface line reads:

Welcome to the neighborhood.

Charlotte from 1C

Caleb heaves a sigh of relief and drops the letter on the dining room table.

"What was it?"

"Ah, one of my neighbors left me a nice welcome letter. Scared me for a second."

"Trust me, it'll all be fine. You gotta learn how to take things one day at a time."

"You're right. Forget this. Let's go out and celebrate."

Drew springs to his feet, and Caleb slips on a pair of tennis shoes and a light jacket. Sliding his hand along the wall, Caleb smiles and goes to shake Drew's hand. To Caleb's surprise, Drew grabs ahold and pulls him in closer. He whispers, "Maybe this is the second chance we should have had all along."

"Could be. You know I always say love overcomes hate. And I am thankful I got you back in my life."

ACKNOWLEDGEMENTS

First, and foremost, I must thank my exceptionally talented editor, Ryan Quinn, for such an amazing job on giving Among the Ashes a chance and helping it shine. He is nothing short of remarkable and I can't thank him enough for his invaluable insight and (many) corrections.

Second, I must thank my amazing close friends for taking time out of their busy lives to read, re-read, and give me feedback on the book well before I released it. Kelly, Jenn, Andera, Josi, and Heather, from the bottom of my heart, thank you ladies for being my cheerleaders and rooting me onward in this journey.

Last, but absolutely not least, I must thank my fans for continuing to support my passion. If you'd asked me five years ago if I ever expected to be on my third novel, I'd have laughed. It's the positive comments and encouragement which drive me to continue following what warms my heart.

www.ingramcontent.com/pod-product-compliance
Lightning Source LLC
Chambersburg PA
CBHW030554180626
46816CB00005B/1533